RE-NAVIGATION

SUE PARRITT

To my dear friend Sue Heward, present at the novel's inception.

ACKNOWLEDGMENTS

Many thanks to Miika Hannila and staff at Creativia for having faith in my writing.

CHAPTER ONE

INTERMINABLE GLOOM ENVELOPED THE SMALL passenger ferry as it ploughed towards the island. Choppy grey sea melded with overcast sky and even the whitecaps seemed soiled to eyes accustomed to turquoise Queensland waters. The sombre atmosphere persisted inside the cabin; all I could see was a host of pallid faces heavy with winter's long shadow. A cacophony of howling wind and clamorous engine made conversation impossible, so I sat back in my seat and waited patiently for journey's end.

The ferry crested a wave, then plunged into a deep trough, evoking cries of alarm from numerous passengers. Beside me, a young woman clutched her stomach, making me thankful for a lifetime of sailing. Even as a small child, I had never succumbed to seasickness on the odd occasion when Dad misjudged the weather and we were caught in a storm far out in Moreton Bay.

'Look to your left and you'll see the island,' shouted Martin, the young staff member from Eden College. I had met Martin that morning in the small Pembrokeshire village adjoining the harbour, where some of us had lodged overnight after arriving late from Heathrow.

I peered out of spray-covered windows, noticed a grey shape shrouded in mist.

'Pity about the weather,' he added, 'there's a glorious view on a sunny day.'

'They have sunny days in Britain?' my bilious neighbour bawled in a thick European accent.

I smiled but made no attempt to answer her. The vagaries of the British weather were of no consequence at this stage of my personal journey. Three months' freedom stretched before me, a welcome break from the pressures of juggling work and home, the demands of husband and children—student would be my only role at Eden College.

———

I almost threw the college brochure away. We received so much junk mail at the suburban Brisbane bookshop where I worked as manager, the bulk of it was consigned to the waste paper basket without a second glance. What caught my eye that day, was the photograph of an old stone church set in the middle of the purple cover like an oval brooch pinned to plush velvet.

Intrigued, I opened the brochure and read an advertisement for a twelve-week residential Spiritual Development course to be held at Eden College, an ecumenical centre situated on a small island off the coast of Wales. The contents appealed, stimulating topics interspersed with photographs of a windswept landscape and joyful students singing. *Out of the question,* I thought and tossed the brochure in the waste paper basket.

In the middle of processing invoices, I remembered my

forthcoming long-service leave. I had considered taking my teenage children, Stephen and Penny, to Europe over the Christmas holidays, convinced they would benefit from a hands-on history lesson, but when I mentioned the idea to my husband Brian, he had pointed out the absurdity of travelling during the European winter. Residents of a sub-tropical city, we didn't possess warm clothing; the children would complain constantly about the weather and half the hotels would be closed. European plans discarded, I had decided to postpone my leave until Penny finished school at the end of ninety-four. By then, Brian, a senior manager in a state government department, would be eligible for his second period of long-service leave. The problem of destination remained. Brian favoured sailing around nearby Pacific islands, while I envisaged walking the streets of Paris, Rome and London. We always spent our holidays on the boat.

My hand strayed to the rubbish bin as I envisaged twelve weeks away from demanding customers, moody adolescents, dull suburban life. *If only,* I mused, reaching instead for another invoice.

During my lunch break, I walked away from the bustle of Brighton Road and headed for the sea, where I sat on a bench reading the crumpled brochure from cover to cover. I knew Brian wouldn't object to my spending three months away, a quiet unassuming man, he never interfered with my spiritual life. Although he didn't attend church or profess faith of any flavour, he was supportive, looking after the children when I had church meetings, cooking dinner every Sunday to save me the trouble after evening service and taking part in social activities I'm certain he found tedious. As for Stephen and Penny, at eighteen and sixteen, they were more than old enough to fend for themselves.

When the time came to return to work, I stood for a

moment watching wavelets dribble over mud and seaweed. Ebb and flow, ebb and flow, continual motion erasing yesterday's pattern. This bay, this island continent I called home had contained me for forty years, but now another island beckoned. It was time to venture into unfamiliar seas.

———

Salt spray decorated my hair as I stepped from the ferry onto a small wooden jetty. Ancient timbers creaked, coils of wet rope slumped at the base of thick bollards, fenders smacked against ferry and dock. Along with several others, I helped Martin to unload the luggage and pile it onto a strange contraption resembling a trolley, which he pulled along metal tracks embedded in the jetty boards. By the time we reached the foreshore, an old truck had materialised out of the mist, so we gathered around to reload our suitcases.

'This is the only vehicle on the island,' the young driver remarked, jumping down from the cab. 'Here at Eden College we do our bit to reduce harmful emissions.' He walked around the truck to open the rear doors.

'What about a tractor or a motor mower?' asked an elderly man with an American accent. 'I understood the college grew most of its own food.'

Martin smiled. 'That's right but we use horses to plough the fields and a hand mower to cut the lawns. The lorry is only used to transport luggage and older people to the house.'

The elderly man grinned and climbed into the truck's passenger seat, while I sighed at the thought of a long walk in unsuitable shoes.

Suitcases loaded, Martin led us away from foreshore

pebbles and windswept bushes into a stand of tall trees. We walked in single-file along a gravel path littered with sodden leaves. Dark moist trunks leant towards the path, raindrops dripped from overhanging branches, plopped onto hair and jackets. Listening for birdsong, I heard only the wind moving mournfully between trees. The absence of sunlight disturbed; the dank trees appeared to edge closer, compressing my flesh. Looking down at my saturated shoes, I shuddered with cold. Then, all of a sudden, we were out of the trees and walking on lush lawn dotted with golden daffodils.

'Wow look at those flowers,' exclaimed an American voice behind me.

I turned around, smiled at a tall African-American woman. 'Yes, they're wonderful. I've never seen daffodils growing before.' I fell into step beside her.

She returned the smile. 'Hi, I'm Donna Jones from New York City. Don't see many flowers at all where I come from.'

'Pleased to meet you, Donna. I'm Julia Mitchell from Australia. Spooky back there in the woods, don't you think?' I shivered even though the breeze had diminished.

'I can't say it bothered me. I was just grateful to be outa that boat. Several times I thought my end was near.'

'Surely not, it wasn't that rough?'

'Well, I'll be real happy to stay on dry land for the next three months.'

'Not me, I'd love to explore this coastline. Martin said there are sheer cliffs on one side of the island and tiny coves on the other. Perhaps I could borrow a boat?'

'I don't imagine the staff would let a student use one of their boats.'

'Why ever not, I'm an experienced sailor?'

'Well I wouldn't count on it. Remember what it said on the last page of the application form.'

I tried to recall details from the sheaf of paper I'd filled in several months before.

'We signed up for three months,' she continued. 'Kinda like the army, except God's the commander here. We can only leave the island in an emergency.' Throwing back her head, she laughed mischievously. 'We're here for the duration, Julia, captives of the Lord.'

'Yes, I remember now. Three months away from the world it said.'

'Sanctuary from a society out of control,' she added, serious now.

We resumed walking at a leisurely pace towards a large house resembling the Victorian mansions I'd seen on BBC documentaries. Three rows of sash windows set at regular intervals, alleviated the monotony of reddish-brown brickwork, sturdy chimneys rose like sentinels from a grey slate roof dotted with seagulls, while at ground level, garden beds filled with spring-green shrubs extended either side of a wide paved entrance. Students milled around open wooden doors.

'Come on you two,' Martin called from the doorway. 'There will be plenty of time later to look at the garden. We're waiting to serve lunch.'

'Comin',' Donna shouted back and began to run.

A cold wind swept across the lawn, agitating golden daffodils. Shivering, I raced after her to the shelter of redbrick solidity.

In the entrance hall, signs directed us to the dining room, a welcoming space filled with rustic wooden tables and benches. A vase of daffodils decorated each table, the glow of seasoned timber and yellow blooms creating a warm friendly atmosphere, reflected in the faces of those already seated. Donna gestured towards empty places near a window, so we hurried across the room, delicious aromas drifting past our noses. As we slid along a bench, I felt an urgent need for food. It seemed days since my last decent meal.

Conversation ceased abruptly, and I looked up to see Martin standing near the servery, arms raised above his head. 'Brothers and sisters,' he began, spreading his arms wide as though embracing the whole group, 'welcome to Eden College. May your stay with us be fruitful, remember the seed of faith grows strong in fertile soil. In this special place, apart from the world, you have a unique opportunity to give your lives over to God. And by so doing, you will be open to whatever you're called to do on leaving the island.' He paused. 'Now let us give thanks for a safe crossing and for the food we are about to eat.'

Head bowed, I made my own small petition, thought momentarily of home and an empty place at a pine table tucked in the corner of our kitchen.

Steaming soup served with crusty brown bread followed by cheese and fruit satisfied my hunger, but throughout the meal I ate as though sitting alone at the table, barely raising my eyes from bowl or plate. Around me conversation hummed melodious and unwavering; strangers became fellow-students as future friendships birthed, but I could only listen and observe. There were too many names to absorb, too many voices, too many faces. I wanted time to assimilate, time to savour each tiny detail, let eyes and ears attune to a different environment.

'Hey Julia, you ok?' Donna asked, reaching out to clasp my hand. 'You've hardly said a word.'

'Bit tired that's all. I guess the jet lag's finally catching up with me.'

'Why don't you have a nap this afternoon?'

'I'd love to, but I must try to stay awake. It's best if you can sleep at the right time after a long flight, helps to regulate the internal clock.'

'Well, I'm gonna take a nap. I'll unpack later. I don't imagine there's much planned for today.'

'Don't forget evening service,' a middle-aged woman opposite remarked. 'After supper in the main lounge. It's a special service to welcome new students. Martin has organised some distinctive music.'

'Thanks, I'll be there,' I replied, and noticing the badge attached to her shirt pocket added, 'the badge is a good idea. I'm terrible at remembering names.'

She smiled warmly. 'You'll find a badge in your room. We suggest you wear them for the first week. I'm May Gordon, New Testament tutor.'

'Pleased to meet you. I didn't realise you were a staff member.'

'Think of me as fellow seeker. We're all travelling the same road here.'

———

My room was situated on the third floor at the end of a long corridor. It had two windows, one facing a small lake, the other looking out over a lawn to tall trees. For several minutes, I stood staring at ducks and reeds, wishing my room were on the opposite side of the house where the sea could be glimpsed crashing against rocky outcrops. All my life I had lived within walking distance of the sea, I loved the sound of waves breaking, gulls cawing, sea-wind singing in the trees.

The lake shimmered in a burst of sunlight and a spring chorus arose from nearby. *No,* I decided, *this room is right.*

Despite airline weight restrictions, my clothes soon filled the small wooden wardrobe. Old-fashioned and shabby, it had a rounded top, forcing me to store my empty suitcase under the bed. All that remained to be unpacked was my new backpack, a gift from Brian. Lifting it onto the old wooden desk in front of the large window, I unzipped its numerous pockets to extract pens, pencils, exercise books, prayer book and bible. In a side pocket, I discovered the tiny koala Penny had given me at the airport. 'To remind you of home Mum,' she'd said, rubbing the furry toy against my cheek. Smiling at the memory, I placed the koala in the middle of the desk, but it kept falling onto its face, so I propped it against the bible.

An inside pocket held the small envelope containing family photographs I had included to remind me of home. Carefully, I placed familiar images on the desk: Brian on the boat, Stephen larking about with a couple of mates, Penny elegant in the blue dress I'd made for the school formal, Dad opening Christmas presents. A pang of homesickness hit me as I picked up the nearest photograph and turned to pin it on the noticeboard adjacent to the desk.

Colour photographs neatly arranged, I opened my wallet to retrieve the faded black and white print I always carried—my mother, hollow-cheeked, her thin pale arms folded against a bright summer dress. She never met Brian, never held my babies in her arms. I pinned her photograph beside the others and quickly dismissed past sorrows.

―――

A knock on the door jolted me awake and for a moment, I wondered why I was lying fully clothed on an unfamiliar bed.

'Julia, Donna here. Are you coming down to supper?'

'Come in, it's not locked.' I sank back on the pillows.

She bounced into the room. 'Get up sleepyhead or you're gonna go hungry.'

'I didn't mean to sleep. I was just trying out the bed. Now it'll take forever to get back on track.'

'Give it a few days, you'll be fine.' She glanced at the noticeboard. 'Family?'

'Yes, that's my husband Brian on our boat.'

She nodded and began to study the other photographs. 'Four kids, you must be run off your feet.'

'Four? Oh no, my Stephen's the one in the middle, the others are his mates.'

'Handsome guy.'

I thought so too, accepted the compliment with a smile, 'Have you got any kids, Donna?'

'Yeah, two little devils, twins going on twelve. Robbie and Jamie, they drive me to distraction.'

'It must have been difficult to leave them for three months.'

'Oh, Mom understood. She's great and the boys love being at her place. She spoils them; heaps of candy and home-baked cookies.'

'Did your husband mind your going away?'

'I haven't seen him in ten years.'

'Sorry.'

'Don't be, he wasn't worth having.'

'It must be tough being a sole parent?'

'Oh, it's not so bad. Besides, I don't remember it any

other way. Anyhow, I've got Mom, plus loads of help from folks at church. There are plenty worse off.'

'I guess so.'

A bell rang in the corridor.

'Supper bell,' she cried, grabbing my arm. 'Hey, this is just like school. Come on Julia, let's go eat.'

———

The afternoon nap had banished reticence, now I felt eager to enter into conversation and take my place in the island community. Glancing around the dining room, I located a large table with seating for eight, six already occupied. 'Over there looks good, Donna.' I gestured towards the table.

'Sure. Lead the way.'

After introducing ourselves, we took the vacant seats at opposite ends of the table, ideal positions for getting to know other students. A bowl of pasta in a rich tomato sauce, followed by one of salad, appeared in front of me; smiling my thanks, I heaped my plate, then poured myself a glass of water. The others were already halfway through their meal but took care to include Donna and me in conversation. Between mouthfuls and listening to friendly chat, I met Sabine, Hannah, Marie-Claire, Hans, Benjamin and Ruth from Germany, Zambia, Belgium, Switzerland, Kenya and Scotland. In the space of one hour, the boundaries of my world had expanded beyond all expectations and my mouth ached from smiling. On a deeper level, I rejoiced in being among other believers and eagerly anticipated our corporate worship and study.

After supper, I helped Ruth clear the table, then made my way to the main lounge, a sizeable high-ceilinged room with pale blue walls and grey carpet. Numerous rows of upholstered chairs were arranged in semi-circles behind a grand piano and lectern. Standing on the periphery, I glanced around for a familiar face, noticed Donna sitting in the front row, a vacant chair to her right. As a rule, I prefer to sit towards the back when faced with a crowded room, but nevertheless made my way to the front. 'Mind if I join you, Donna?'

'Of course not.'

'Hi, I'm Marceline from Rwanda,' said the young woman to my right as I slipped into the chair.

'Julia from Australia.'

Brown eyes flashed friendship, white teeth gleamed. 'Delighted to meet you, Marceline.' Her ankle-length floral dress rustled as she settled back in the seat.

I made a mental note to look for an atlas in the college library. I knew Rwanda was an African country but had no idea where it was located in that vast continent.

Seated between two women clad in colourful clothes—Donna had changed into a scarlet skirt and dazzling white top since supper—I felt as faded as the well-worn chairs in my stonewashed jeans and light-blue sweater. Around the walls, the flags of our many nations hung from bunting pinned to the picture rail, while in the centre of one wall, a huge multi-coloured crepe paper crucifix shimmered in pale evening light above a grey stone fireplace. Rainbows swirled before my eyes and I wanted to leap from the chair, dance across the floor, dip my fingers in a gleaming pot of gold.

Music halted absurd thoughts. Hands resting in my lap, I listened to the familiar strains of a favourite hymn. Martin played without music his face tilted to one side as though receiving the notes from another place. I contemplated his words of greeting before lunch, his exhortation to be fruitful, to give our lives over to God. Clearly the seed of faith flourished in him, but I couldn't help pondering how a young man coped day in, day out with an island existence. Perhaps he simply preferred a secluded environment, the warm intimacy of life in community?

The hymn concluded, and I noticed that May Gordon had left her seat at the end of the front row and was standing behind the lectern.

'Can you all hear me?' she asked, adjusting a microphone.

'Yes,' we chorused.

On her right, in the far corner of the room, I noticed a man I hadn't seen before sitting behind two large African drums. Head bowed, his face was in shadow, only a circle of tightly curled black hair visible in the fading light. I hoped this was the distinctive music May Gordon had mentioned during lunch.

Martin rose from the piano stool and stepped forward. Raising his arms, he cupped his hands, drawing us together as he had done a few hours earlier in the dining room. Obedient, I closed my eyes, turned thoughts inward. The silence thickened with expectation, minutes passed, and I felt desperate for air as though I had dived deep and the pressure was squeezing my lungs. A cough pushed me skyward; I opened my eyes as our collective breath rippled the surface.

'Tonight, we celebrate our faith and praise God with music,' May exclaimed, her gaze encompassing the whole room. 'But don't expect familiar melodies and rhythms. Our music will be loud and exuberant, it will stir your very souls. Tonight, we praise the Lord with the music of Africa!' She turned and flicked a switch on the wall behind her.

Light enveloped the motionless drummer. Reaching

out, he flexed long thin fingers, then brushed taut skins, sending a protracted growl rolling across the room. I waited eagerly for further sound but almost leapt out of my seat when next he struck the drums. Fire blazed from his fingertips, he flung back his head and for instant, black eyes flickered ensnared in harsh artificial light. Eyes closed, full lips parted, he began to sway, back and forth, back and forth until the bold patterns of his African clothing became swirls of scarlet and gold caught like bright butterflies in a luminescent cone.

The mounting tempo drew me away from the tiny Welsh island to an immense continent teeming with unfamiliar wildlife. Enchanted, I pictured a million hooves pounding vast savanna, deep forests resounding with birdsong and the chatter of monkeys, wild rivers roaring as they raced to the sea. Donna's warm thigh pressed against me; her hands slapped the evening air. Behind me, I heard the thunder of other palms and we sprang to our feet, nimble as gazelle. Over our heads distinctive song surged as Benjamin, his voice ascending in praise, pushed through the crowd to join the drummer. I recognised only the word 'Jesu' but the message was crystal clear. Diverse homelands, one God, we were gathered here to celebrate our faith.

———

Night settled over the redbrick house. I lay in my narrow bed exhausted but exhilarated by over two hours of worship. We had sung and clapped and stamped our feet until our bodies crumpled with weariness.

Somewhere a clock struck midnight. Hugging the pillow, I tried to conjure up tranquil images to quiet my churning mind. My thoughts turned to childhood nights, waves washing a sheltered shore, sliding into sleep wrapped in the ocean's endless rhythm. Cool blue water dribbled over my face; I inhaled salt air, listened for familiar night sounds: possum and frog, cicada and fruit bat. Instead, I heard monkeys chatter, hyenas howl, a lion roar in the distance. Perspiration beaded my forehead and trickled down my flushed cheek. Over-heated, I pushed back the blankets, gulped cool air. My body temperature soon returned to normal and I was forced to admit jet lag and excitement had scrambled my senses. African fauna had no place on an island off the coast of Wales.

Familiar words surfaced, and I sighed with relief. '*He makes me to lie down in green pastures, he leads me beside the still water. He restores my soul, he...*' Sleep beckoned, unable to finish the psalm I whispered, 'Amen.'

But as I sank into slumber's deep well, I saw the drummer's face mirrored in clear water above me and heard the distant echo of his drums. Closer, closer, soon his music displaced all other sound and I was falling, falling, the rhythm of African fingers dancing in my head.

CHAPTER TWO

SOMEONE WAS CALLING MY NAME; I STRUGGLED TO raise heavy eyelids, blinked in bright sunlight. 'Come in,' I called, realising the voice was coming from the corridor outside my room.

'I brought you some coffee,' Donna said, closing the door behind her, 'I thought you might be sick and need a hot drink.'

Reluctantly I raised myself on one elbow. 'Thanks, but I'm fine. I could easily have come down to the dining room.'

'It's a bit late for breakfast and if you don't get a move on you're gonna miss morning service too.'

'Is it that late?'

'Thirty after nine.'

I groaned and reached for the coffee. Donna perched on the end of my bed her face turned towards me. Sleek black curls brushed her shoulders, smooth cheeks shone in morning light. Unlike me, she seemed perfectly prepared for the day's devotions, her inner and outer worlds composed as Mother's had been during those brief, untroubled years. My sister and I were never late for school, always had clean socks and shoes, neatly wrapped sandwiches. Why had Donna brought me coffee? A friendly gesture or a yearning to play mother? I wanted to tell her I don't need a mother, I'm grown up now, in control of my life, mothering others.

'Great worship last night,' she remarked dreamily. 'It transported me to another world.'

I glanced at the dark hands folded neatly in her lap. 'To Africa?'

'No, my grandmother's place, gospel singers and soft southern nights.'

'Do you ever think about your African heritage?'

She shook her head. 'Too many years gone by, too much white blood running in my veins.'

I nodded. 'My mother always called England home even though she was only two when her family emigrated to Australia. On Sundays, we struggled through roast dinner whatever the temperature and at Christmas we sat sweating in our hot little house, eating turkey and plum pudding while other families went to the beach.'

Donna smiled. 'My mother always cooks grits. The boys hate them.'

My travel alarm clock flashed nine four zero as I placed the empty cup on the bedside table. 'I'd better get going. Thanks for the coffee.' I swung my legs out of bed. 'See you downstairs.'

'Oh Julia,' she said, getting to her feet, 'I forgot to tell you worship's in the chapel today. You take the dining room exit and then turn right. It's down the path a bit, pretty little place.'

'You've been there already?'

'Yeah, I spent a few minutes in there before breakfast. See ya.'

———

Conventional words and melodies resonated through the stone chapel as I slipped into a pew close to the door. May Gordon, standing nearby, reached out to hand me a hymn-book. I smiled my thanks before bowing my head to hide crimson cheeks. This was the first time I'd been late for church.

Music restored my equilibrium and soon I forgot about oversleeping and distant drums. Secure in my faith, I knew God would forgive my inauspicious beginning, but during the few moments of silence before the sermon, I prayed for diligence and punctuality, just in case.

The minister, a short, rotund, middle-aged man with a shock of unruly brown hair, took Genesis I as his text. First day words, a new world unfolding. Pilgrim sailor, I felt elated by the prospect of twelve weeks' exploration.

After delivering a short sermon on beginnings, he moved away from the lectern and placed his hands on the edge of the pulpit. 'At Eden College we encourage diversity.' His eyes skimmed over the entire congregation. 'It's no accident our students come from all parts of the globe, so don't be afraid to embrace new experiences, explore different ways of worship, cultures, languages. By learning from one another we can help create a new earth where all people live in harmony.' He smiled, then clasped his hands together. 'I dream of a new Genesis.'

But what happens when we leave this ordered garden and return to a chaotic world? I wanted to ask, watching him descend from the pulpit and stroll down the centre aisle?

Standing outside the chapel bathed in spring sunshine a few minutes later, misgivings evapourated as his warm hand enfolded mine.

'Julia,' he read, peering shortsightedly at my badge. 'Delighted to meet you. I trust your stay with us will exceed your every expectation.'

'I'm sure it will.' I looked for his name badge but couldn't locate it. 'Er, sorry I don't know your name.'

'You weren't at early morning prayers?'

'No, I slept in. Jet lag, I'm afraid.'

'Did you have a long journey?'

'Yes, I travelled from Australia.'

'A long journey indeed; the very end of the earth.'

I waited to hear his name, but at that moment the wind caught the open chapel door and slammed it against the wall.

'Damn wind,' he muttered and hurried away to secure the door.

———

We spent the remainder of the morning in the main lounge, May and Martin handing out timetables and answering general questions, so it was lunchtime before I had an opportunity to ask Donna if she knew the minister's name.

'Choddy,' she answered.

'Don't you mean Reverend Choddy?'

'No just Choddy. It's short for Chodbury. His Christian name is Clive, but he said he detests it and as we're all friends here, there's no need to stand on ceremony.'

'Suits me.'

'Me too.' She touched my arm. 'I love it here, Julia. Early this morning out walking in the garden, I just knew this place is real special. We're so lucky to have been chosen.'

'Chosen?'

'By God I mean. I believe he put that winning ticket in my hand. I don't usually gamble, can't see any sense in it but the guys at work bought a lottery ticket for my birthday. It won first prize.'

I recalled the purple brochure, a brief discussion with Brian, a bank draft organised almost without thinking. 'I'm glad you won,' I said, squeezing her hand.

Martin's announcement of an afternoon walk prevented further conversation and for this I was grateful. I didn't want Donna to ask how *I* came to be spending a term at Eden College. Naive, I had believed we would all be equals here. 'I'll just go and get my jacket,' I told her.

By the time I returned to the dining room, a large group had assembled by the doors, those from cooler climes sensibly dressed for the variable spring weather. Others, including Hannah and the drummer, Jeremiah had to be sent to a nearby storeroom to rummage among left-behind clothing for suitable coats.

'Are we ready now?' Martin asked impatiently the moment they reappeared.

'Yes Martin,' we chorused like schoolchildren. He opened the door and stepped outside.

We followed meekly, two by two.

Beyond the lake, a gravel path led through woodland. As we followed him, Martin pointed out oak, ash, laurel and holly, trees that in Australia had been planted by home-sick settlers. I tried to commit the names to memory for inclusion in my journal, made a mental note to bring my camera on my next walk. My eyes were everywhere, drinking in the lushness of a northern hemisphere spring and for the first time in my life mourned the absence of distinct seasons in Southern Queensland. Flowers bloomed year-round in my sub-tropical garden and grey-green gum leaves littered the lawn whatever the date. Weathered and ancient, my land simply grew older, rebirth an impossible concept.

All of a sudden, I heard the sound of water trickling over rocks. Leaving the path to investigate, I discovered a small creek meandering through the trees. Standing close to the edge, I watched ribbons of emerald weed float in clear water. Spring flowers clung to the banks, shades of lemon, blue and white fluttering in the breeze. Abundant growth; promise of a new garden already fulfilled.

'It is so beautiful,' a deep voice said behind me.

Startled, I turned to see the drummer gazing at the water. 'Hi, yes, it is beautiful. Is this your first experience of a British spring?'

'Oh no, I have been to university in England many years ago, but I do not think I noticed flowers and trees. My study window looked out on a brick wall and my head was full of engineering.' He threw back his head and roared with laughter, the vibrations hanging in the cool air, thick and sweet as treacle.

Laughter faded as he squatted to stroke a pale-yellow flower. 'There is no excuse for ignorance,' he said, his tone serious now. 'I shall have to learn their names.'

'Me too, after all it's my heritage. My maternal grand-parents were English.'

'You are not English?'

'No, Australian. Julia Mitchell, Brisbane Australia.' I held out my hand and he shook it vigorously.

'Jeremiah Ajuwon, Lagos Nigeria. Is this your first visit to this country?'

'No, I came over when I was a child, with my grand-mother and sister. But I don't recall much about the land-scape. We spent most of the time visiting relatives.'

'I am thinking there is perhaps a book in the college library to inform me about this landscape?'

'Very likely, we could have a look after the walk.'

'Thank you, but I am busy at that time.'

'I'll let you know if I find anything useful.'

He walked away from the water, pausing to stroke spring growth on a nearby tree with long thin fingers.

'Martin won't be too pleased if we get lost,' I called out, realising that the rest of the group were no longer in sight. 'We'd better hurry and catch up.'

'I am a good runner,' he announced and sped away through the trees.

Before long I caught up with the others, Martin having stopped to wait for stragglers only a short distance away. It seemed Jeremiah and I were not the only ones to have lagged behind.

Beyond the woods, flat fields rolled to the cliff edge and an icy wind blew in from the sea to sweep across freshly tilled earth. Seagulls soared in a gunmetal sky, spring sunshine had vanished, rain threatened. Surely it was time to return to the house.

Martin had other ideas. 'It's about ten minutes to the cliff,' he remarked cheerfully. 'We'd best get a move on if we're going to beat the rain.'

A narrow track dissected the fields, so we walked in single file, heads bowed against the wind. Hard-packed earth beneath my feet led me to ponder how many before me had trodden this path and what thoughts absorbed them as they walked towards the edge of land.

Perched on the rim, we stared in awed silence at a boiling sea. Huge waves battered white cliffs, jagged rocks emerging at intervals to gleam briefly before disappearing beneath the ensuing onslaught. Raw gusts of wind captured my breath and I felt immense agitation as though I too was churning like the sea. Inexplicably for a seasoned sailor, I wanted to turn around, run away from perpetual motion, back to the placid creek, the peaceful chapel, the solid brick house.

'You look a bit pale, Julia,' Martin said, taking my arm. 'Come away from the edge.'

'Stormy seas,' I murmured. 'What a contrast from ordered fields.'

'All part of God's earth, there's no need to be afraid.'

'I'm not afraid, the wind just took my breath away.'

'That's not all,' Hannah said beside me. 'My blood's frozen solid.'

'Mine too,' Benjamin echoed.

Martin laughed. 'Guess I'd better get you hothouse plants back in the warmth. How about soup by a roaring fire?'

'Great,' we answered in unison and turned our backs on the angry sea.

After walking for only a few metres, a trailing shoelace forced me to stop and when I straightened up, I noticed a lone figure still standing on the cliff edge. His borrowed jacket vibrant against the darkening sky, Jeremiah stood arms outstretched as though poised for flight. Afraid to call out in case it spooked him, I contemplated a safe way to steer him away from danger, but before I could take a step forward, he spun around and began shouting at the sky. A gust of wind whipped his words away, so I couldn't tell whether they were praise or anger.

———

Back at the house, soaking in a hot bath, I remembered the library. It was too late to search for a book on British flora, supper would be served in half an hour. I decided to look the following day after class.

When supper had been cleared away and I'd taken my turn at washing up, I wandered into the main corridor to read the multitude of notices pinned to cork boards along the walls. There were plans of the house, potted biographies and photographs of the staff, lists of tutor groups, extra-curricula activities. Sign up here: painting prayer pottery singing gardening tapestry; a plethora of choice. Pencil in hand, I hesitated, loath to encroach on the alone time I had promised myself. Moving on, I headed for the main stair-case and the sanctuary of my bedroom, but as I approached one of the small sitting rooms, the sound of a guitar slowed my progress. Curious, I paused by the open doorway, saw Jeremiah sitting in front of a log fire, strumming and singing softly, a small group gathered at his feet. Alone time dismissed, I tip-toed into the room and sat quietly on the edge of the rug.

'Welcome Julia,' said Jeremiah, barely altering the rhythm of his song.

I blushed and raised my hand in greeting. Why was I always turning up late in this place and drawing attention to myself?

'Well that's the end of my repertoire, friends,' he declared after a few minutes. 'Anyone else care to play?' He held out the guitar.

Benjamin from Kenya leant forward. 'I'd love to teach you all a song from *my* country. Do you think you could pick up the tune Jeremiah?'

'You don't play?'

'No, but I sing.'

'Ok, try me.'

'Ji bo tu, ji bo tu, mu mo yo, mu mo yu,' he sang. 'Ji bo tu, ji bo tu, mu no yo.'

Jeremiah repeated the tune perfectly.

'Great. It's a simple song but beautiful lyrics. In English, the words are: It is well, it is well, in my soul, in my soul. It is well, it is well, in my soul.'

'Once more and then everyone else join in,' Jeremiah instructed, motioning Benjamin to sit beside him.

Evening slipped into night as we taught each other songs and hymns from our various traditions, and I realised Choddy had been right about the benefits of learning from one another. At home, my fellow-worshippers were white, mostly middle-class Australians and the beliefs espoused in our small weatherboard church answered, or appeared to answer, all our late twentieth-century spiritual needs.

'Why search elsewhere for religious guidance?' my sister Karen, a confirmed atheist, had asked when I told her about the course.

'To deepen my spirituality,' I'd answered, meaning I wished to delve further into my own tradition. Now, I understood the narrowness of that explanation. Living at 'the very end of the earth,' to quote Choddy, I *was* isolated from other cultures and faiths. Multiculturalism might be a nineties' media buzzword, but it barely touched *my* life. I moved in a tight circle of first or second-generation Australians whose ancestors came from Britain, the only Italians I knew ran the local fruit and vegetable shop, the only Chinese, the restaurant Brian and I favoured some Saturday evenings. I had never spoken to an Aboriginal Australian and had little notion of indigenous spiritual traditions. Dreamtime for me conjured up images of Uluru, rainbow serpents and desert dot painting.

Benjamin tapped my shoulder. 'Goodnight Julia, I hope you enjoyed this evening as much as I have.'

I looked up at him. 'Yes, it's been wonderful. Goodnight Benjamin.'

All except Jeremiah rose to leave, but still contemplating the constrictions of life in a close-knit, self-absorbed community, I found myself moving closer to the fire. In the dying embers, I saw the red centre of my land, remote, ancient, her secrets concealed beneath rock and sand.

'Penny for your thoughts,' Jeremiah said softly.

'I was thinking about Australia.'

'Homesick?'

'No, I was thinking about Aboriginal Australians. Their culture is just as foreign to me as yours.'

'You do not learn the history of your country at school?'

'Not in my day, it was all British history. It's different now.'

'Yes, it is different now.' Leaning forward, he picked up a poker lying on the hearth and stabbed at the coals. 'They taught British history in my school too and they taught us well. I can recite a list of monarchs from Edward the Confessor to Elizabeth.' The poker pitched into the coals, smashing the red centre. 'Elizabeth the Second I mean, not that proud virgin who sent her ships across the seas to plunder and subjugate. Britannia rules the waves, long live the Empire!' He pulled out the poker, then spat into the fire. 'They ruined our land and dismissed our culture, but they could not destroy our souls.'

Truth bit deep, my own country a prime example of the destruction wrought by colonisation. He continued to stare into the coals and I questioned whether he wanted to be alone. A curtain had fallen between us, the evening's cheerful camaraderie cooled like night air. 'Goodnight, Jeremiah,' I murmured, and padded towards the door.

'Please stay,' he called after me. 'I do not want to be alone when the fire dies.'

Reluctantly I re-traced my steps.

'Thank you,' he whispered, his eyes still fixed on the glowing coals.

A long discomfiting silence ensued. I yearned to speak, heal the rift widening between us but words eluded me, and in their place, guilt surged to the surface. White guilt for forty years lived in blissful ignorance, staying away, as instructed by my mother, from the wasteland near the railway line where Aboriginal children played; crossing the road to avoid the black drunk lying outside the post office, never asking why? What could I say to this black man whose country and people had suffered under British rule, what good were my little white words?

Then, the words of a psalm reached my lips: '*God is our shelter and strength, always ready to help in times of trouble. So, we will not be afraid, even if the earth is shaken and mountains fall into the ocean depths; even if the seas roar and rage, and the hills are shaken by violence.*'

The last embers flickered and died.

'God bless you, Julia,' he said quietly and taking my hand, pressed it between his warm palms.

CHAPTER THREE

Choddy droned on about temptation, sin and suffering. The first class, the beginning of our spiritual journey together and already waves of disappointment were dousing anticipated delight. Impatient, I wanted to move beyond the genesis, deepen the well of knowledge not return to the rhetoric of schooldays. I began to fidget.

'Something wrong, Julia?' Donna asked when Choddy left the room to collect some papers.

'Not really, I just didn't think we'd start with Adam and Eve.'

'Why not? Begin at the beginning. It makes sense to me.'

'But we're all familiar with the creation story, it's standard Sunday School fare. I was hoping for something new.'

'We may get something new.'

'How?'

'Fresh insight.'

I nodded. 'Guess I'd better pay attention.'

'I should think so.' She slapped my wrist playfully.

Contrite, I sat up straight facing the front, wondering

what on earth was the matter with me and why my customary patience and acceptance had evaporated.

'I'm dying for a cup of coffee,' she whispered, leaning towards me. 'And my bum aches something awful. I'm not used to sitting still for hours on end.'

'I'm pleased to hear you're not a goody-two-shoes after all.'

'Goody what?' she queried, but Choddy had reappeared and was handing out sheets of pale green paper.

'Homework children,' he announced as we bent our heads to read the few lines of typed text.

I suppressed a groan. Had Choddy forgotten his students were adults? Perhaps he'd been a primary school teacher before taking up his island post?

'Linguistic truths or falsehoods?' He threw the question like a spear.

'In the creation story?' someone behind me asked.

'No, what I just said. Is it homework, is it work? That's debatable, but the second word was undoubtedly a lie. You are not children. I know that, and you know that, but no one challenged me.'

'You're the teacher,' Ruth called out.

He grinned. 'So that means I have absolute authority or else you're all too polite to confront me.'

'Something like that,' Ruth agreed.

'Two simple words,' he continued, 'and already we have confusion. Such is the nature of language. No doubt you're all wondering what this has to do with Genesis, so now I'm going to challenge you. Write your own creation story. Seek within for the source of your faith and write about the birth of your spiritual life. No set number of words.' He grinned again. 'This isn't school.'

We all laughed with him.

———

Shadows crept across the lawn and breeze cooled on my windowsill as I sat at my desk by the open window, writing neatly on Choddy's pale green paper:

'Long ago somewhere deep within, a seed germinated and produced tiny green shoots. A careful gardener, I tended the fragile plant, moistening the soil, adding compost and tearing away weeds. The plant grew strong. Flowers appeared with the coming of spring and I delighted in their beauty. But before long the petals withered and died. Saddened by this demise, my tears fell to the earth.

Soon hot sun shrivelled sorrow and I realised I had been so preoccupied with showy splendour, I'd overlooked the formation of tiny fruits. So, I gave thanks for new growth and eagerly awaited the yield of my labour.

Some fruits fell to the ground before ripening, others withered on the branch and once more loss perturbed me. But the remaining fruit continued to ripen, and I rejoiced, understanding at last that a young plant can only support a limited crop. When the season altered, I gathered a small but sweet harvest.

Thus, began the cultivation of my garden.'

———

Choddy pushed my green paper across his desk. 'What are you afraid of Julia?' He peered over the top of his glasses.

'Sorry, I don't follow you.'

'This is well written with excellent use of metaphor, but you haven't done as I asked.' A plump finger reached out to prod the paper. 'Your creation story seems to me to be a Garden of Eden narrative with the Parable of the Sower thrown in. There's nothing original here. Oh, sure I can read between the lines, but I wanted *your* experience, *your* truth. What have you actually written about the birth of your spiritual life?'

'Nothing much I suppose.'

'Why not?'

I hesitated before admitting quietly, 'it was too difficult to peel away the layers. I didn't want to expose the core.'

'There you go again.'

'Sorry, I mean...'

'No problem,' he interrupted, 'two can play the metaphor game. I say your plant is strong, so it can endure a little exposure.'

'But I'm scared of damaging it.'

'I'm not asking you to dig up the roots.'

I managed a small smile. 'I realise that, it's just, well, I'm reluctant to revisit that period of my life.'

He nodded and began to rummage in a pile of papers to his left. 'Ah, here it is.' He pulled out a folded sheet of paper and pushed it towards me. 'Truth, Julia, that's what's important.'

I picked up the college brochure, focused on gold lettering rather than a photograph of the church where I had worshipped that morning. 'Come to the Island and Open your Heart to the Truth,' I read slowly, determined to fully digest each word. Text faded, memory surging uninvited through the long tunnel of years, bringing a flush to my cheeks as I recalled the day a gardener caught me vandalising hibiscus bushes in a church garden. 'You haven't been abandoned,' he'd said when I burst into tears following a brief exchange. 'If you open your heart to the truth, you will hear God's message of love.'

A troubled and grieving adolescent, I had seized his

words, repeated them over and over until they became as much a part of me as blonde hair and blue eyes. Soon after that embarrassing encounter, I had plucked up the courage to attend a service at his white weatherboard church tucked into the bend at the end of Flinders Parade. Perched on an old wooden pew at the rear of the church, I'd heard him tell the congregation that warm winds embrace God's words, carry them far beyond our small church beside the bay and our two large islands and our immense Pacific Ocean.

Months later, when I had attained a modicum of spiritual confidence, I imagined beads of islands strung across the globe and me island hopping, a faithful messenger spreading the word. Youthful aspirations supplanted too soon by work, marriage and children, potent truths of the adult world.

Memory receded, I refocused on the minister sitting opposite, watched him remove his glasses and place them carefully on the desk. 'Sometimes we need to return to the past in order to move forward,' he said, leaning towards me. 'It's easy to become comfortable with our spiritual lives, even complacent. We worship regularly, say our prayers, do good works and think this is all that's required of us. But God may have other plans, so once in a while it helps to return to the beginning, rediscover the spark that ignited our faith and let it show us the way.'

'Do you think God has plans for me?'

'I do, otherwise you wouldn't be here. Eden College isn't a holiday camp.'

Anxious to escape his penetrating gaze, I averted my eyes. 'The thought of an unplanned future is alarming.'

He made no comment. 'Let the world drift away, sink down to that place where God dwells and be open to the truth however painful it may be. Don't be afraid of what God asks you to do, we're never asked to do the impossible.'

The rustle of thin paper drew my attention away from the desk's scratched surface.

'Every test that you have experienced is the kind that normally comes to people,' he said, reading slowly from his well-worn bible, *'but God keeps his promise, and he will not allow you to be tested beyond your power to remain firm; at the time you are put to the test, he will give you the strength to endure it.'*

Despite apprehension, the words seeped into me and found their place. 'Thanks, Choddy,' I said, after a protracted silence.

'I hope it helped. Remember, I'm always here if you need to talk.' Twisting his chair around to face the window, he appeared to be studying a tree clouded with pure white blossom. 'Changing direction isn't easy, Julia. Initially I came here to recharge my spiritual and emotional batteries. Ten years in South Africa had taken their toll. When I was asked to stay on as resident minister, I thought maybe I needed a longer break. Conducting services and Old Testament teaching seemed such uncomplicated duties. But helping other people sort out their souls isn't an easy task and sometimes I think life was less complex in Soweto.'

Soweto, a township on the outskirts of Johannesburg, subject of brief bulletins on ABC news, dusty streets, ramshackle houses, police brutality. Footage observed from the safety of my family room half a world away; commentary heard but not digested. 'I have a lot to learn, thank you for pointing me in the right direction.' I rose quickly, moved away from his desk. The creak of his chair stayed my steps; I heard a sharp intake of breath, waited for further insights. Nothing stirred save blossomed branches, tossed by summer breeze. I slipped out of the room, leaving substandard home-work on the desk.

———

Later that day, sitting by a window in one of the small lounges, watching petals float like pink snowflakes to the green lawn, I felt a sudden compulsion to rush outside, gather handfuls of blossom and seal them in a jar. This first northern spring seemed too precious to lose to the wind.

'I miss the dazzling bougainvillea and the scarlet hibiscus flowers,' a voice said behind me.

Swinging around, I saw Jeremiah standing in the doorway hugging his thin body. 'Come and see the blossom. It's beautiful, a pink carpet.'

'I miss its perfume potent in the hot night.' He walked towards the window.

'Are you feeling homesick today?'

'Don't *you* miss warm winds and golden sun?'

'Sometimes, but I didn't come here for the weather.'

'I feel alienated.' He turned away from the window. 'These grey skies are subduing my spirit. Surely *you* under-stand, Julia, Australia is a land of sunshine?'

'Yes, it is, but we must look beyond the clouds.'

'See what, a silver lining?'

'I was thinking of God.'

He sighed. 'God is the reason I came here, but I am finding it difficult to worship in that cold chapel.'

'It is rather draughty. Why don't you sit down and tell me about your country, it might help to dispel the home-sickness?'

He nodded, ambled over to a second easy chair posi-tioned against the wall opposite, lowered himself slowly.

Long thin legs encased in faded blue denim stretched out in front of him, he tilted his head back and stared at the ceiling.

I thought perhaps he had changed his mind, but before I could return to pink blossom, he gave a slight cough and lowering his head, began to speak, his tone reminiscent of a lecturer. 'Nigeria is not a great country, it is corrupt, dirty, noisy. My home is the city of Lagos; it is hot, smelly, ugly. The lagoon is full of untreated sewage and wrecked cars. Children dressed in rags hawk cheap goods to motorists trapped in traffic. Exhaust fumes fill the air and there are beggars on every street.' He leant forward, looked directly into my face. 'Why do I stay you may ask when I have an English education and have been offered good jobs in other countries?' He paused as though waiting for my response, but I sensed his question was rhetorical, so remained silent.

'I stay because Nigeria is my country and I love it.'

'What brought you to Eden College?' I asked, relieved to have something to say.

'A few months ago, I was challenged in a dream to use my engineering skills for the benefit of others less fortunate, especially those in the inland villages where life is so hard. My church sent me here to consider this calling.' He sighed, a long, muted exhalation that hung in the mild atmosphere like gossamer threads. 'It is not easy to obey God's will; I can't just rush off into the interior. I have my family to consider.'

'You have children?'

'Yes, two boys. Luke and Matthew, thirteen and eleven. A handful.'

'I know.'

'You have boys?'

'A boy and a girl. Stephen and Penny, eighteen and sixteen.'

'They are not children; they are grown up.'

'I'm sure they would agree with you, but I believe they still need plenty of care.'

'We all do,' he murmured, 'whatever our ages.'

I nodded in agreement. 'What does your wife think about leaving Lagos?'

'Elizabeth is a doctor; she would be happy to heal the sick any place.'

'Not many obstacles then. You'll have it all sorted in no time.'

He responded by easing his lean frame out of the chair and walking over to the window where he stood gazing out at the garden. Suddenly the palms of his hands thumped the glass. 'I must get out of here,' he cried. 'I am being suffocated by these walls.'

'It is a bit stuffy. How about a walk on the cliffs?'

'Cliffs?' Lifting his hands from the glass, he twisted around. 'Yes, yes, I can see the white water again.'

'How about we meet by the back door in five minutes? I have to fetch my jacket.'

'Me too.' He grinned. 'I won't forget warm clothing this time.'

———

Wind lashed the fields, my ears ached, and dampness invaded thin-soled shoes. Rain threatened, but Jeremiah, like Martin a few days earlier, remained determined to reach the cliffs.

'I am going to stand on the edge and shout,' he informed

me as we left the fields behind and stepped into the full force of the wind.

'Why?' I asked, but he was forging ahead and either didn't hear me or refused to answer. My ears were screaming in pain, so I stopped to release my parka hood.

When I reached the cliff path, he was propped against a large rock tugging his tuft of beard and crooning in what I assumed was his native tongue. Desperate to find some protection from the incessant wind, I ran forward and collapsed beside him. When he hadn't acknowledged my presence after several minutes, I sat hugging my knees, concerned I had interrupted prayer.

All of a sudden, he sprang to his feet and without a glance at me, ran to the cliff edge, stood arms outstretched shouting at the sea. Even if I had understood the language, I was too far away to hear clearly, so once again could only speculate whether his words were prayer or anger. But there was no mistaking how close he stood to the edge; one false step would send him crashing onto the rocks below. Shuddering at the thought, I reminded myself he was an adult and knew the risks. Why then did I feel responsible for his welfare?

At last he stopped waving his arms, pulled something from his coat pocket and threw it over the cliff. Then, as though such actions were an everyday occurrence, he turned around and walked nonchalantly back to the rock.

'They are content now,' he announced, looking down at me.

'Who?'

'My Yoruba ancestors. I have fulfilled my obligations.'

'Why practice Nigerian rituals on a Welsh island?' I scrambled to my feet. 'I thought you were a Christian?'

Without further explanation, he spun on his heel and

set off down the chalk path. Shaking my head, I hurried away from crumbling cliffs and disconcerting behaviour.

Heavy rain began to fall as I turned off the cliff path to follow the track leading to the fields. Slippery ground slowed my pace, but before long I caught sight of Jeremiah, so called out his name. For a change, he stopped running, stood staring at rows of crops waving in the wind.

'Bloody climate,' he shouted when I came within earshot. 'No wonder so many of you emigrated to warmer lands. I can't think why anyone in his right mind would want to live in this sun-forsaken place.'

Rain pitted my face like shards of ice. I shouted back in agreement.

Lightning flashed in the darkening sky; distant thunder rolled in from the sea. *At least ten minutes hard running to reach the house,* I calculated, hurrying towards him. Heads bowed, we raced along the track, Jeremiah several paces ahead. We were in sight of the woods when he halted, almost mid-stride it seemed, and twisting around, declared in a loud voice, 'I am not walking through those trees in a storm.'

'But we'll get soaked if we stay here.'

'Better wet than dead.' He pushed past me.

'Where are you going?' I called as he turned onto the cliff path. I had assumed he would seek shelter behind the row of thick shrubs planted as a windbreak at the cliff end of the fields, not head for an exposed rock.

There was no response.

'Bloody idiot,' I muttered, but nevertheless plodded after him, conscious of his vulnerability and my self-imposed responsibility. 'Jeremiah, wait,' I yelled, as the distance between us lengthened.

His pace slowed, and hunched shoulders straightened. 'What is the matter now?'

'I've just remembered there are some old stables around here,' I said, on reaching his side. 'I saw them marked on a map in the library. If we retrace our steps and follow the path for a few hundred metres, we should come to another track. The stables are at the end of it.'

'We must find these stables without delay,' he replied, taking my hand and pulling me along the path. 'You may think it strange in a grown man, but I am very afraid of storms.'

And primitive gods and being alone by a dying fire, I thought, recalling his plea last evening.

Almost blinded by rain, we pushed forward, searching for signs of another path. Lightning blazed over the sea illuminating iron-grey waves tipped with white, thunder edged closer. Jeremiah tightened his grip and I felt as though my fingers were about to break. Ahead, the chalk path stretched around the cove, a single white line leading nowhere.

'This is ridiculous,' I shouted, after several violent gusts had all but halted our progress. 'We should take our chances in the trees.'

'No way!' He jerked my arm.

Shoes slipped on the sodden ground, I stumbled over a lump of chalk sticking out of the path and fell against him. Caught off balance, we tumbled to the ground and rolled towards a windswept bush.

'Now I have hurt you with my foolishness,' he cried, sitting up and burying his face in his hands.

'It's all right, I'm not hurt.' Brushing damp soil from my clothes, I noticed blood oozing from small tear in the right knee of my jeans, so fished a tissue out of my pocket. The wound soon stopped bleeding, but as I pushed the bloody tissue into the bush, my hand touched something hard. Parting the branches revealed a row of white rocks similar to the one I had tripped over. 'Hey, what's this?'

Jeremiah turned around and bending over, caressed a rock with his fingers.

'They seem to have been deliberately put here. What do you think they mean?'

'They are signs,' he answered, his tone confident.

'Religious symbols?'

'No, a message from the sea.'

Before I could seek an explanation, he had jumped to his feet, backed away from stones and bush. Letting go of the branches, I struggled to my feet, brushed dirt from the back of my jeans. When I rejoined the path, he had vanished.

'Jeremiah,' I yelled, fearing the worst.

No answer.

'Jeremiah, where are you?' I scanned the cliff, saw nothing but flattened grass edged with white chalk. A scream swelled in my throat, I swallowed it fast as hands materialised and clutched the edge.

A grinning face appeared. 'Come Julia,' he said, calmly, 'I have found a cave. There are steps cut into the cliff here, the message in the stones has saved us from the storm.'

Rough-hewn steps led down to a narrow ledge. Flat against the cliff face, a cave mouth yawned, dark and uninviting. Jeremiah stepped inside without hesitation, but I lingered in the entrance, loath to enter absolute blackness. Gathering courage, I searched for a chink of light, found nothing, not even the whites of his eyes. Alarmed, I screamed out his name and stepping forward, tripped over his crouched figure.

'Julia, you want to hurt me?'

'Sorry, I couldn't see you, I was scared you'd fallen.'

'I am trying to light a fire. Someone has been here before, and recently. I found fuel and matches over in the corner.' A match flickered, illuminating his face for an instant. He lit another, held it against a pile of kindling until flames licked thin twigs. Next, he added larger pieces, taking care not to smother the blaze. Framed in firelight, his damp face gleamed polished onyx, smooth and hard. Spreading out his hands, he warmed them briefly before turning to me. 'Now my friend, we have light and warmth.'

'Thank you.'

Eyes fixed on my face, he cradled my cold cheeks in his hands.

For many minutes, we sat in silence staring at the fire. Small twigs collapsed into the red centre; the violent outer world retreated as perfect peace pervaded the tiny cave. He slipped his arm around my waist, an ordinary action that comforted. I rested a hand on his thigh, felt the warmth of his skin ease my ice-cold palm. Tiny blue flames danced along a log, reminding me of raindrops sparkling in bright sunshine. Velvet lips brushed my forehead, meandered over eyes and nose and cheeks. Taut skin relaxed, I parted my lips to inhale fire-warmed air. Hot breath entered my mouth; I savoured the sweetness and warmth of long summer afternoons. Soon, the atmosphere grew thick with honey; breathless we raised our heads, gulped cooler air.

Spellbound, I watched gleaming white teeth clasp my parka zip and swiftly separate cold metal. Nimble fingers unfastened coat buttons and with a flourish he spread our outer garments beside the fire. Remaining layers of wool and cotton flew over our heads, lifelong inhibitions abandoned like a caterpillar's carapace. Cushioned by the quilted lining of a borrowed jacket, I lay limbs languid, firelight flickering over bare skin; transitory pigment destined to fade. Beside me, enduring blackness leaned towards the fire, absorbed its many-hued heat.

Long fingers drew drum circles on my breasts, then progressed towards the dark centre, pressing gently. Mystical music pervaded my head; I rippled and rolled to primeval rhythms. On and on the drummer played, until my surface cracked, and my cries drowned every beat.

CHAPTER FOUR

Outside my bedroom window breeze murmured through fresh green leaves and birdsong welcomed new dawn, but I lay rigid beneath thick blankets, trapped in yesterday's tempestuous environment. Sleep had evaded me throughout the night; I couldn't quiet turbulent thoughts, escape graphic images. Over and over again I had asked myself why?

Two decades of fidelity, an enduring relationship, never before had I desired another man. Brian and I were content with one another; our marriage glided along a smooth path, arguments rarely ruffling the surface. We had a good life, considered ourselves blessed. Around us, friends and colleagues terminated partnerships with increasing regularity. We listened to their stories, offered tea and sympathy but failed to understand the real reason behind the frequent demise of contemporary marriage.

'They have no staying power, that's the trouble,' Brian had said, following news of yet another separation. 'One big blue and they call it quits. It's just the same at work, the going gets tough and they chuck it in. That's another reason the country's going to the dogs. There's no real commitment to anything these days.'

Ten days ago, I had readily agreed with him, secure in the knowledge our marriage was strong, impenetrable. I had underestimated the power of passion. Trapped in a cave with a mysterious companion, the awesome energy of desire had smashed all my defences. Exposed to such intense heat, little wonder my soft centre had melted.

All through the night I had prayed for forgiveness, asking repeatedly for a second chance, the opportunity to prove myself a worthy disciple in this holy place. But to my dismay, no still small voice had offered a modicum of empathy, or even the chill of chastisement. Silence intimidated, what could I do to restore contact?

Sunlight filtered through the curtains, creating patterns of warmth on the worn grey carpet. Grateful, I raised weary limbs, reached out for yesterday's crumpled clothes.

———

Chapel stone pressed against my knees, cracking the scab on my grazed skin. Pain disrupted prayer, desperately I tried to retrieve lost words. At last they returned, flooding my tense body with relief. Hands clasped tight, I began anew, but the words drifted away, floated just beyond my reach, taunting me with their presence.

'No forgiveness without repentance, no forgiveness without repentance.' The Gospel message echoed within me and still I found nothing to say.

A single tear slid down my cheek, splashed onto impermeable stone. I closed my eyes in a vain attempt to prevent other tears falling. Prayers drowned. Bereft of familiar language, I plummeted into a void where darkness viscous as treacle enveloped me, clinging to my skin and swelling the silence. Then, an unwelcome question wormed its way into the stillness and I struggled to the surface, disbelief clinging to my lips.

What if God has stolen all my words and left me empty as that Sunday tomb?

Distraught, I fled from failure to a world where daffodils tilted yellow heads to a cloudless sky, turned tear-bright eyes to a gentle sun.

———

Preoccupied with prayer disaster, I sat head bowed on the old wooden bench positioned to the left of the chapel door, oblivious to morning's increasing warmth.

'Glorious day, isn't it?' Donna remarked.

I jerked upright, cricking my neck.

'Sorry, I didn't mean to startle you.' She sat down beside me. 'You're up early this morning.'

'I couldn't sleep.'

'I'm not surprised; it was real cold last night. I'm going to ask for another blanket.'

'Good idea.'

'I didn't see you at supper, where were you sitting?'

'I wasn't there, didn't feel like food.'

She leant towards me. 'Julia, are you ok?'

'Fine, just a bit tired.'

'It's so peaceful in the chapel first thing in the morning.'

'I found it lonely today.'

'Then come back in with me.'

'That's not what I meant.'

She frowned, and I felt a sudden compulsion to explain my early morning need for solitude.

'I had something important to say, but I couldn't find the right words. Not that it would have made any difference, God wasn't there.'

'Perhaps you just couldn't feel his presence?'

'I'm telling you God wasn't there.'

'Ok, ok I believe you.'

What on earth was the matter with me? She was only trying to help. 'Sorry, I didn't mean to snap.'

'Don't let what happened in the chapel get you down. We all find it difficult to pray sometimes.' She patted my hand. 'Go and have some breakfast, it'll lift your spirits.'

———

In the dining room, I sat alone at a small table near the door, poised for a quick exit. Jeremiah didn't show, for which I was thankful. What could I say to him? How could I explain my behaviour? I had no idea why I'd allowed him to make love to me. But it couldn't have been love; we had only known each other for a few days. I imagined he would be feeling rather smug having made a conquest with so little effort. Who was next on his list: Donna, Hannah, Ruth? I envisaged a stream of visitors to the cave, smoke from myriad fires blackening the roof. Of course, he'd known the cave's location, his fear of storms a ploy to entice me inside. And the fire and his warm hands and his hot breath and his music burrowing beneath my skin—how could I have resisted?

A bell rang. I gulped hot tea, then hurried to class.

———

New Testament studies occupied the entire morning; Jeremiah's continuing absence proving helpful. Immersed in familiar text, John's Gospel had always been my favourite, guilt and weariness retreated to a corner of my mind. May Gordon's lively interpretation and encouragement of class discussion soon transformed the printed word into living images that seemed to dance before my eyes. Delighted and relieved, I saw Jesus heal the sick, talk to his disciples, turn water into wine.

A college clock struck twelve, prompting May to close her bible and return to her desk near the whiteboard, where she placed textbooks in a neat pile. Determined to revisit the chapel before lunch, I stuffed pen and books into my bag and was about to pick up my bible when she said, 'Before you all disappear for lunch, I'd like to hear one of my favourite passages from John.'

Damn, an unnecessary delay, I thought, unaware her eyes had alighted on me. 'Julia, would you please read John fifteen verses five to nine.'

Pages rustled as I hastened to find the place. '*I am the vine and you are the branches,*' I began, trying not to rush. '*Whoever remains in me, and I in him, will bear much fruit; for you can do nothing without me. Whoever does not remain in me is thrown out like a branch and dries up; such branches are gathered up and thrown into the fire, where they are burnt. If you remain in me and my words remain in you, then you will ask for anything you wish, and you shall have it. My Father's glory is shown by your bearing much fruit; and in this way you become my disciples.*'

She smiled. 'Thank you, Julia. Tomorrow we'll discuss the whole of John 15.'

Grabbing my bag, I raced out of the door.

———

Alone in the chapel, I re-read the gospel text aloud to quiet my mind before attempting prayer. Then I remembered Choddy's reassuring words, 'I didn't ask you to dig up the roots,' and before I could close the bible resting on my knees, metaphors employed in my hybrid creation/parable homework swam before my eyes. *I am the vine, and my Father is the gardener,'* I read slowly, concentrating on every word of the fifteenth verse. Once more a gardener had offered me hope, wise words to contemplate when all seemed bleak. Clasping my hands together, I began to pray.

A breeze blew through the open window and I shivered as confidence cooled. Leaning back against the wooden pew, I waited for further words. Minutes passed, perhaps I had said enough. Whispers arose, gathered pace, swirling around my head like clouds whipping up a storm. 'Test,' I blurted out, 'you have tested me.'

Breeze freshened, petals quivered, tumbled from altar flowers.

'But I failed the test,' I cried. 'I am the branch that doesn't bear fruit; I've been cut off and thrown into the fire. And it's your fault because you broke your promise. You didn't give me the strength to endure the test and now I'm finished, nothing but grey ash.' Tears streaming down my face, I ran from the dim chapel into bright sunshine.

When I had recovered my equilibrium, I retreated to the dining room to fill the hollow space with food. Around me, fellow students chatted and laughed; I nodded at intervals to appear sociable, but kept moist eyes firmly fixed on my plate.

Martin approached when I was putting my used cutlery

into the relevant bucket on the trolley near the door. 'Hi Julia, have you seen Jeremiah today?'

'No, and he wasn't at May's class this morning.'

'It seems no one's seen him today.' He frowned. 'I'd better go up to his room and check he's all right.'

'I'll go if you like,' I offered, grasping the opportunity to confront him in a private space. 'Which room is it?'

'Number thirteen on the second floor. Thanks Julia. Let me know if he needs anything.'

'Sure.' I headed for the door.

———

Outside number thirteen, I hesitated before knocking lightly, half-hoping Jeremiah wasn't in or wouldn't answer.

'Who is it?' a gruff voice demanded.

'Julia. Are you sick?'

'Come in, the door is not locked.'

I found him sitting cross-legged on the floor, wrapped in the red blanket I had seen him wear at morning prayers, an open book on his knees. Unsure whether to approach, I lingered in the doorway, said quietly, 'Jeremiah, I came to er, to explain.'

'I'm the one that should explain.' He looked up. 'Please come in and sit down.'

The door closed automatically as I stepped forward. Ignoring the easy chair opposite the bed, I sat on the floor in front of him. Uncertain what to say next, I stared at the floral pattern on the carpet and fiddled with a loose thread on my sweater. 'I think I know why it happened,' I said, addressing my feet.

'I know for sure; it was lust.'

My head jerked upright. 'It was a test, God testing me. I failed miserably and now he won't listen.'

Jeremiah frowned. 'What on earth are you talking about?'

'I've been to the chapel twice today. Each time I prayed over and over for forgiveness, but it was no use.'

Leaning towards me, he grabbed my shoulders and shook them roughly. 'Stupid woman, God has nothing to do with what happened in the cave or in the chapel. That was the Devil's work.'

I shuddered. 'I don't believe in the Devil.'

Sighing, he removed his hands. 'Then you'd better start believing 'cos he's all around us on this island.'

'Don't be ridiculous!'

'Don't you contradict me, woman,' he shouted.

Scrambling to my feet, I headed for the door, but as I reached for the handle, he gripped my shoulder.

'Please don't go. I'm sorry. I shouldn't have spoken to you like that. Let me try to explain.'

I hesitated before retracing my steps, sat primly on the easy chair, hands folded in my lap.

Resuming his position on the carpet, he pulled the red blanket tighter around his body before turning to face me. 'I had to escape from that stuffy lounge, my head was full of cottonwool, so when you suggested a walk it seemed a good idea.' Shoulders slumped, he sighed deeply. 'I went for a walk with you to clear my head. Clear my head, Julia not screw you.'

I squirmed, not so much at the word—he could have used a much cruder verb—but the sordidness it implied.

'If I'd wanted that,' he continued, 'I would have picked a better place. But I didn't have any choice; that Devil-man got under my skin, pushed away all my defences.' He turned away, focused his attention on the wall above my head. 'I saw his face in the dancing flames, heard his voice all over the cave. "You can have her," he said, "you can possess her soft warm body." So, I touched your skin and it was like velvet. And there was no protest, no white hand raised to slap my black face.' Lowering his head, he looked directly into my eyes. 'Don't you see, that Devil-man had got under your skin too?'

I grasped the arms of the chair to still my shaking hands.

'Now I don't know what to do,' he cried. 'I can't just pretend it didn't happen.' The red blanket sagged on his drooping shoulders.

Eager to allay his distress, I leant towards him. 'It was a stupid mistake Jeremiah, but it's over now.'

'How do we know it's over? You could be carrying my child.'

'No, that's not possible, I had my tubes tied years ago.'

'Oh, end of story then.' He rose stiffly and walked over to the window.

Images from the grim reaper advertisement flashed before my eyes. 'Is it? Sterilisation doesn't protect me from AIDS.'

He twisted around. 'What are you implying?'

'How do I know you haven't got AIDS? It's rampant in Africa.'

'How dare you,' he hissed, black eyes blazing, 'I don't sleep around. How do I know you're clean? It's common knowledge white women are promiscuous.'

Leaping to my feet, I ran towards him, one hand raised as if to strike. 'I've never been unfaithful before, not in twenty years. Never, never, I swear.'

He caught my wrist, held it high above my head for a moment before dropping it as though it was burning him.

Then, his head sank to his chest and he began to whimper like a wounded animal.

'I shouldn't have come to see you,' I stammered, forcing my feet backwards. I had to get out of his room.

'I'm sorry Julia,' he called out as I reached the door. 'I'm not angry with you, I'm mad at me for gettin' sucked in by that old Devil-man. I should have known better at my age. Please forgive me.'

Once more the door handle turned beneath my fingers. 'I, I need some fresh air.' The door opened; I headed for the stairs.

Footsteps pounded down the corridor after me. 'Wait, Julia, please wait.'

Two steps down I stopped and turned to face him. 'Go back your room, Jeremiah. I'm going to the cliff top to shout at the sea.'

'Whatever for?'

'God refuses to help so I thought I'd ask your ancestors for assistance.' The words were out of my mouth before I'd considered their significance.

Black eyes widened. 'I don't think you should do that.'

My left hand tightened around the banister. 'Why not?'

'You don't understand the complexities of Yoruba culture. Your people may have practiced Christianity for two thousand years, but we Yoruba prefer to be flexible about religion. Some of us are Muslim, some Christian, some worship the ancient ancestral gods.'

'But I thought *you* were a Christian?'

'I am.'

'Then why worship your ancestors?'

'Haven't you been listening? I'm keeping my options open.'

'That's a cop-out, Jeremiah.'

'Not in my world.'

I shook my head, turned to scurry down the stairs.

———

High above crashing waves we stood together hurling petitions into a grey sea, but the wind flung every word back in our faces and I quickly realised the futility of appealing to long-dead Yoruba. Even if it were possible to communicate with spirits, would they be interested in our misdemeanour? I didn't even know if we had broken tribal law. 'Jeremiah, it's useless,' I said, tugging at his arm. 'They're not listening.'

'I know, they have abandoned me.' Defeated, he crumpled to the ground.

'Perhaps it's because I'm here? I'll go back to the house.'

'No, don't go.' He clutched my leg. 'Don't leave me alone with my demons.'

Obedient, I sat beside him, slipped my arm around his waist and drew him close. Huddled together, we looked out to sea, the slap of waves on rock and wind rippling short grass the only movement, the only conversation.

After a long silence, he shifted his gaze to my solemn face. 'Africa is too far away, Julia. Her hills and valleys are no longer visible. I must turn my eyes from the sea face the wrath of my Christian God and the mocking laughter of his Devil. Lead us not into temptation and deliver us from evil we ask daily in the chapel, but do we really understand what we are saying? No, they are merely familiar words recited without thinking, empty as sea-shells tossed on the shore.'

'Empty as sea-shells,' I repeated, devoid of original thought.

'I must dig deep.' He scratched the chalk with a thick fingernail. 'I must unearth new language.'

'Do you think we could explore together?' I asked tentatively. No words emerged. Saddened, I placed a hand on the ground and prepared to rise.

Bending his head, he sealed our new alliance with his lips.

CHAPTER FIVE

IN CLASS WE TURNED FAMILIAR PAGES, LISTENED TO familiar language, debated familiar theology. Anticipating fresh insight, I made every effort to immerse myself in the texts, but words and phrases drifted away, vanished in the summer sky. Like clouds they had no substance, could offer me nothing except rain.

Beside me, Donna's face radiated confidence and faith. Each day she wrote copious notes, asked pertinent questions, took a leading role in class discussions. Jealous of her diligence, I began to avoid her both at mealtimes and after class. Most evenings I spent in the library wading through one book after another, desperately trying to find a way forward. Sometimes, I encountered Jeremiah sitting in a corner, hunched over a book or writing in his notebook. He always looked up and smiled as I passed but made no attempt to whisper a greeting or suggest a meeting elsewhere. I convinced myself he was obeying the library notice on silence.

After seven days, I feared he'd forgotten our pledge to search for new truths together, yet I seemed unable to make the first move. The previous day I had spotted him in the dining room, but as I approached his table felt colour tinge my cheeks and the words I'd intended to say evaporated before I could open my mouth. All I could do was smile timidly and scurry away like a frightened child. Oblivious to my distress, he laughed and talked with all around him. Longing to discuss my atypical behaviour, I considered visiting Choddy's office but quickly dismissed the idea. How could I articulate what I didn't comprehend?

Donna might have been able to help, but I had snubbed her and lacked the courage to apologise. On several occasions, I'd taken the coward's way out and written her a note. None ever reached her pigeonhole in the lobby.

———

On the eighth day, I abandoned my evening visit to the library and returned to my room straight after supper. Staring at bedroom walls seemed infinitely preferable to staring at pages of bewildering text. What seemed like hours later, I was sitting at my desk, running a finger over its scratched surface when someone knocked on the door. 'Come in,' I called, relieved at the prospect of conversation.

'I thought I'd catch you in the library,' Donna remarked, closing the door behind her, 'but Jeremiah said you hadn't been there this evening.'

I blushed at the mention of his name and quickly turned my head.

'Overdoing it with the study, aren't you?' she continued. 'Why don't you leave some time for socialising? We haven't talked in a week.'

'You seem pretty busy yourself.'

'Sure, but I can always make space for a friend.' A warm arm hugged my shoulder.

Guilt swam to the surface. 'Donna I owe you an apology. You probably realise I've been avoiding you. It's nothing you've done,' I added hastily, grasping her free hand. 'I'll try to explain if you'll let me.'

She disentangled herself and moved towards the bed.

'You seem so absorbed and confident in class,' I began when she had settled, legs straight out in front of her, back against the wall. 'It's obvious your faith's increasing. I should be pleased for you, instead I'm jealous.'

'Why, no one could be more immersed in study than you are, Julia?'

'But I'm a fraud.' Tears threatened to spill over flushed cheeks. 'I read and read until my eyes sting and my head aches, but nothing sinks in, not one word. I came here to grow spiritually but I'm shrinking fast.' I sniffed. 'Soon I'll disappear altogether.'

'Something else on your mind?'

I hung my head.

'I understand Julia, he's an attractive man.'

'Is it that obvious?'

'It is.'

'I feel like shit,' I murmured, raising my head slowly.

'Why, what's wrong with falling in love?'

'This isn't about love.'

'You could've fooled me. I've watched you when he's around. Why not admit your feelings, it's not a sin to love someone?'

'But it couldn't have been love, we hardly knew each other.'

'So, you had sex,' she said calmly. 'Never a good idea when you've just met someone in my opinion. But there's nothing you can do to alter past events so why don't you enjoy the falling in love?'

Why no mention of sin? I couldn't believe it, had she forgotten the man whose photograph was pinned to my noticeboard? 'I feel so guilty.'

'It's normal to feel desire.'

'But I'm married, adultery's a sin. It says so in the bible.'

'So that's what this is about; you're waiting for the wrath of God. Are you afraid of expulsion from Eden?'

'I did eat the apple.'

A mischievous smile danced on her lips. 'I bet it was sweet.'

She's applied the wrong adjective. Ice-cream and chocolate cake are sweet, sex with Jeremiah was intense, pungent. I risked a half-smile.

'That's better.' She leant forward, took my hand in hers. 'Aside from the creation story, if you feel it was a mistake, put him behind you and move on.'

'I can't, I'm stuck in a hole. I can't even pray now.'

She looked thoughtful. 'I don't think you want to move on.'

'I don't know where to go next.'

'You can't think straight because you're in love.'

'Please don't keep harping on about that.'

She dropped my hand and sat back against the wall. 'But don't you see Julia, love explains everything: why you can't concentrate on your studies, why you can't pray, why you can't look him in the eye. If you didn't feel anything for Jeremiah you could walk away, dismiss the sex as a foolish mistake. Love is an all-consuming emotion; it blocks everything else. Don't you remember the first time you fell in love?'

'That was different, I was only sixteen.'

'So?'

'It was an innocent affair. We held hands on the school bus, shared lollies and chewing gum. Love was light and easy, only tiny ripples of desire. Passion wasn't part of our vocabulary.'

'But you're grown up now, Julia, passion is a normal emotion. My life is full of it. Passion for my kids, passion for God, even for my job occasionally.'

'Passion of that kind poses no threat, but this, oh God, the violence terrified me.'

Her eyes widened. 'Are you trying to tell me he raped you?'

'No, no, I mean the violence within *me*. I've never experienced such frenzied emotion. I couldn't get enough of him; I was totally out of control!'

She took a sudden interest in the hem of her sweater. 'I had a similar experience years ago. Do you want to know what a friend of mine said when I was full of regret?'

'Yes, if it's not too painful to recall.'

'No way, can't remember the last time I even thought of the guy.' She looked up. 'My friend said, "Lust such as you've described swells swiftly, but it lacks substance and soon deflates when removed from the source of heat."'

'Sound advice.'

'Sure, but I'd like to add something. I don't believe your entire life has been altered by an isolated act. Think of it as an experience, perhaps one you had to have. But you do need to remember this island existence is only temporary. Brian and the kids are your real life.'

Silenced by truth, I re-focused on the noticeboard, fragments of life captured in photographs, smiling faces to remind me of home. If only I could connect with them for a few minutes, but students weren't supposed to request use of the telephone unless the matter was urgent.

'There is an alternative,' she added in a low voice.

I turned away from poignant photographs. 'What?'

She rummaged in her pocket, pulled out a crumpled piece of paper and pressed it into my palm. 'You and Jeremiah could be just friends.'

Hands trembling, I smoothed out the note. 'Dear Julia,' he had written in large red letters. 'I am lonely. Please be my loving friend. I remain yours. Jeremiah.'

Tears flowed free as the island stream winding through woods, where Jeremiah and I had shaken hands and engaged in that first brief conversation. A chance encounter; two summer term students admiring an unfamiliar environment. Loving friendship offered an opportunity to make amends, to begin again. 'I can't thank you enough for...'

'No need.' Donna wrapped her arms around me and rocked me gently until tears diminished.

Later that evening, I attended 'day end prayers' for the first time in over a week, sensed my spirit stir as Choddy blessed us and bade us goodnight. Afterwards, I looked for Jeremiah but couldn't find him in the library or any of the small sitting rooms. Disheartened, I headed for the main staircase, too weary from lack of sleep to join others in the dining room for a warm drink. I began to climb, each step an effort as though I had just completed a marathon. At the second floor, I stopped altogether and sat down, loath to attempt another flight. Leaning against the banister, chest heaving, I glanced down the corridor. One, two, three doors to pass before I reached number thirteen.

Jeremiah answered my knock with a faint, 'Who's there?'

'It's Julia. I hope I didn't wake you?'

'I wasn't asleep, come in, the door is not locked.'

Wrapped in his red blanket, he sat on the bed, a pen in his hand, a notebook balanced on raised knees. 'Have a seat.' He gestured towards the easy chair opposite the bed.

'I don't want to interrupt your writing, finish what you're doing.'

'No problem, I can write tomorrow.' He closed the notebook and pushed it aside. 'Friends are more important than words.' He flashed a brilliant smile.

'Your friendship brought me here,' I replied, sliding into the chair. 'And God.'

'He has returned then. I am pleased for you.'

'What about you?'

'Still I struggle with my demons.'

'I'd like to help you banish them.'

'Really?'

'That's what friends are for, to be there when the going gets tough.'

He leant forward to clasp my hand. 'I thank you with all my heart, Julia but I don't believe anyone can banish *my* demons. They remain to remind me of sin, to punish me.' He hung his head. 'Oh, I am so ashamed.'

'So am I, but we can't go back and change anything. Why don't we begin our friendship again, make this the first day?'

'The first day,' he murmured and releasing my hand, twisted around to retrieve his bible from the bedside cabinet. He flicked the flimsy pages with a practised hand. '*In the beginning,*' he read softly, '*when God created the universe, the earth was formless and desolate. The raging ocean that covered everything was engulfed in total darkness, and the power of God was moving over the water. Then God commanded, 'let there be light' and light appeared. God was pleased with what he saw. Then he separated the light from the darkness and he named the light 'day' and the darkness 'night'. Evening passed, and morning came—that was the first day.'*

The bible slipped from his knees onto the floor. His hand brushed my leg as he bent over to retrieve it. I trembled at his touch. Oblivious to my distress, he placed the bible back on the bedside cabinet and rearranged his blanket.

'Come, sit beside me,' he said softly, making space for me. 'We can pray together.'

Slivers of apprehension crawled across my skin. Trying to ignore them, I moved over to the bed and perched on the edge, my attention focused on the wall opposite.

'You look cold,' he said. 'Come let me warm you.'

I shuddered as if to confirm his comment, then inched further up the bed. Thick red wool enveloped me; I sank into safety.

Silence suffused the room, safe comfortable quiet, awash with peace and the first flickers of re-emerging faith. Later, much later, he broke the silence with a kiss that barely touched my cheek.

We began to talk of our countries, our children, our hopes and fears for the future. Hours passed, down in the foyer the grandfather clock struck midnight. I kissed his cheek, one small kiss well away from his sensuous mouth. His blanket fell from my shoulders as I slid off the bed. So, the first day ended.

CHAPTER SIX

Loving friendship germinated in the damp soil of our temporary island home, broke through to the light and flourished in temperate summer warmth. Destructive heat remained a distant memory, safely contained within the cliff cave.

Grateful to be sharing a unique experience—in mid-life most people couldn't take three months away from careers and family—we also played tourists on occasion, taking photographs of one another beside the lake or on the cliffs.

Africa loomed large in our new relationship. United by a mutual fascination for its complex complexion, the immense continent seething with humanity and bedevilled by political and economic problems, provided us with endless topics of conversation. Far into the long light evenings, we sat on a bench by the lake, or in one another's rooms, discussing diverse landscapes, countries and peoples.

This was my second love affair with Africa. The first had taken place beneath blue Queensland skies during my final year at primary school, when the African continent, once inert on atlas pages, came to dominate my days both in and out of the classroom. The impetus for my burgeoning devotion was a new pupil fresh from the wilds of northern Nigeria.

One overcast Monday morning when winter rain spattered the classroom's louvre windows and a cold breeze blew in from the bay, our teacher, Miss Eliot, informed us that a new girl would be arriving the following day. She went on to explain that Dorothy Green had spent the whole of her short life in Kenya, Zambia and Nigeria, accompanying her doctor parents on their mission of healing, so she knew nothing of the Australian education system. We were asked to help her settle in.

Most of the girls and a few boys complied, but after a couple of days all of us had exhausted our supply of local knowledge and yearned to hear exotic tales of far-away places. So, following a brief discussion in the playground, a small group of girls gathered around the new classmate and asked her to tell us about the mysterious world she had left behind only weeks earlier.

We knew from the start that Dorothy's stories would eclipse all other schoolyard conversation. Wide-eyed and open-mouthed, we absorbed vivid descriptions of her difficult birth in a mud hut on the shores of Lake Victoria, her almost-drowning as a toddler in a crocodile-infested river and her recent narrow escape from marauding warriors who wanted to sell her to the highest bidder as a virgin-bride. Day after day, fascinating narratives carried us away from a monotonous suburban existence to an enchanted land where every excursion proved exhilarating.

Inevitably, the excitement of schoolyard tales waned, and my classmates reverted to customary games, inviting Dorothy to join them. I, on the other hand felt cheated and spent many solitary hours in a deserted corner of the playground contemplating ways to become part of Dorothy's world, share more of her kaleidoscopic memories. After a week, I decided there was only one way to achieve my goal: I had to become her best friend, the only person to whom she would confide her deepest, darkest recollections.

Our families moved in very different circles, so becoming Dorothy's best friend required immense effort. Although her parents were exiles from a crumbling colonial world and, according to Dorothy, had been forced to abandon all their worldly goods in Africa, they now lived in white-brick splendour high on a hill overlooking Moreton Bay. My family inhabited a small, shabby weatherboard house situated on marshy ground near the water. Low tide exposed our home to the stench of mudflats, while high tide, especially during stormy weather, threatened to submerge us in a stinking stew of seaweed.

One lunch break, just before school finished for the summer holidays and I lost sight of Dorothy forever—she was going to a private high school the following year, I to the local state school—schoolyard conversation turned to sailing in Moreton Bay. In her customary dramatic fashion, Dorothy expressed great longing to experience Australian wind in her hair, the blue Pacific beneath her feet and yards of gleaming canvas above her head.

'My Dad needs an extra deckhand next Sat 'day,' I remarked casually. 'My sister can't come 'cos Aunt Muriel's taking her to the dentist to get her braces fixed.'

Dorothy noticed me for the first time since her flamboyant entry to our classroom several months before. 'Oh, if only Daddy would allow me to sail again,' she said wistfully, 'but he won't hear of it ever since that dreadful episode with the pirates.'

'There aren't any pirates in Moreton Bay,' I said hurriedly before anyone could urge her to elaborate.

'I suppose I could ask Daddy. After all, the worst he can say is no.'

'I'll get my Dad to come and explain how safe our bay is,' I heard myself say. 'If that would be all right?'

'Would you, Julia darling?'

'Of course, that's what friends are for.'

———

Moreton Bay water scudded beneath the bows and hot sun heated the forward deck where Dorothy and I sat close together, our brown summer legs dangling over the side cooling in salty spray. Dad was heading for St Helena Island, intent on introducing our guest to a little local history. I was eager for African tales, but politely answered Dorothy's convict questions before steering the conversation across the continent and the vast Indian Ocean. Fixing her eyes on distant shores, Dorothy took several deep breaths and clasping my hand, embarked on a new African tale. 'One night when the silver moon hid behind cloud curtains and the breeze had dropped to a whisper,' she said, her voice quivering with emotion, 'two huge lions entered our village and began to stalk anything that moved.'

After several lurid descriptions of gruesome deaths, mostly village dogs, I made appropriate comments and asked if she had ever encountered headhunters.

'Once,' she answered, her lower lip trembling.

A long silence followed. I saw terror mirrored in her turquoise eyes, heard a sharp intake of breath, felt pain as sharp nails dug into my soft palm. Then she sighed and together we drifted along wide rivers towards the dark heart of Africa. Rainforest hugged the banks, monkeys chattered in massive trees, birds shrieked and swooped over our flimsy canoe, scaly shapes slithered across mud to disappear beneath murky water. Leaving the river, we followed herds of elephants across vast shimmering plains, stood in the dust on a high Kenyan plateau in the place where, according to Dorothy, humans had first walked upright on the earth.

Later, reliving those glorious tales as I settled down to sleep, I remembered reading an article in National Geographic about the discovery of hominid fossils in a place called Olduvai Gorge, which was somewhere in Africa called the Rift Valley. Niggling doubts began to burrow in my head, leaving holes in my new friend's African tales. Before closing my eyes, I decided to borrow the magazine the next time I visited the library, for if I remembered correctly, the fossils had been found in Tanzania not Kenya.

———

Childhood memories drifted away as a fishing boat skimmed over grey-green waters. Mild breezes and temperature had prompted Jeremiah and me to venture beyond the lake; this afternoon we sat on the cliff top staring at the sea. There had been no shouting at ancestors or throwing gifts into the waves; our prayers late twentieth-century Christian, spoken in low voices, followed by long periods of comfortable silence broken only by the caw of seabirds. The day lingered, light and warm as the hours marched towards night. I had twice suggested we return to the house, but Jeremiah appeared reluctant to leave.

'Sailing across Moreton Bay, drifting in my dreams towards Africa,' I mused, turning my head and raising one hand to stroke his cheek.

He looked puzzled by this juxtaposition of place, so I gave a brief account of my short-lived friendship with Dorothy. She had soon persuaded her wealthy grandfather to buy an ocean-going yacht, so our sea-paths never crossed again.

Jeremiah smiled broadly at my youthful naivety and lightly brushed my arm with cool fingertips.

'But at least her tales took me away from a lacklustre world,' I added, aware of an arm sliding around my shoulders. 'In the sixties, everything interesting happened far away in London, Paris or New York. Australia was still an outpost of empire, stuck in a pre-war mindset.'

'But at least the mother country possessed a familiar face.' His tone was bitter, the smile past tense.

'Familiar?'

'White.' He spat the word into the grass.

'Your country gained independence in nineteen-sixty,' I offered.

'We were delivered from colonial bondage, but freedom did not last.'

'I know,' I said, well-versed in the history of the period. 'It was an appalling civil war.'

'What do you know of war?' he demanded, gripping my shoulder.

'Australians fought in Vietnam.'

'Was your village drenched in blood? Did you watch family and friends die of starvation?'

Images on a small screen, children with bloated stomachs, flies clustered around mucus-encrusted months, the tragedy of Biafra, the clarity of black and white television. Jeremiah would have been about ten. What could I say to take away his pain?

'Talk of war is inappropriate here,' he announced,

following a protracted and uncomfortable silence. 'Come Julia, night beckons, it is time to return to the house.'

I rose quickly, overtly aware of failure. I shouldn't have raised the issue of Biafra. My eagerness to demonstrate knowledge of his country had soured our bright summer evening. How well I knew the history of his continent, how little I understood the psyche beneath his skin.

We walked briskly along the chalk path to the fields, dissension palpable between us. Soon the woods were in sight. I watched thin shoulders rise and fall as he increased his stride. Embracing the night, he disappeared into dark trees.

———

Morning brought heavy showers interspersed with bursts of brilliant sunshine. The garden glowed. Abandoning my pre-breakfast walk, I studied raindrops from my window. Bright bubbles, they clung to leaf and petal. Idly, my fingers drew circles on the wet windowsill.

'Good morning, Julia,' Jeremiah called from the path below my window. 'How beautiful the earth is after rain, come share it with me.'

'Good morning, Jeremiah.' My wave scattered rain-drops. 'I'll be down in a minute.'

His smile was warm as I stepped onto the path. Relieved, I took the proffered hand. The ghosts of civil war had vanished in the night.

Before long we were walking through dripping woods, negotiating puddles and boggy ground. Mud stained my light-coloured sandals. When would I learn to wear appropriate footwear, instead of grabbing the nearest pair of shoes?

'Oak, ash, laurel, holly,' Jeremiah declared, pointing to various trees. 'See, I have done my homework.'

'I'm afraid I forgot all about Welsh flora.'

'Bad girl,' he scolded and slapped my bottom playfully.

Childlike, I pouted.

'Don't spoil a beautiful face.' He lifted my chin with his fingertips.

Obedient, I smiled up at him.

'That's better, now the sun shines in your sapphire eyes.'

Pale cheeks reddened.

'And now you glow, a scarlet hibiscus.' Lips brushed my smiling mouth.

Colour flooded face and neck. How I coveted his dark skin; my lack of pigment betrayed all secrets. Laughing, he danced away from me and disappeared behind a huge oak tree. I considered running back to the house, but soon dismissed such a foolish thought. Games were meant to be fun.

'Boo,' he shouted, jumping out from behind the tree as I passed.

'You'll have to do better than that. I knew you were there.'

'Close your eyes, count to twenty, then come and find me.'

'One, two, three, four...' Raindrops tumbled from a nearby leaf. '...twenty.' After walking a few paces, I stopped to scan the trees. No movement, no sound, wet leaves enfolded me.

'Over here,' he called.

I jumped at the sound of his voice but had no idea which direction it was coming from. Taking three steps forward, I paused once more to look around.

'Gettin' warm.'

Mud invaded my sandals, squeezed between my toes, spongy and cold.

'Warmer.'

Ahead, a small branch waved. The wind misleading me, or was he hiding behind that sodden trunk? I approached cautiously, shivered as the branch anointed my head with water.

'Warmer still.'

Catlike, I crept towards the tree, arms outstretched ready to grab him. The thick trunk hid no one.

'Hot.'

Arms encircled my waist; his breath was warm on my neck. If I were facing him, would I see mischief brewing in his dark eyes?

'Time for breakfast,' he announced and released me.

Game over, I trudged after him to the house.

CHAPTER SEVEN

FOUR WEEKS HAD PASSED SINCE THE BEGINNING OF term and yet today was the first occasion I had opened the notebook intended as a daily journal. Faced with a mass of conflicting and unfamiliar emotions, I had been reluctant to put pen to paper, record for eternity the minutiae of my island disintegration.

When I awoke this morning, the last of a momentous month, I felt sufficiently calm to attempt a few lines. Not that I intended to share these words with anyone, memory and the photographs I took when alone would have to serve when family and friends requested island information. Eight weeks of term remained, an insufficient period when I thought of all I wanted or hoped to achieve at Eden College, so I decided to get up earlier, maximize study time with an hour's work before breakfast. Early morning walks seemed an unnecessary luxury; I would forego them, observe the garden from my window in between reading or writing.

I could have set the alarm for an hour before dawn, studied and then gone for a walk. But I was never an early bird, even on bright December mornings when plovers called their greetings a little after four and sunlight streamed through curtains drawn back a little to catch night breeze. Dawn would be later on the other side of the world, as the winter solstice drew near.

Still tentative, I began by writing about the natural world around me, the delight tempered with disorientation as I adjusted to northern hemisphere flora and flora. Here on the island, we were approaching the longest day of the year, but I still thought of June the twenty-first as the shortest day! For a woman from down under, Britain seemed a topsy-turvy land. Down under what, I wrote, drawing a line under the question to emphasise my confusion. Under or over, what difference did it make on a sphere spinning in space?

Next, I wrote about harmony, sun and moon spinning together, each performing a necessary function. This led to a few lines about wholeness, again from a naturalist perspective, with no mention of spiritual matters. Or perhaps God was there, hiding behind metaphor? Too many questions, I decided and closed the journal.

———

I need not have worried about morning walks, sunshine soon faded and for several days all I could observe from my window were sheets of rain sweeping across lawn and lake. Low cloud further diminished the green panorama, so I withdrew to an inner world where words supplanted weather.

Most evenings I spent with Jeremiah. We both felt the need to fully explore the spiritual world, each acknowledging the advantage of companionship during what was proving, at least for me, an arduous journey. But more than friendship, we had discerned a common goal, a desire to move far beyond the Genesis of Choddy's first lesson.

The Old Testament portrayed a harsh God judging and punishing those who sinned, forgiveness and mercy rarely found in that bloody history of the Jews. Inappropriate doctrine for the post-industrial age, we believed, we were unable to sanction an eye for an eye. So, we abandoned Jehovah and turned our attention to the unconditional love of Jesus. Together, we embarked on a journey through parable, miracle and prayer. In Cana, we supped wine and rejoiced in the first miracle; in Judea, we were baptised; by the Sea of Galilee we witnessed the miracle of the loaves and fishes. Text became truth, past present; the pages of my journal were no longer bereft of Christian symbols.

Outside in the garden, leaves and petals drooped sodden and still, unable to stir in the viscous atmosphere. Sea mist hung in voluminous flounces over flowers and trees, thick curtaining still closed at noon. Sky had merged with earth, the landscape folded inwards. Becalmed on grey seas, the island resisted the pull of time.

Behind sombre drapery, loving friendship continued to blossom, its sweet perfume permeating the farthest corners of our world. As day drifted unnoticed into evening, we sat on his red blanket in his room or mine, our heads almost touching, the bible open before us on the floor. When we turned each page, our fingers met, linked for a second and moved on. At the end of each chapter, we raised our eyes from the text and held each other tenderly. His soft body pressed against me offering comfort and warmth; in his eyes I saw only love, undemanding and true.

Days ended as they began, in prayer. Afterwards, we said goodnight, secure in the knowledge that nothing would have altered in the morning. Feather-light kisses stroked our skin, arms rested lightly around our waists, a tender embrace. God smiled at his children; perfect peace enveloped us.

———

After seven days of rain, we longed for a glimpse of sky, a breath of fresh air. Stillness chafed now, and a roar of discontent ballooned in our throats. In the early evening, we opened the window wide and leant out to touch the cloud. Raindrops ran over outstretched hands, soaked sleeves, dampened hair.

'This British rain seeps into my skin,' Jeremiah declared. 'There is no escape from it, even in this room I breathe it.'

'Not like *our* summer rain teeming from the sky. Three inches in an hour, children standing in the street, rivers of cool water swirling around bare feet.'

He beamed. 'Next minute hot sun blazes from a clear blue sky and the earth steams.'

Warm lips nuzzled my damp hair. 'I love playing in the rain,' I whispered.

'Come on then, let's forget this dampness and pretend we are children again.' Grabbing my hand, he propelled me towards the door.

At the edge of the woods, weak sunshine welcomed us. Delighted, I lifted my face to the sky, but no heat warmed my skin. Instead, a cool breeze stirred leaves, sending raindrops scudding across my cheeks. 'Race you through the trees to the fields. Ready, steady, go.' I powered along the waterlogged path, Jeremiah close behind. Beyond the big oak tree, I turned left as usual, but was forced to stop after a few metres. Orange safety netting had been slung between trees to block the path, black letters on a yellow sign declaring, 'Path closed due to wet weather.'

'Rubbish,' Jeremiah shouted. 'I am not defeated by a little Welsh rain.' Pushing the sign out of the way, he walked around the netting and sped away.

'Wait for me,' I called after him.

Around the next turn, I almost tripped over his abandoned shoes and quickly discarded my own. Barefoot, he would have an unfair advantage. Ignoring the cold mud splashing my feet, I raced on towards the sea. Trees pressed against me, the path barely visible as I searched for footprints among leaves and branches littering the ground. After a few minutes, I stopped, convinced I'd taken a wrong turn. 'Jeremiah, Jeremiah.'

'Julia,' he answered from somewhere up ahead.

'Where are you?'

'Julia, Julia, Julia.'

My name bounced around the trees, each syllable striking a different note. I pushed through dense undergrowth to what I hoped was the sound source, emerged in a small clearing, where Jeremiah perched on a large tree stump, hands clasped around his knees

'Ah there you are,' he said, without raising his head. 'It seems we can go no further. A huge tree has come down.'

I plodded towards him, wet grass brushing muddy feet. 'You win then.'

He shook his head. 'Race abandoned. No winner or loser.'

Warm arms encircled my waist and drew me towards him. Comforted, I pressed my lips against the smooth skin above his beard, felt frizzy black hairs tickle my neck. I wanted to laugh and wriggle away as I used to do years ago when Dad's shaggy beard brushed my child-cheeks, but

Jeremiah held me close, his lips sinking into my skin. Rain-drops clung to his hair like diamonds gleaming in black earth; I flicked them away with my fingertips.

Sunlight enveloped us as clouds parted, heat radiated from moist soil, humid air permeated the clearing. Caught in a funnel of fog with my face pressed against his damp wool coat, I had difficulty breathing. My body sagged like a rag doll.

When I opened my eyes, wisps of cloud hung in a washed-out blue sky. Damp leaves lay beneath my fingers although the padded gabardine of my jacket cushioned my back. Beside me, Jeremiah knelt on moist soil, fingers unfastening the top two buttons of my tight-fitting shirt. Liberated, I inhaled deeply, cleared the fog clogging lungs and throat. I struggled to sit up.

'Lie still awhile,' he murmured, his breath cooling my clammy skin, his hands tenderly caressing. 'There is no hurry, it will be a long evening. We are moving towards the summer solstice.'

'I still expect darkness at seven,' I mumbled sleepily.

Lifting his head, he inspected the eight o'clock sky. 'Darkness will not find us here.' He shivered.

'You're cold, we should return to the house. I'm all right now.'

'No, this is the right place.'

For what, I wanted to ask, but his kiss erased all deliberation. Imprisoned by warm earth, I lay defenceless, as he moulded soft skin to the desired form.

When at last he surfaced, the sun was low in the sky and sheer ribbons of light filtered through deep green leaves. Air cascaded over bare flesh, smooth silk. Languidly he peeled off his clothes, layer after layer of bright cloth falling away into the long twilight. Then, he loomed over me, dark shadow. Together we eased into sunset.

———

Sunrise roused me from slumber. I turned to impart a morning embrace, but my beautiful lover had vanished with the night. Dreams lingered, filling my empty arms with stars that morphed into dust specks as the room slowly materialised in soft morning light. I recalled damp leaves, humid earth, burrowing. *When hearts and souls have already bonded, the union of bodies is inevitable,* I mused, lying back on the pillows, eyes half-closed. Sleep-slowed limbs bent and stretched; I inhaled new day through parted lips. A draught of cold air drifted across my face, forcing me to reach for yesterday's shirt folded on the floor. Swinging my legs out of bed, I padded across the carpet, slid into the narrow space between desk and wall. Birdsong greeted me, the window wide open. There remained ample time for a walk in the garden before morning prayers.

As I turned away from the window, the crepe-paper cross I'd made two days earlier in the art room, fluttered against the wall in early morning breeze. Rainbow bright, it drew me towards other images pinned on the noticeboard below. Trembling, I barely resisted the overwhelming urge to tear blank pages from a nearby exercise book and pin them over familiar faces.

Less than five minutes later, I was hurtling down wide stairs, the buttons on my shirt fastened incorrectly, socks bunched at the ankles. Outside, I noticed the spring flowers planted in the small garden bed beneath my window had wilted, their stalks already turning brown. Picking a small bunch, I spread withered petals over my palm. Regret surfaced swiftly, it was too late to learn their names or inhale fresh fragrance; they would not bloom again while I walked these paths. Petals fell through my fingers, littering damp gravel. Unable to face further decay, I abandoned flower-fringed paths and ran across the lawn to the lake.

Prayer arose unexpectedly as I sat mesmerised by tranquil water, unaware that shafts of sunlight had carried me far from chill depths and reed-fringed banks. Cradled by a temperate ocean, I drifted with familiar currents, words dribbling over me, lace-edged wavelets lapping a sandy shore.

Ebb and flow, ebb and flow, God with me, God with me.

Sweet slumber, sweet slumber, God with me, God with me.

Shoes crunching damp gravel returned me to lakeside haven. Delighted to share the morning, I waved to a faithful friend walking along the nearby path. 'Come and join me,' I called. 'It's so peaceful here.'

Donna joined me on the bench, her bare brown legs glowing in the sun.

'You were right,' I acknowledged, 'God *is* here.'

She smiled.

'And you were right about love.'

She squeezed my hand. 'A gift from God.'

'Rather unexpected.'

'But not unwelcome I trust?'

'No. I accept this love in the spirit it is given and in return give *my* love unconditionally.'

'*Love is patient and kind,*' she said, and I swelled with joy, hearing the beginning of my favourite passage from Corinthians. '*It is not jealous or conceited or proud; love is not ill-mannered or selfish or irritable; love does not keep a record of wrongs; love is not happy with evil but is happy* with the truth. Love never gives up; and its faith, hope, and patience never fail.'

We slipped into silence. Down, down I sank to the place where tides never turned the waters and sunlight could not penetrate. Black seas entangled me in a silken embrace. Somewhere in the distance a bell rang. I responded to the sound, but my cry drowned. The bell rang again, but by then I was mute, mind and body numbed by cold water. Only my spirit remained alert, darting hither and thither seeking guidance. *No one to turn to down here,* I thought, *no life at this level.* Patient, I waited in the blackness, silent, motionless. Water flowed above and beneath and through me.

The rustle of her skirt reached inky depths. Immune to pain, I surfaced quickly. She offered her hand and pulled me to safety.

'We've missed morning prayers,' she said softly.

'Yes,' I mouthed through frozen lips.

'Sometimes it's good to ignore the bell. Anyhow, God is all around this blessed place.'

I tried to smile, but my body trembled with cold.

'Such changeable weather over here.' She buttoned her cardigan. 'Why didn't you bring a jacket?'

'Forgot where I was, I guess.'

She laughed. 'You folks from the tropics are all the same. Come on, let's run back to the house, the exercise will warm you up.'

I trailed after her along the lakeside path. Ribbons of weed decorated placid green water. Stopping for a moment, I peered into the lake. No reflection, no movement; still waters ran deep.

CHAPTER EIGHT

MORNING CLASS PROVED DEMANDING AND BY NOON, I was hoping for early dismissal, Choddy having overlooked the usual break for morning tea. We were studying the Old Testament prophet, Jeremiah, a biblical figure I knew little about, given my usual focus on the four gospels and other New Testament books. Apart from the heading 'Jeremiah the Prophet,' Choddy had written three sub-headings on the whiteboard attached to the classroom's rear wall: 'Sin,' 'Worshipping idols' and 'Punishment.' Serious topics that had engendered deep and at times, divisive discussion throughout the morning. When the slap of rubber soles on wooden floorboards signalled imminent release, I closed my bible and reached down for my bag. No one else appeared to be making a move, so I looked up and realised with a tinge of embarrassment that Choddy was adding a fourth sub-heading to the whiteboard, this one in large capital letters. The red marker pen—he had abandoned his usual blue for this final missive—squealed as he underlined each letter and I winced, discomfort increasing as I read the finished word. Underneath 'Punishment' four letters pulsed 'FEAR.'

'Jeremiah's terrified,' Choddy pronounced, glasses wobbling on the end of his nose as he twisted around to face us, 'and his fear is a double-edged sword. He's scared of the task God has set him and he's scared of God. For if he fails, surely God will destroy him.'

On my right, Donna declared, 'Catch twenty-two.'

'I agree, Jeremiah has no choice but to obey.' He pushed his glasses further up his nose with the marker pen. 'But what about us, would we have any choice if God made demands?' Blue eyes scanned the room, but no one risked a response. 'Very well, let's try this. Of course, *we* have a choice, this is the late twentieth-century, we have moved beyond ancient superstitions, think logically before we act.' He stepped away from the board. 'Now, I want you to consider this scenario, based I assure you, on actual events.' Shoulders hunched, he began to pace back and forth in front of the whiteboard, shoes squeaking with every turn. We waited expectantly for elucidation, faces forward, myriad eyes following his footsteps. Suddenly, he stopped pacing, straightened his shoulders and turned to face us. 'Black night, a voice hammering in your head.' The words reverberated around the room like thunder. 'I command you to leave your employment, family and friends and journey to another land where you will work in my name. This task is not finite, so you must trust me to release you when I see fit.'

Fingers gripped my arm. Glancing to my left, I saw a familiar mouth twitch as dark eyes refocused on an open notebook.

'You try to muzzle the words,' Choddy continued, his

voice restored to its usual pitch, 'present a thousand excuses but God will not be silenced.' Still grasping the marker pen, he bowed his head.

We followed suit, expecting prayer. Tension ranged around the room, we sensed the force of his inner struggle, the price he had paid for obedience. Lifting his head, he pointed the pen in our direction to pose a final question. 'What would you do if faced with this dilemma? Think about it carefully, we'll discuss your conclusions tomorrow.'

Beside me, a red pen careered across a blank white page, tracing the outline of fear.

———

A pool of sunlight bathed my feet as I sat in the middle of a small clearing, scribbling responses to Choddy's question. An old oak tree provided support for my back; a nearby stump a flat surface for my books. During the lunch break, Martin had told us the heatwave wouldn't last, so I'd decided to make the most of it and study out of doors. Above my head, leaves wilted, unaccustomed to hot sun and insects hung in the humid air, lethargy precluding swift movement. Jade jewel in an azure sea, the island shimmered.

Jeremiah had chosen to study on the cliff top, declaring the sea breeze would clear his head. I assumed he wanted to spend time alone, consider his reaction to Choddy's class well away from the intensity of our relationship. I too, felt grateful for a tranquil interlude. Since our passionate encounter in the woods, we had spent every spare moment together. Early morning walks took us to the lake or into the garden, after lunch saw us head for the cliff path or the tiny stream, destinations guaranteed to delight. But now we had little interest in beauty, natural or man-made, preferring instead to discuss a multitude of serious topics as we walked hand in hand or sat side by side, arms around each other's shoulders. There was no place for small talk in this volatile environment. At sunrise and sunset, we prayed together on bended knees in one or other's room, pouring out our souls to the God who had given us new love, new life.

Late each evening, as light began to fade, and a hush fell over the island, we abandoned the warmth of food and friendship to run through the woods, ignoring fresh summer growth in our quest to discover new destinations for love. Jeremiah dismissed any suggestion of intimacy in either of our rooms, asserting that the red-brick building imposed boundaries, held him taut in a white world. Away from the house, he claimed we could be uninhibited, God's children playing in paradise.

———

The pen fell from my fingers as I recalled the field where yesterday we lay hugging the dying rays of day. Around us, feather-topped grasses waved in warm wind as his tongue flicked over my face, his woolly beard tickling my skin. Mischievous, I plucked a blade of grass and brushed it across his chest. Laughter bubbled to the surface, brimmed over and filled the field with foam. Light as summer breeze, we rolled together, dancing till all the bubbles burst.

A faraway voice jolted me back to present day occupation. My name ricocheted from tree to tree, but although I listened carefully, no other sound filtered through leaves, no feet pounded the path.

'Julia, Julia, Julia,' his voice seemed closer now.

'I'm in the clearing,' I called, jumping to my feet and running to the path. There was no sign of him. 'Jeremiah, Jeremiah, where are you?'

'Julia, oh thank God,' he said behind me.

He shook violently as I held him, perspiration streaming down his face. 'Come and sit down,' I urged and led him into the trees, where he collapsed in a heap beneath green foliage, lay shivering bathed in dappled sunlight.

'What's happened?' I asked, when his laboured breathing had returned to normal.

'I, I saw her again,' he whispered, leaning towards me.

'Who?'

'The white woman.'

'Which white woman?'

'The one on the cliffs, near the cave. She was in front of me, so close, so close this time I could have touched her.' He raised himself to a sitting position. 'The first time, I thought she was an island spirit conjured up somehow by Yoruba rituals. So, I called out in the old language, used all the right words to banish her. But the wind carried my words away and I knew then she had come from *my* world to haunt me.'

'Did she say anything?'

He shook his head. 'She reached out as if to grab me.'

Perturbed, I stared at my feet, then lifted my head and looked directly into his eyes. 'Did you slip up there on the cliff?'

Pushing me away, he leapt to his feet. 'You don't understand the power of the spirit world. She wants me to step over the edge.' He fumbled in his pocket, pulled out his small bible and thrust it towards me. 'He saved me. Without him I would have obeyed her.'

I reached up to touch the faded red cover. The shock

was immediate, a bolt of fear surging through my fingers. 'Could the white woman be me?' I asked tentatively.

Sighing, he raised his eyes heavenward. 'Of course not. This woman is ancient, her skin cracked like old leather.'

'So, who do you think she is?'

'I don't know. She can't be an ancestor and who else would haunt me?'

'Why couldn't a white woman be your ancestor?'

'Don't be ridiculous, woman. I am one hundred percent Yoruba.'

I'd had enough; he was the one being ridiculous. Scrambling to my feet, I retrieved notebook and pen and hurried towards the path.

'Don't leave me, Julia,' he called after me. 'I'm sorry. It doesn't matter who the woman is. Her presence is the issue.'

Reluctantly, I waited for him to catch up. 'I'll stay but only if you calm down.'

'Promise.'

I glanced at his face, smiled when he reached for my hand. 'You're safe now,' I assured him as we walked back to the clearing.

Side by side, but with sufficient space between us to forestall intimate touch, we leant against the tree stump, eyes closed. A tranquil setting, yet the force of his continuing distress intruded on my prayers for serenity. Part of me wanted to believe the apparition he'd described had been nothing more than a resurrected childhood memory, perhaps a weary white teacher at a mission school determined to punish a disruptive student. It wasn't difficult to envisage an impish Jeremiah disturbing class calm. Another part queried whether inbred white superiority prevented acceptance of matters beyond my experience. If asked, I would have said hallucinations belonged to the superstitious past or were induced by present-day drugs; they had no place on a Welsh island where educated international students gathered to study Christianity. But somewhere within, a sliver of doubt invisible to the inner eye made me dread the thought of an evil being haunting the cliffs, intent on causing unwanted death. Jeremiah had come to the island to deliberate on his immediate future, determine whether the calling that had come to him in a dream had been the genuine article. Suicide couldn't be part of the process.

Opening my eyes, I focused on sturdy tree-trunks securely anchored in deep soil. Minutes passed, at last I felt ready to resume answering Choddy's question, so lifted notebook and pen from their bed of fallen leaves. And as I began to write, the nearby rustle of thin pages reassured. Silence had restored his equilibrium.

———

Homework completed, I closed the notebook, looked up at puffy white clouds gathering beyond the woods. Sunlight had lost its intensity, it filtered through leaves, gentle, benign.

'Oh, where is it?' Jeremiah demanded.

'What?'

'Choddy's text this morning.'

'Jeremiah four,' I answered, still focused on clouds.

'Found it.'

'Good,' I murmured, hoping for a return to peace and quiet.

'*The Lord says,*' he read aloud, '*People of Israel, if you want to turn, then turn back to me.*' He stabbed the text with his finger. 'The answer is clear, Julia. I must abandon my tribal gods. One God, one faith, then I will be strong like my namesake the prophet, an iron pillar, a bronze wall. What a fool I've been, thinking I could have it all. Why do I cling to a past that's dying?'

'It's always difficult to let go,' I said softly.

'No, it's dead not dying,' he cried, the words flying skyward, piercing cottonwool clouds. 'All the old ways ejected, dried up like shit two days on the ground. The white woman is dead!' Grabbing my shoulder, he forced me to abandon sky and trees. The bible fell from his hand, lay open between us on dry grass. Tears gathered in his frightened eyes, spilled over to stain his cheeks.

I held him close, a weeping child, weary and distraught. 'Cry all you want,' I said, recalling the day a golden childhood collapsed around me. 'It's part of letting go. If we don't grieve, the hurt devours us.'

———

My eyes stung but tears refused to fall, my lower lip trembled but words refused to form. Beside me on the sofa, Karen's tears splashed my brown legs. I held her tighter, tighter.

'Mummy, Mummy,' she cried, 'I want my Mummy.'

I remained mute, the brave older sister, comforting, comforting.

'It's all right darling, Mummy's safe in the arms of Jesus,' our grandmother pronounced from the safety of her armchair.

I wanted to jump up, clap my hands over her mouth. How could she tell such lies? Our mother was not with Jesus; our mother was lying in a hospital bed, her thin fingers clutching the sheet, her skin whiter than the sheet and cold.

———

'The white woman is dead,' Jeremiah repeated in a calm voice.

'I know,' I sobbed.

His warm brown body absorbed my tears.

CHAPTER NINE

AFTER SUPPER, RELAXING IN MY ROOM, I THANKED God for an evening of solitude. Jeremiah had retired to bed long before the late-setting sun, physically and emotionally drained by the cliff top experience, engendered, I believed, by the morning's discussion of his namesake the Prophet and Choddy's atypical outburst. Sleep, if deep and dreamless, would bring him peace.

I too craved sleep, dealing with my overwrought lover an exhausting task, but right now, I needed to pray, alone, to *my* God, our father who art in Heaven, the familiar, the uncomplicated.

———

I woke from sound sleep coughing, my throat sore and dry as though I had spent the night shouting. Water from the glass on my bedside cabinet soon eased the irritation, so I lay back on the pillows, watched specks of pale light filter through the curtains. Island light remained gentle on the eyes; its delicate hues unchanged by several days of exceptional warmth. Daybreak beckoned, I slipped out of bed, stepped over discarded clothes and drew back the curtains a fraction. A thin film of mist covered lawn, lake and flowerbeds. Little by little, the lake emerged, dark green depths tinged with gold. Water birds floated over its smooth surface, then disappeared among the reeds. Breezes stirred leaves; cool air drifted through my open window. Bare flesh tingled as I inhaled new day.

A tap on the door roused me from contemplation. 'Come in,' I called, knowing it was Jeremiah come to share the sunrise.

Sleep lingered on his lips and his eyes were wrapped in dreams. I held his warmth against my cool body.

'You're not ready for our walk,' he remarked, as though only just aware of my nakedness.

'I'm watching the earth. See how she breathes, gently, evenly and then a sigh. She's releasing the night and retrieving the morning.'

He dropped a kiss on my forehead and taking my hand, led me away from the window.

'Breath with me,' I implored.

Together we knelt on the carpet, our backs straight, hands resting on thighs, chests rising and falling in unison. Sunlight licked smooth morning faces.

'It is good,' he said, 'cool and fresh. I greet the day.' Cupping his hands around his mouth, he blew a breath towards the window. 'And I greet you Julia.' He paused and turning his head towards me added in a low voice, 'I greet you with my love.'

I resisted the urge to smother him with kisses. We had spoken of love many times, analysed its moods, discussed its shortcomings, but I had not said 'I love you' for fear he would flee, threatened by the image of commitment that phrase evoked. Today, he had broken free from rhetoric and spoken from the heart.

'I accept your love and offer mine in return.'

'Bless this day,' he whispered and covered my mouth with his lips.

When I opened my eyes, every corner of the room was filled with amber light. 'Oh no, we've missed the sunrise.'

'No, it is here in your golden skin.' Warm fingers stroked my thighs, meandered to the edge of softness.

'Jeremiah, I thought you didn't want to make love inside?'

'Hush,' he murmured, 'I claim this dawn for us, to celebrate our love.'

Desire inflamed me; my breath came in short sharp bursts that pierced delicate morning sunshine. His mouth hovered above my face. 'You are the rays of the sun,' he said, edging closer. 'Your flesh is a honey stream, rich and sweet.'

'And you are the bee.'

'No, I am treacle, thick dark syrup.'

'Strong sweetness.'

Suddenly he sat back on his heels and dug his fingers into his thighs. Had he changed his mind? I reached for my shirt lying crumpled on the floor.

'Do not hide from me, I need your sweet warmth.'

Throwing the shirt aside, I laid warm fingers on his abdomen, but he shook his head and began to remove his clothes, methodically folding each garment in a neat pile beside my desk. Then, he slithered across the floor until our bodies almost touched.

'Treacle and honey,' he pronounced in a confident tone, 'warmed and softened by the sun, blended together, a taste sensation.'

I bent to kiss him, but he pushed my head away, grasped

my waist and with no concern for pain or pleasure, plunged into me. Confused and disturbed, I clung to him, longing for a return to the sweetness of unity. Physically connected, we remained emotionally separated, as if a barrier had been erected between us. I sensed it building higher and higher, pushing up and over our heads, into the ceiling, into the room above, into the roof. Truth stung bruised flesh; boundaries inside the house were holding him taut in a white world, a society he despised, *my* world, *my* culture. Shocked, I tried to stuff irrational thoughts back into my subconscious. Muscles tensed as I fought to liberate him, whisk him away to that other world, the tender land of our desiring. Depleted, he rolled away from me.

Echoes of last night's dream free-fell over my fast cooling flesh and a landscape unfolded, amorphous as though painted hurriedly. Vibrant colours—green red blue yellow—ran to the edges of a cream canvas, congealed in thick ridges. I pondered the meaning, tried to recall if words had accompanied my dreamscape. Nothing emerged. I turned to my silent lover but when I opened my mouth to speak, he brushed my lips with his finger and with that small gesture the barrier between us began to crumble.

———

Alone again, I lay still. Morning sounds streamed through the window, voices called out in greeting, breezes stirred lush foliage. Get up, I told myself, but my limbs refused to obey.

'Julia, Julia,' I heard Donna call from the garden below.

How could I answer her? I was a honeycomb lodged in a hollow tree, sweet sap dripping over dry timber.

When footsteps on the path below receded, I threw on

some clothes, splashed cold water on my face and took several gulps from the tap without even bothering to fetch my glass from the bedside cabinet. My hair remained tousled, my body unwashed, the aroma of sex lingered on my skin. I had no desire for breakfast or company. Island breeze blew through the open window, cooled hot skin, but inside I burned, heat and glare sapping my strength. Tranquility was a forgotten state possessed only by others: Donna, Hannah, Benjamin, Martin. They inhabited a serene world; they experienced the peace that passes understanding.

And yet, I would not, could not abandon the place of passion. For the first time in forty years I felt fully alive.

———

For several hours, I sat at my desk writing in the back of an exercise book, trying to interpret my abstract dream. After numerous attempts, at last I was making some headway, having decided to concentrate on colour.

Green: the island/me, the spring promise of new life growing to completion during summer.

Red: (this one's easy) Jeremiah's blanket, his borrowed wool jacket, the faded cover of his bible.

Blue: ocean currents carrying me across open water far from familiar coastlines.

Yellow: sunshine, sand, the colour of my hair?

I had to admit yellow stumped me. Sunshine and sand were so obviously Australian, the first things that had entered my mind, but despite lengthy deliberation, I couldn't think of anything else. Yellow hair was a misnomer, at forty I was more faded blonde with streaks of grey around the temples.

Questions followed each interpretation. I felt relieved to have exposed them at last—they had been rattling around in my head for days—but remained unsure how to proceed. They were, I believed, the sum of numerous island dreams, night questions resurrected and blinding in noonday light.

Green: What happens at the end of this northern summer? Does new life
require different soil?

Red: Is God asking me to travel to Nigeria with Jeremiah and help him improve life for his people?

Blue: If so, how can I justify leaving Brian and the children? Is God really asking me to abandon my family, my home, my country?

Yellow: What, where, why? (One-word questions, is yellow still troubling me?)

At last I had something concrete to work with, a starting point. My head ached, and my stomach rumbled but I dared not leave my room. Was I afraid the paper would be blank when I returned? My bible and prayer book remained closed; I had no wish to cloud the issue by absorbing more words. Questions had arisen, therefore I sought answers. Was that too much to ask?

'Julia are you there?' someone called, outside my door.

I closed the exercise book before getting to my feet. The door opened, and May Gordon stepped into the room.

'We were concerned about you,' she said, closing the door behind her. 'No one had seen you today, we thought you might be ill.'

'No, no, I'm good. I just have some important work to finish.'

She nodded. 'Lunch is in five minutes. Would you like to walk down with me?'

'I'd prefer to stay here, thanks.'

'Are you sure there's nothing wrong, Julia?'

'Everything's fine but I must finish this work.'

She headed for my desk. 'Perhaps I could help you with it?'

'No, it's private,' I answered curtly.

She backed away. 'Sorry, I didn't mean to intrude.'

'I'm the one who should apologise. I should have told someone I was working in my room today. It's,' I hesitated, reluctant to voice what I believed was the reason for unplanned seclusion. 'It's something I have to work out with God.'

'I see. Would it help if I brought you some lunch?'

'No thanks, I've got an apple in my desk, that'll do.'

'See you later then.' She retreated hurriedly.

Contrite, I raced to the door. 'Sorry, I didn't mean to cause concern,' I called after her, but the lunch bell drowned my apology.

In need of a change of scene, I picked up my pen and exercise book and sat cross-legged on the floor, my back resting against the bed. Suddenly eager to jot down answers or suggestions, I realised my head had cleared, the brief interruption beneficial after all.

The day lengthened and pain began to gnaw at my stomach. Hunger, I assumed, getting up to rummage in the desk. The apple filled a space but within minutes the pain had reignited, spread out over my abdomen and up into my chest. Breathing became difficult, twinges became knife thrusts, puncturing lungs. Was I having a heart attack? I tried to call out, but my voice sounded thin as the reeds fringing the lake. Alarmed, I scanned the room for something, anything that could offer immediate assistance. The washbasin was within reach; I grasped cool porcelain with one hand, stretched out the other, turned on the tap. Cold water doused blazing fire. Exhausted, I crawled over to the bed.

Lying still on top of the covers, I endeavoured to control erratic breathing—inhale, exhale, concentrate, calm down. Ash fell through me, settled in the pit of my stomach. When it cooled, I sensed vocabulary assembling in my head. Answers to impossible questions? The reason for an unforeseen anxiety attack?

No time to fetch pen and paper; the words had already formed a coherent sentence. I received it eagerly, but it solved nothing. 'Is God really asking the questions?' I repeated in a small voice.

————

Walking through shadowed trees three days later, Jeremiah declared his own spiritual dilemma. 'I don't understand what God wants,' he protested. 'I've kept my promise, rejected all the old gods and what does he give in return? Nothing.'

'What were you expecting?' I asked cautiously.

'Peace of mind, an indication that I'm moving in the right direction.'

I yearned to offer helpful advice, but how could I, when I had known nothing but spiritual silence for three whole days?

'It was easier when I had Yoruba gods to turn to. At least they provided some comfort, took me back to the old days of harmony.'

'Back to the ancestors and their world?' I queried, relieved to have thought of something to say.

He smiled wistfully. 'No, back to childhood, secure in my mother's arms, listening to her honey voice tell stories of our people immortalised in song. She said I hummed tunes before I learned to speak.' He paused, raised his eyes to a patch of pale sky. 'When I grew older, I discovered drums. One night I waited until everyone was asleep, then crept from our hut and ran over to the big hut where the drums were stored. Oh, the skins were so smooth when I brushed them with my fingers. They came to life and I made music; the night resounded with *my* music.' He grinned. 'The drummer was furious; he said I could have damaged them. But I wouldn't have done that, I just wanted to feel their texture and make them live.'

'You make them live now. I was transported to another world the first time I heard you play.'

He looked down and smiled at me. Linking arms, we walked on in comfortable quiet, conscious only of soft tree-breath and gathering harmony.

We were in sight of the sea when he stepped in front of me and seizing my hands asked excitedly. 'Would you like to go to Africa?'

'Yes, I'd love to,' I answered without hesitation, adding by way of explanation, 'it's been more than twenty-five years.'

'I thought you said you hadn't been to Africa?'

'It was only a brief visit on the journey to and from England. My grandmother took my sister and me for a holiday a few years after our...' I hesitated, unable or unwilling to finish the sentence.

'Where did you go?'

'Cape Town. The ship stopped there for a couple of days. The Suez Canal was closed after the sixty-seven Arab-Israeli war, so instead of travelling through the Mediterranean, we had to go around the Cape.'

Snorting, he released my hands. 'Cape Town is not *my*

Africa. Not while de Klerk is still in power.' A volley of spit flew from pursed lips.

We resumed our walk, disharmony dogging each step. Soon, we reached the cliff path, but did not linger to stare out to sea, as was our custom. A fresh breeze swept over stunted grass and chalk, dislodging a handful of tension.

'At least there's talk of democracy in South Africa,' I remarked, determined to resume disrupted conversation. 'I heard de Klerk and Nelson Mandela are negotiating.'

'What about Chris Hani? Negotiations didn't do him much good. I don't understand why they don't rise up and overthrow the white government, reclaim their land, their languages, their dignity? All this talk of democracy is getting nowhere.'

'Give it time, I'm sure Mandela knows what he's doing.'

'Mandela, what do you know of Mandela?' Black eyes blazed.

I struggled to remain calm. 'I didn't come out here to argue with you, Jeremiah.'

'Bloody politics,' he muttered. 'Never a safe topic of conversation, even between lovers. Please forgive me Julia?'

I reached out to squeeze his hand.

'Now what was I saying before we got embroiled in politics?'

I hesitated, unsure whether I should repeat such a weighty question. 'You asked me if I'd like to go to Africa and I said I'd love to.'

He tugged at his beard. 'We could go now.'

'Now? Don't be absurd.'

'Don't you want to come with me?'

'Yes but...'

'But what?'

'We can't just up and leave an island. Besides, we signed up for three months, didn't you read the fine print?'

'This isn't South Africa, Julia. I'll tell Choddy we've had enough, he'll soon organise a boat.'

'Do you really think he would?'

'Yes, and if he refuses, we can board the next supply boat.'

'Supply boat, I thought the farm provided all the fresh produce? When we arrived, Martin said the boat wouldn't be returning for three months.'

'The passenger ferry, silly. I've seen the supply boat several times.'

'Where?'

'Down by the jetty of course.' He leant towards me. 'And always at night.

'But it doesn't make sense docking at night, it's only a short run to the mainland.'

He shrugged. 'I imagine they want us to believe we're isolated for three months. Anyway, I think the ferry is due next week.'

'I thought you said we could go immediately?'

'We can if we speak to Choddy today.'

'Why don't we just wait for the supply boat?'

'Why wait, an extra journey won't be a problem?'

'He'll think we're crazy.'

'Why should he? I'm sure we're not the first students to want to leave before the end of term. We can speak to him after lunch, he's usually in his office at that time.'

'I can't believe we're doing this.'

'Out of Eden,' Jeremiah cried, dancing down the chalk path. 'Exodus, exodus. Freedom, freedom, freedom!

CHAPTER TEN

CHODDY WASN'T IN HIS OFFICE AFTER LUNCH AND inquiries failed to locate him, so we decided to go for a walk and try again later. We took our usual route through the woods, intending to spend an hour or so traipsing the cliff path, but when a strong wind began to twist the treetops, we felt reluctant to continue. Jeremiah suggested a walk on the other side of the island instead, where it would be more sheltered.

A fresh breeze cooled our faces when we arrived at the jetty, but the sun felt warm and the sea sparkled. After pounding weatherworn boards, we stood at the end with our backs against the rail, gulping mouthfuls of salty air. Tendrils of loose hair drifted across my glowing cheeks, obscuring the view, I pushed them behind my ears to survey the island. Away from the land, there was a different perspective, and I felt a welcome detachment as I scanned the pebbled shoreline, small waves washing, receding, leaving behind a trail of white foam that sailed skyward. Further along, a patch of green and gold caught my eye. 'Is that a beach over there?' I pointed to a small stretch of yellow sand just visible behind low windswept vegetation.

Shielding his eyes from the sun, Jeremiah peered into the distance. 'Could be, why don't we explore?'

'It's strange that Martin has never mentioned a beach, when he appears to know every part of the island,' I remarked as we set off along the jetty.

'Well, it's hardly the climate for swimming.'

'You wouldn't catch me in that sea.'

'Nor me. Come on, let's get warm, race you to shore.'

The path petered out a short distance from the jetty leaving tufts of thick grass dotting sandy soil. Before long, we reached the vegetation I had noticed from the jetty, masses of shrubs and a few wind-twisted trees. There was no sign of a path leading to the beach, but Jeremiah pushed through dense foliage without hesitation, holding branches aside so I could proceed unhindered. Beneath my feet, the ground felt spongy and I could hear the sea lapping the shore close by.

We emerged onto a tiny strip of coarse sand strewn with seaweed. At the far end, I noticed a clump of trees with what looked like a large rock in front of them. When I pointed it out to Jeremiah, he took off at once, sprinting along the beach, his red shirt flapping in the breeze. In no hurry, I followed at a slower pace, pausing now and then to pick up shells.

'Julia, come quickly' he called.

Pocketing the shells, I ran towards him, taking care to avoid piles of stinking seaweed.

'Look what I've found,' he announced as I drew near. He was kneeling beside an old wooden dinghy that lay upside down on the sand. The painter, frayed rope intertwined with strands of seaweed, had been tied to a nearby tree.

Leaning over, I ran my hand over planks grey with age and neglect. 'What a waste.' I looked down at him. 'Give me a hand to right it.' I dropped to my knees. 'Put your hands under the gunwale.'

'The what?'

'The edge of the boat.' I pushed away sand, then gripped the gunwale. 'Right, one, two, three, heave!'

The dinghy crashed onto the beach. Brushing sand from my hands, I peered inside. A pair of oars and rowlocks had been tied to the forward seat with rope. Delighted, I untied them carefully, slotted rowlocks into place. 'Why don't we find out if it's seaworthy?'

Jeremiah looked apprehensive, but I had no intention of letting the opportunity slip through my fingers, so quickly rolled up my jeans and pulled off trainers.

'Come on, let's have some fun.' I moved to the stern, pushed the dinghy over the narrow strip of sand and into the water. Up to my knees in cold water, I jumped aboard, sat down heavily on the centre seat and grabbed the oars. 'Hurry up Jeremiah, I can't hold her for long, the wind's too strong.'

Kicking off his shoes, he splashed through the shallows, clutched the stern and levered himself aboard. 'It's a good thing you know about boats.'

Waves lapped the small arc of beach, unimpeded by jagged rocks. *Such a contrast to sheer cliffs and pounding waves on the other side,* I thought, recalling Jeremiah's gift falling into foam. *Here the water is clear, green, benevolent.*

Several hundred metres out, I shipped the oars and lifting my head to the sky, gulped salt air like a swimmer surfacing after a lengthy dive. The dinghy bobbed on a gentle swell, her timbers creaking and groaning. Automatically, I checked the boards for moisture, but except for a few drops clinging to a patch of faded red paint, they remained dry. *Run-off from our feet,* I concluded, grateful to find she remained watertight. I'd always taken care of *my* boats, a lesson learned early in life from a strict seafaring father.

Memory surfaced, smooth as silk. A sultry December morning, Mother and Dad leading Karen and me away from discarded wrapping paper and winking lights to Granddad and Grandma's place two streets away. After depositing Karen and Mother upstairs in the living room, Dad took me back downstairs into a corner of the slatted area under the house, where a diminutive dinghy, her red and white paint-work gleaming, lay on an old piece of carpet. Inside, was a small pair of oars and a rolled- up sail.

'J-U-L-I-A,' I read slowly, stroking the bold black letters adorning her prow.

Dad beamed. 'Happy Christmas to the best swimmer in Grade Two.'

My seven-year old voice whooped with delight.

———

Face flushed with memories of another sea; I began to sing a favourite childhood song. 'The owl and the pussycat went to sea in a beautiful pea-green boat, they took some honey and plenty of money wrapped up in a five-pound note.'

'Oh Julia,' Jeremiah sang, 'oh Julia my dear, what a beautiful pussy you are.'

A blush stained my cheeks. 'I don't think those are the right words,' I said, irritated by adult intrusion.

'So what, you are beautiful.'

'And we're crazy.'

'Why, for being in love?'

'No, for paddling about in an old boat talking about escape and freedom.'

'Have you changed your mind about coming to Africa with me?'

'Of course not.' I dipped the oars and began to row back to the beach.

'Julia, I must go soon.' He uttered the words through gritted teeth, his forehead furrowed.

'Be patient, didn't you say the supply boat's due next week?'

'I won't be here then,' he said sadly, 'there's no one to save me now.'

'What on earth are you talking about?'

'God. He has abandoned me; I know that now.'

'Maybe he has, but how does that affect our leaving the island?'

'She'll bewitch me next time, I'll step over the edge.'

Oars froze mid-stroke. 'You've seen the white woman again?'

'Four days ago, after we made love in your room. I went to the cliffs to...' He picked at the frayed cuff of his jeans.

'I thought you'd stopped believing in ancestor ghosts?'

'She won't die.'

'Perhaps you won't release her?'

'Immortality is forever.'

'Jeremiah,' I began, but the words I wanted to say died in my mouth. His face was an empty page, his black eyes glassy as the lake at dawn. He had already left.

———

Words spoken on the jetty came back to haunt me as I wrote the day's unexpected events in my journal before retiring to bed:

 I AM CRAZYI AM CRAZY
  I AM CRAZY I AM
  CRAZY I AM
  CRAZY CRAZY
  CRAZY CRAZY CRAZY
  CRAZY CRAZY CRAZY CRAZY

It seemed no matter how many times I re-read the words they remained blurred as though the ink had run. I would have liked to add names: Jeremiah, Brian, Stephen, Penny, draw a box around each one in heavy black ink. But my pen ignored cerebral directives and besides, there wasn't enough room left. Tomorrow's blank page was available, yet I baulked at the thought of encroaching on another day, one day at a time all I could manage at present. Sometimes, even that felt burdensome.

Leaning back against the chair, I focused my attention on the ceiling. Hairline cracks meandered across the plaster; I tried to follow their path, but they disappeared, swallowed by blobs of white paint. My eyes connected with an unbroken white cord, ascended to the white plastic light fitting, swaying in evening breeze. Devoid of colour, the panorama remained vacuous as tomorrow.

Long after midnight, I still sat at my desk. Having abandoned my journal, I had decided to concentrate on writing a letter to Choddy. Although I knew my private life was my own affair, I felt reluctant to leave Eden College without supplying a reason. Choddy had helped me a great deal during the first few weeks of term; the least I could do was rationalise my sudden departure.

The first words formed effortlessly, love, passion and commitment easy to explain. Choddy would understand my desire to go to Africa and assist Jeremiah in his work among Yoruba villagers; ten years in the Cape had sealed his affection for all Africans. But how could I justify leaving only a few weeks before the end of term? Such irrational behaviour defied explanation.

The pen fell from my fingers as my gaze alighted on milky stars and a lemon moon. Why did I want to leave this place of peace, this sanctuary? The island shielded me from a harsh world, a world that waited to judge and condemn. There would be no clemency; I had broken all the rules.

Distant thunder rumbled through the summer night, promising rain and renewal. I watched for streaks of lightning, saw only the shadow of clouds. Thunder intensified, a million drums disturbing the darkness, luring me towards a throbbing sky. Feather-light, I danced over buildings treetops and clouds, silver moonlight licking my limbs, stars slipping through my fingers, a thousand sequins adorning a black velvet gown. Aching for Africa, I skipped through space seduced by his marvellous music.

CHAPTER ELEVEN

Next morning, I attended chapel as usual, anxious to present an ordinary face to the college world and perhaps, reassure myself that this was just another day.

'Beautiful day again,' Donna remarked as we walked in the garden after the service. 'I expected a terrible summer. At home, everyone joked about the British weather.'

'Summer was on August the fifth the year I left England, I once heard my grandfather say.'

She laughed. 'Martin thinks the weather will break soon. We had some rain in the night.'

'Yes, and I heard some thunder.'

'I didn't hear a thing.'

'I hope we don't have a storm tonight,' I said half to myself.

'Yes, it would ruin the celebration.'

'What celebration?'

'The one for the summer solstice. May's organising a bonfire on the cliffs tonight after evening prayers. Didn't you listen to the notices?'

'Yes, but obviously the words didn't sink in.'

Donna leant towards me. 'I understand. Lovers inhabit another world.'

I blushed.

'Don't be embarrassed, love is a beautiful experience, make the most of it.'

'You speak as though it won't last.'

'Well, how can it?' She put her arm around my shoulders. 'You can't stay in paradise Julia. Genesis is only a beginning.'

'And after Genesis?'

'Exodus, of course. We all have to return to the real world.'

———

I was ready to leave, everything tidy, books piled neatly on the desk, papers clipped together. Despite the hour, my bedroom remained dim, for I had closed the curtains and felt it would be wasteful to turn on the light. Sitting on the bed, I re-tied my shoelaces for the fifth time. Why was I stalling, when I knew he waited downstairs in the hall? I rose slowly, smoothed my clothes, took a deep breath.

At the top of the stairs, I paused to look over the banister. He stood stiffly, hands clasped behind his back. I resisted the urge to call out, but when I was halfway down, he turned around and raising his eyes from the floor asked, 'Julia, what took you so long?'

'Shoelaces,' I mumbled, hurrying down the remaining stairs.

'Don't be afraid,' he soothed as I reached his side, 'I'll be right beside you.'

'I'm not afraid Dad,' I replied, taking his proffered hand.

Together we left the house and headed for the car, where Karen sat on the backseat clutching a favourite doll.

Outside the church, jacaranda blossom dusted the pavement, reminding me of confetti falling over a snowy gown. The last time I'd stood here, cousin Dawn and her new husband had been posing for photographs. No photographer here today, but I guessed it wouldn't be appropriate at a funeral. Then, I spotted Aunt Muriel rushing towards us, holding on to a ridiculous hat. When she arrived, I lifted my cheek for the inevitable kiss. She smelt of soap and talcum powder.

'Such a brave girl,' she said before moving to Dad's other side where my sister stood looking down at her new shoes.

We filed into church and took our places in the front pew. The priest smiled down at us. I tried to return his smile, but my mouth muscles refused to move, someone had pasted my lips together with the white lumpy glue we used at school. It tasted of flour. Looking beyond the priest, I noticed wreaths clustered around an open coffin. A scream rose in my throat, pushed against the hard line of my teeth. Now I understood the need for glue.

The organ began to play, so I opened my hymnbook, stared at unfamiliar words. Beside me, Aunt Muriel sang loudly as though making up for my silence. My father's voice faltered after the first verse and he dabbed his eyes with a crumpled handkerchief. After the hymn, we had a reading from the bible and a prayer. Listening to the priest, I felt less troubled; he spoke of love and *his* voice stayed strong, unwavering.

'Come Julia,' my father said suddenly, reaching for my hand.

Had the funeral finished? I shuffled along the pew and out into the aisle, eyes fixed on floorboards.

'Kiss your mother goodbye,' my father commanded.

Vomit filled my throat; I thanked Jesus for unyielding glue.

'Come on Julia, you must say goodbye.'

Horrified, I clutched white satin, leant over, brushed dead flesh with rigid lips.

———

Out on the blue water, I lifted my damp face to the sun. A trail of vomit stained the sea, but I was free at last to scream and scream and scream. Salt air filled the sail, I grasped the tiller and steered the 'Julia' out into my beloved Moreton Bay.

———

We were ready to leave. I had packed a few clothes, bread, cheese, fruit and water bottles in my backpack and stowed it under the small seat at the stern where it should stay dry. Passport return airline ticket to Brisbane and my wallet had been sealed in a plastic envelope and zipped into an inside pocket of my parka, in case the rest of our luggage didn't arrive on the next supply boat.

A short time after my conversation with Donna in the garden, I finished the letter to Choddy. In the end, I elected not to give a concrete reason for leaving early, wrote instead of Genesis and Exodus. Choddy could read between the lines.

From the moment I sealed the envelope, the island receded as though I had already left. Woods and lake and buildings merged with sky to become a swirling mass of pale blue and white. Faces faded before me, voices diminished into silence, by afternoon nothing remained except the sun, riding high on this the longest day of the northern hemisphere year.

Jeremiah had been unusually quiet since we'd retrieved the dinghy, which made me wonder if he was having second thoughts. Feet planted firmly on hard sand, he stood staring at the sea, one hand gripping the gunwale, the other pulling his tuft of beard. Another phobia? No, I told myself, the question was ludicrous, he must be familiar with the ocean, Lagos is a coastal city. A glance beyond the shallows reassured; the stretch of water between island and mainland appeared unruffled by waves or wind.

'Jeremiah,' I said gently, 'it's time we were going.'

'What?'

'Time to leave if we want to be on the mainland before nightfall.'

He nodded, directed his attention to the dinghy, helped me drag it into the water. I clambered in and seized the oars. Knee-deep in cold green water, he lingered, head turned towards the shore.

'Get in, Jeremiah.'

The small craft rocked as he levered himself into the stern, but I soon steadied her and began to row away from the island. An unfamiliar sea held no trepidation, I had checked maps in the library, knew it was only a short crossing to a small cove east of the harbour where we had caught the ferry weeks earlier. Tide and wind were in our favour; I'd calculated we should reach land before the light faded. But Jeremiah's silence alarmed, and his face remained a closed book. Crouched on the narrow seat, he diminished before me, a thin body retreating into thick

English clothes. How I longed for blue water, hot sun, bare brown limbs.

'Freedom on the other side,' I said brightly.

'Not over there,' he answered, staring straight ahead.

'I mean Africa. We only need stay in the village until our luggage arrives. Then we can head for Heathrow. It won't take long to organise a flight to Lagos.'

He looked wistful. 'Africa is a long long journey.'

'Not by jumbo jet.'

He ignored my comment and continued to stare at the distant horizon. 'It's inexplicable our need to return to the mother country,' he mused, after a long silence. 'Only a few weeks' absence and yet I yearn for her soil, moist and warm between my toes, her hot sun burning my neck.'

'Don't forget summer storms,' I said, relieved he was thinking of the future.

He blinked, looked up at the evening sky. 'Thunder and lightning, the wrath of Olodumare.'

'Who?'

'The divine ancestor, the one who lives in Heaven, Olorun-baba, God our Father.'

'Who watches over us.'

'Who determines our destiny.'

Leaning on the oars for a moment, I watched evening sunshine soften the contours of his face.

'Wait for me beloved country,' he cried. 'Wait for me.'

CHAPTER TWELVE

ALL I COULD SEE WERE CLOUDS AND SKY. PUZZLED, I turned my head and realised I was lying in the bottom of the boat. 'Oh, shit that hurts.'

'Lie still,' Jeremiah ordered, bending over me, a blood-stained handkerchief in his hand.

'What happened?'

'You hit your head.'

'How?'

'You fell backwards and hit the seat.' He stroked my cheek. 'A piece of wood broke off. This boat's rotten, it's been too long lying on the sand.'

'Did we lose the rowlock?'

'The what?'

'The metal bit where the oar sits.'

'Yes.' He shifted backwards, eased himself onto the stern seat, threw the handkerchief over the side.

'What about the oar?' I asked anxiously.

'That too.'

'Oh my God.'

'There's no point in appealing to him, he has deceived me.'

'What on earth are you talking about?'

'This boat was put on the beach to tempt me. And once again I fell for it, took the easy way out. This accident is the result of disobedience.'

'Disobedience?'

'Don't you remember Choddy's words? We really don't have any choice. God makes the rules; he decides who stays in the garden and who departs. You can't just up and leave. His silence was a warning, I should've realised that. Now I hear nothing but Devil-man laughter.'

'Are you sure you didn't hit *your* head?'

'No.' He raised a hand to silence me. 'Listen, it's all around, Devil-voice, mocking me.'

Irritated by nonsensical statements, I reached out to grab his leg and pulled myself up to a sitting position. 'Mixed up that's your trouble, Jeremiah. Tribal gods, ancestors, devils, Christianity, it's all intertwined in your head. Why don't you try being an atheist for a change, it would be a lot simpler?'

He covered his face with his hands and began to moan; eerie sounds, spilling over the sea. I held out my arms, but he would not be comforted, recoiled from my touch.

'Don't worry, with this breeze and the incoming tide we'll soon drift into shore. No devil will claim you, you're free now.'

Thin shoulders sagged. He fell forward, a hollow man.

Day hung in the sky squeezing patches of light from the setting sun. I held him close, prayed that the tide would carry us to shore before darkness descended.

———

Wrapped in the warmth of my thighs, Jeremiah slept soundly as the longest day of the year drew to a close.

My dreams were full of water, translucent turquoise, unfathomable depths. Buoyed by a gentle swell, I swam effortlessly across a vast ocean. In the distance, I could see a landmass, an ancient continent, layer upon layer of rock crushed by millennia. Strong currents carried me forward, I caught a glimpse of red waves rolling across endless plains. No moisture out there, nothing to hold the soil together, this was a landscape governed by desert wind.

'I have so much water,' I cried, 'take what you need.'

'No,' said a harsh voice above my head, 'salt water burns the earth.'

Mist rolled over the sea, smothering dreams. I searched for a shoreline, found nothing but wisps of cloud suspended from a sleepy sky. Baffled, I pushed up my sleeve to glance at my watch. Oh no, I'd slept all night!

Jeremiah dreamed on. I stroked his smooth cheek and pondered the absurdity of falling in love. Middle-aged lovers, one an African schooled in ancient ways, the other Australian, product of a young nation, bold and brash; an improbable alliance. But I couldn't desert this curious man I hardly knew, he alone held the key to my future, for I had given him far more than heart and body. Unwisely perhaps, I had also given him my soul.

Sunlight began to penetrate the grey curtain, incredulous I stared at looming white shapes. 'Jeremiah, Jeremiah,' I called, shaking him roughly, 'wake up.'

'What do you want?' he mumbled.

'I can see cliffs.'

He raised his head. 'Cliffs, I thought you said we would land on a beach?'

'We should have. We must have drifted during the

night, the wind's changed.' Lifting the heavy oar, I grasped it like a paddle and sliced through smooth green water. The dinghy jerked forward. 'There's not much of a swell, we'll soon be on dry land,' I said in a confident tone, intended to convince myself there was little danger, rather than reassure my nervous companion. Patches of brown materialised, we were close to rocks. Anxious, I scanned the shore for a strip of sand.

'Oh, Jesus Christ this is the end,' Jeremiah cried. 'This is what the white woman wanted my body smashed on the rocks. But not you as well, not you, Julia. It's my fault, it's all my fault. Oh Olorun-baba, what have I done?'

I stopped paddling and turned to face him. Dark eyes wide open, lips trembling, he clung to the seat like a terrified child. 'Calm down, we'll be fine, the current will take us well past the rocks.' I could see he didn't believe me. 'Look to your right, there's a small beach.' I leant forward, grasped his wrist. 'If there's any danger of a collision, we can abandon ship and swim to shore.'

'I can't swim.'

'You can hold on to the oar. We'll make it Jeremiah, have faith.'

'In what?'

'Oh, I don't know. God, Olorun-baba, what does it matter?'

He shuddered and turned away from menacing rocks.

I lifted the oar. Minutes passed, the dinghy surged towards the beach, green water slapped the hull, liquid drumbeats steady, soothing.

'Help, help,' he yelled behind me, breaking my paddle rhythm.

Annoyed, I glanced over my shoulder, noticed his arms rising and falling like waves. 'What is it?'

'There's someone on the cliff,' he said between further shouts for help.

Resting the oar on the seat, I turned to search white chalk. 'Where, I can't see anyone?'

'Just above that dark patch. It looks like a man in a blue jacket.'

'Yes, I see, about a metre from the top. He must be standing on a ledge.'

The man began to scramble up the cliff face.

'Oh no, he's going. Shout, Julia, shout.'

'Help, help, over here, over here,' we called in unison.

The man reached the top, heaved himself onto firm ground and got to his feet.

'Coo-ee, coo-ee,' I yelled, hoping the call that helped locate someone in the Australian bush might work half a world away.

The man turned around, scoured the sea, waved.

'He's seen us,' Jeremiah cried. 'Oh, thank God. Help, help we've lost an oar.'

'Stay calm,' the man shouted, hands cupped around his mouth. 'I'll get help.'

The voice seemed familiar; I clutched the seat to steady myself. 'It's Martin,' I said, trying to disguise my disappointment. 'We've returned to the island.'

'Back to Eden,' Jeremiah said wistfully.

Our boat bobbed on the swell; we focused on the cliff top until the blue jacket became too small to track.

'Do you think Choddy will give us another chance?' I asked, envisaging his displeasure when he learnt of our attempted escape.

'Yes, if we ask forgiveness.' And as if on cue, Jeremiah raised his eyes heavenward and began to recite the Lord's Prayer.

'Amen,' I managed to say when he'd finished, but my voice lacked conviction. I resented this interruption to our journey, returning to base a backward step, an unnecessary delay. Africa remained a distant continent, unknown, unexplored. How long would she wait for me?

No time remained for further contemplation, the breeze had freshened and in the few minutes spent alerting Martin to our plight, I noticed we had drifted some distance from land. Paddling furiously, I tried to steer the dinghy towards the shore, but wind and waves thwarted my efforts. Water began to seep through the ancient boards, gathered around our feet in icy puddles. Morning sunlight evaporated; grey clouds scudded across the sky; I felt the swell carry us back into deep water. Defeated, I shipped the oar and slumped on the seat, chest heaving.

'This was a stupid idea,' Jeremiah admitted.

I twisted around. 'Not just stupid, hazardous.'

'Then why did you go along with it?'

'Because I love you,' I said breathlessly.

'If Choddy has already opened our letters, we've got a fair bit of explaining to do,' he said, resting one hand on my knee.

'With a bit of luck, they'll still be in his pigeonhole.'

'If we do retrieve the letters, we'd better say we found the boat and decided to explore. A wave washed an oar overboard, we have been drifting ever since.'

'But they'll know we weren't in the house last night. We didn't go to supper or breakfast.'

'Not a problem. I told May we were going to have a picnic on the cliffs before the summer solstice celebration. I doubt we were missed at the bonfire and no one worries about breakfast.'

'I suppose not.'

'You're not convinced?'

'It seems such a feeble explanation.'

'Don't worry, they'll swallow it. No one in their right mind would try to cross to the mainland in a broken-down boat.' I turned my attention to the water pooled in the bottom of the boat, trying to decide whether it had deepened. I had a couple of shirts in my backpack, perhaps they could be put to use? Mop up, wring out over the side, repeat until dry. Movement in the stern drew my eyes away from the water. 'Careful,' I warned as he wriggled around on the seat.

Hands reached out, clasped my knees. 'Julia, I've been a bloody fool. I'll understand if you want to end our relationship.'

'Why would I want to do that?'

'I just thought...' His voice trailed off as he turned his face into the wind.

'Jeremiah our journey hasn't been abandoned. A slight delay that's all, you'll soon see the beloved country.'

His eyes remained fixed on white cliffs.

———

We sat in silence waiting for rescue, the dinghy's aged boards creaking as we drifted slowly south. I prayed help would arrive before the rain.

Jeremiah stiffened. 'I can hear something. It sounds like a motor.' He peered into the distance. 'It's a boat, we're going to be rescued, we're safe at last.' He waved furiously, both arms pumping. 'Hello, hello, over here, over here. Wave Julia, wave.'

CHAPTER THIRTEEN

Anxious to delay what promised to be an awkward meeting, I shuffled along a familiar corridor towards Choddy's office. Finding the door closed, I took several deep breaths before knocking lightly.

'Come in,' Choddy called.

I turned the handle, lingered in the doorway, reluctant to step inside.

'Ah Julia. I see you got my note.'

'Yes. I'm so sorry for all the inconvenience we caused yesterday. We were very foolish taking out an old boat like that.'

Choddy smiled warmly. 'There's no need to apologise, it was an accident. Thank God Martin was on the cliff. Another couple of hours and the incoming tide could have swept you onto the rocks, there are strong currents on that side of the island. It has happened before, so I'm told, a local fishing boat lost in fog, smashed to pieces. There were no survivors.' He gestured towards the chair on the other side of his desk. 'Sit down will you, it's time we had a talk.'

'About yesterday?'

'No, about Jeremiah.'

I walked forward, slid into the chair.

'You're pretty close to him, aren't you?'

'I'm an adult,' I answered defensively. 'What I do after class is no concern of this college.'

'I want to talk about Jeremiah, your relationship with him is your business.'

Embarrassed now, I focused my attention on the desk.

'Did Jeremiah tell you why he came to Eden College?'

'Yes, his church sent him.'

'So, you're aware of the situation?'

'Of course.' I looked up, met Choddy's gaze. 'Jeremiah needed time to consider his calling.' Eager to show my familiarity with my lover's plans, I prattled on about building bridges and sinking wells in poor Nigerian villages; his need to be away from family and work in order to determine if the calling was indeed the will of God. 'After all,' I concluded, 'it won't be an easy task leaving the city he's called home for so many years. Although I must admit I don't like the sound of Lagos.'

Choddy shifted in his seat, then leant forward. 'Jeremiah doesn't live in Lagos, Julia. He lives in Bournville, a suburb of Birmingham, England. He moved there at the age of nine with his parents. The family fled Nigeria during the Biafran war. To my knowledge he has never been back.'

'I think you must be mistaken,' I replied, refusing to admit Choddy might know more than I did. 'Jeremiah has told me all about his life in Nigeria: people, places, politics, graphic descriptions of corruption, poverty and filth. They weren't a child's memories. One phrase stuck in my mind, although I'm not sure he meant me to take it seriously. He said, "only a masochist with an exuberant taste for self-violence will pick Nigeria for a holiday."'

'That's a line by Chinua Achebe, the Nigerian writer,' Choddy said quietly.

'Are, are you certain?'

'Yes. The quote is from Achebe's book 'The Trouble with Nigeria.' If I remember correctly it begins, "Nigeria is not a great country."'

'That's exactly how Jeremiah began.' I sniffed back tears. 'Why did he lie to me, Choddy?'

'He finds it easier to surround himself with illusion.'

'I don't understand.'

Choddy sighed and sat back in his seat. 'Jeremiah suffers from severe depression and has done so for many years. At present, he's recovering from a prolonged episode that began over six months ago.'

'I see.'

He began to fiddle with a pen. I watched it roll between chubby fingers, wishing he would resume the sorry tale, yet dreading unwelcome truths.

After a lengthy silence, he placed the pen on the desk. 'In March this year, I was approached by Jeremiah's pastor who felt that a term at Eden College would be more beneficial than another period in a psychiatric hospital. I agreed and subsequently contacted Jeremiah's psychiatrist. He was happy for Jeremiah to come here, provided a member of staff could administer his medication and monitor his general health. May Gordon worked as a nurse before coming here to teach, so after consulting her, I was able to reassure the psychiatrist Jeremiah would be well cared for here.'

Truth destroyed *my* illusion. I bit my lips to stifle dismay.

'I realise this must come as a shock, Julia, but I thought you should know before you become too involved.'

'It's too late Choddy, I love him.'

'I see.' He picked up the pen again, held it taut between index finger and thumb.

'I'm not sure you do,' I retorted, immediately regretting my sharp tone.

'Then perhaps you could explain,' Choddy said mildly.

'Love can help Jeremiah find the way forward,' I began, gripping the arms of the chair to bolster flagging confidence. 'He hungers for Africa and reading books or spinning tales won't ease his pain. He needs to make that journey to Nigeria, return to where he belongs. Naturally he's apprehensive, God knows it will be a very different life over there, but with a loving partner beside him he can move towards a meaningful future. He is an African, Choddy, there is no other truth.'

'Africa is a dream, Julia, he will never return.'

'That's your opinion. I happen to hold a different view.'

Leaning forward, he stabbed the pen into a pile of papers. 'Please listen to me, Julia. Jeremiah takes refuge in the past, ancient gods, ancestors, village life long before the Biafran war. It's a retreat to an imaginary childhood, life before bloodshed, starvation and poverty. According to his psychiatrist, some victims of childhood trauma believe denying the 'real' past enables them to cope with whatever the present demands. Jeremiah has never come to terms with his horrific childhood. He suffers from recurrent nightmares, which impact on both his physical and mental health and probably triggered the depression in the first place.' He paused, carefully placed the pencil in a tubular container. 'You must try to understand you're dealing with a clinically depressed person.'

How dare he address me in this manner. I'm not a child, I understand the meaning of depression and don't need his advice on how to handle my lover. 'No wonder Jeremiah's depressed,' I snapped, conscious of reddening cheeks. 'Who wouldn't be in his situation. Living in a society he despises, playing the role of pseudo-Englishman, mortgage, school fees, high-profile job; all the demands of Western culture. What's more he can't see a way out or couldn't until he came here and realised he can do anything if he has faith.'

'In God?'

'In himself,' I stammered, wary of a quiescent deity.

Silence descended, a thick blanket amplifying embarrassment. I contemplated making a run for the door.

'If you don't mind my asking, Julia, when you mentioned a loving partner accompanying Jeremiah to Africa, were you referring to yourself or his wife Elizabeth?'

'Marriages end,' I answered, deliberately avoiding the question. 'I told you before, I love him, and he loves me. Nothing is impossible under those circumstances.'

'And is this what you were sorting out with God the other day?'

Furious that May Gordon had reported a private conversation, I jumped to my feet. 'I'm sorry Choddy, but I really don't wish to discuss this matter any further. If you'll excuse me.'

I fled from probing questions and all-seeing eyes.

CHAPTER FOURTEEN

CLEAR MORNING LIGHT DISPLACED THE THICK FOG OF dream, but no matter how hard I tried, the irrational mono-logue that had haunted pre-dawn hours, refused to end, the narrative repeating over and over like a damaged disc stuck in a cd player.

I shall lead you out of exile, give me your hand and don't look back, the sun has set on yesterday. People and places belonging to those hours are but a memory now. Come raise your eyes from this cold island earth and walk with me towards a golden tomorrow. The Promised Land waits for you, waits to embrace your wounded spirit. Your name is spoken in wide rivers, in the depths of dense forests, along palm-fringed shores. Don't disappoint your homeland; she desires your return. Move forward; see how easy it is with someone close beside you. Someone who truly loves you, who can help you attain your goal.'

'Even in dream, gullible Julia imagines she can find refuge in allegory,' a second interior voice mocked.

Crushed, I sank back on the pillows, stared vacantly at a much-studied ceiling. My eyes stung, a burning itching sensation that sleep, albeit not much, had failed to alleviate. Hours earlier, exhausted from exodus and re-entry, I had wept copious tears, though whether for myself or Jeremiah or thwarted plans, I still had no notion.

Africa had seemed an imminent possibility as I rowed away from the island. A short hop to the coast, a bus ride to London, a flight to Lagos; in less than twenty-four hours I could be standing on unfamiliar ground, a brand-new future unfurling before me. But my dream of expanding horizons remained unfulfilled. I had returned to a series of diminutive circles: red brick walls surrounded by green lawns, surrounded by brown tree trunks, surrounded by white cliffs, surrounded by grey-green water. Unbroken circles, ropes coiling around my body, digging into soft flesh, binding me to a place I yearned to leave. Blinking, I refocused on the desk, tidied prior to yesterday's escape attempt. Next to the pile of books I'd failed to return to the college library, lay a pair of scissors borrowed from the art room. Scissors designed to cut paper or a single thread, so even if I could reach out and grab them, what use would they be when dealing with thick rope?

Wind and tide had brought us back to the island, or was it God, determined to return recalcitrant pilgrims? As we drifted towards the cliffs, Jeremiah had spoken of disobedience, but I dismissed his fears with foolish talk of freedom. The know-it-all white woman: educated, sophisticated, confident. A sharp contrast to the Julia who lay huddled in her bed, diminished by failure and so, so alone.

Following our rescue, Jeremiah had retired to his room, refusing to speak to anyone, at least according to what Martin told me over supper. I presumed his silence was a defensive device, a way to avoid humiliation. Confessing he'd been spooked into fleeing the island by a spirit-woman who haunted the cliff-top could be viewed as evidence of severe mental breakdown. Or was he simply ashamed of his actions, his manipulation of a gullible woman? But how could I speculate on his current state of mind, this man I loved passionately yet barely knew? And what about my state of mind? For weeks, he had stirred in me emotions so raw, so extreme they induced interminable periods of pain as body and soul screamed for release. How long could I bear such torment? Even the ecstasy of physical union seemed fraught with agony, for his withdrawal left a void deep within. Cracked in two, I was coming apart at the seams. Only when he filled me again, could I experience wholeness.

A small voice wormed its way through muddied thoughts. 'Walk away,' it advised, 'return to your own land, known places, familiar people.'

Obedient, I rose from my bed and walked over to the noticeboard where family faces hung smiling and silent. Brian, Stephen, Penny, Dad: four names, four photographs embodying countless days of love and laughter. Soon, three of them at least would be waiting in the arrivals area while I scanned the carousel for luggage and cursed the lengthy customs queues. Concealed behind opaque sliding doors, would I hesitate, knowing it was only a few steps to their waiting arms? A few steps to hugs and kisses, a few steps to warm sunshine and the clear blue sky of a Brisbane winter day. Could I really return as if nothing had changed?

Cold summer rain spattered the windowpane, smudging potential answers. Turning away from the notice-board, I pulled on yesterday's clothes, fled from solitude and the gaping wounds of my own rhetoric.

———

Donna welcomed my visit; she was feeling down, missing her own familiar faces. Sitting side by side on the floor, backs against the bed, we discussed our children and the challenge of motherhood in a world where traditional values seemed to have been swept away. Her boys, Robbie and Jamie, lay in her lap, shiny photographs dog-eared from excessive handling.

'I can't wait to see their cheeky faces,' she said for the umpteenth time, clasping the photographs to her breast.

'I feel ambivalent about returning home,' I ventured, unsure whether to broach a complex subject. 'Part of me longs to be back with my family, performing everyday tasks and chatting about ordinary things, but I'm scared as well.'

'About settling back into the same old routine?'

'Maybe, but I think there's more to it.'

'Want to talk about it?' she asked, her brown eyes tender with concern.

Grateful, I nodded. 'The problem is I'm not the same Julia they said goodbye to all those weeks ago. I've been changed by my experiences here, so I wonder if they'll accept me?'

'If you don't mind my saying, I think it's more a question of whether *you* can accept the new Julia.'

Uncertain how to respond, I stared at my feet.

'When we first met,' she continued, reaching out to take my hand, 'I thought your view of life naive. Follow the right path and all will be well, you seemed to be saying. Your path was a highway, straight and wide with no deviations. You knew where you were going, had no need to look in the rear-view mirror.'

'It didn't take me long to crack.'

'Don't interrupt, I haven't finished.'

'Sorry.'

'Forgiven.' Gently she released my hand and lifted my drooping chin. 'It looks to me like God wanted to throw a spanner in the works, 'cos everything was just too darn perfect.'

'To make me grateful for a happy marriage and great kids?'

'No, to help you understand yourself.'

'Care to elaborate, I promise to be a good listener?'

'Good. Well, how I see it, there's a shadow side to everyone, thoughts and feelings that often we refuse to acknowledge. We push them away or bury them deep, convinced we can banish them forever. But sooner or later they surface, give us a nudge and remind us that we're human after all.

'Take me for instance. I wanted to be the perfect mother, show the world that a black woman from the wrong side of town could rear two kids single-handed and hold down a good job and take Sunday school classes and help out at summer camp during vacation. I managed fine for years and folks at church just shook their heads and said, "My, Donna Jones, how you do it?" I would smile sweetly, answer that the Lord gave me strength. But he kicked my butt one day and when I'd gotten over the shock, the humiliation really, I sure was thankful.'

'What on earth happened?' I asked, unable to remain silent any longer.

'Oh, I should have seen it coming. The boys had been acting strange. You know, secretive, whispering and giggling together. They'd taken to playing down in the old parking lot while I made supper. It was summer, so I didn't see any harm in it and Jimmy and Pete from the church, they were 'bout fifteen, well, they were always around to keep an eye on them. The twins were keeping me sweet, flowers some days and candy too. Bless 'em, I thought, they're spending their allowance on me. I didn't even catch on when they gave me a silk scarf for my birthday. You could've knocked me down with a feather when Officer Jardine called round and told me the boys had been caught stealing from the drug store.'

'Oh my God,' I exclaimed without thinking, added quickly, 'Did you find out why they were stealing?'

'Oh yeah, it seems they had a bet with some kids at school.'

'A bet?'

'Yeah, they wanted to beat me at my own game.'

I shuddered. What on earth was Donna trying to tell me?

'Apparently the boys had a month to prove themselves.' She laughed. 'They did well, three weeks thieving before they were caught.'

I swallowed hard.

'It sure put me in my place,' she continued, unaware of my discomfort. 'Made me realise I'd been too busy being Superwoman, to notice what my own kids were getting up to.'

'Donna,' I said tentatively, 'you've never told me what sort of work you do.'

'No, I thought I'd leave all that behind in New York City, it can alter the way folk relate to me. I wanted to be plain Donna Jones here.' She leant towards me. 'But I guess I should tell *you* Julia, seeing as we're such good friends.'

'Whatever it is, it won't make any difference to our friendship,' I assured her.

'Here goes then. At work I'm known as Officer Jones, juvenile crime. I made the highest number of arrests in the precinct last year. Now you know why I felt I'd been kicked off my perch.' She laughed again, a rich throaty sound that filled the small room.

'Oh Donna,' I blurted out, 'I'm such a fool. I thought you were going to say you were a thief.'

'And what were you going to do, absolve my sins?'

'Something like that,' I murmured.

For a few minutes, we sat together, arms wrapped loosely around one another's waists, the only sound summer rain beating against the window.

CHAPTER FIFTEEN

FIVE DAYS HAD PASSED SINCE OUR FORCED RETURN, BUT I hadn't seen Jeremiah at meals or in class or in the chapel. Notes pushed under his door remained unanswered and my knocking was ignored. Brooding on possible reasons for his prolonged silence occupied my mind a great deal, especially during the night. Was he on hunger strike as a protest against the white world, was he sick, or unable to face me after the failure of our escape? After five restless nights, I determined to uncover the truth, so decided to pay another visit to the third floor and risk his wrath by trying the door handle.

In the corridor leading to Jeremiah's room, I encountered Martin carrying a tray. 'Hi Martin,' I said from behind him. 'Is someone sick?'

'Yes, Jeremiah. Your little adventure the other day has brought on an attack of nerves. Don't worry, he'll be fine in a few days. It's probably delayed shock.'

'I'll take the tray if you like. I was going to visit him anyway.'

'Thanks, I am rather busy.'

I quickly relieved him of the supper tray.

'Oh Julia,' he said, almost as an afterthought, 'be gentle with him, won't you.'

'Of course, I do understand the situation.'

But I failed to understand the man. Loving Jeremiah was easy, fathoming the complexity of his psyche almost impossible. The remaining weeks of term would be difficult, now that I had accepted the inevitable ending of this all-consuming relationship.

Outside his door, I hesitated before knocking. 'Supper, Jeremiah.'

'Come in it's not locked.'

Pushing the door open with the tray, I stepped inside.

'Julia,' he exclaimed, as though I was the last person he expected to see.

'I was coming to visit, so thought I'd bring your supper. I'm sorry to hear you're sick.' Clutching the tray, I stood by the door uncertain whether to approach the bed where he sat cross-legged, swathed in his red blanket. Only his face remained visible and his eyes were half-closed, so I couldn't gauge his reaction to my presence.

'Shall I put the tray on the desk?'

'Yes please.'

I felt more at ease with my back to him, but realised I would have to turn around before long. Meanwhile, I went through the motions of setting out cutlery and condiments. Soon, a shuffling sound alerted me to his presence, thin arms encircled my waist and warm breath agitated the hairs on the back of my neck. Unwilling to participate, I remained bent over the supper tray. Fingers burrowed into my shirt, progressed slowly around my abdomen and up to my breasts. Nipples strained against white cotton.

No, I wanted to shout, we need, I need to talk first. My

head was teeming with a hundred and one questions, questions that required answers. Words pushed to the surface: why the silence Jeremiah, why the solitude, why the lies? He squeezed my breasts and the queries died on my lips. I struggled to voice others, but his hands were everywhere, pressing soft flesh, pushing towards my liquid centre. Lips nuzzled my neck, blood rushed to my temples as I tried frantically to cool burning desire and recover the language of protest.

'Jeremiah,' I cried out at last, but my tone contained no hint of dissent. He pressed against the crack of my buttocks.

'No talk,' he commanded and spinning me around, began to remove my clothes.

The red blanket lay crumpled on the floor and his hardness danced as he released me from cotton and denim. Cool evening air assaulted my skin and I shivered uncontrollably. Oblivious, or indifferent, he grasped my waist and we sank to the floor, our faces almost touching. Compliant, despite my need for answers, I sat astride him, and we rocked together, one flesh, one spirit, disparate selves reunited by the power of passion.

———

Lush flora surrounded us, protection from a world grown dry with discord. Summer fragrance filtered through the open window; soft light lingered long into evening. We had returned to an unsullied garden. Quiet and content, I sat beside him as he ate his meal. No need for conversation; the atmosphere teemed with loving greetings. Fingers broke brown bread, dipped chunks into warm red soup. He offered a piece but no longer hungry, I declined with a shake of the head. When he had finished, I slipped on my clothes and descended to the kitchen to fetch coffee.

Facing the window, our hands clasped around thick brown mugs, we watched the earth compose herself for sleep. I offered a few parting words, then tilted my head to receive a goodnight kiss. His response was unexpected. Placing two fingers on my lips, he took my arm with his free hand and led me to bed.

Sleep came swiftly, remained sweet, dreamless.

———

'Tuesday,' Jeremiah announced the moment I opened my eyes. 'Choddy's class. It should be an interesting one today. If I remember correctly, he's going to discuss life after Eden.'

'What?' I asked, still half asleep.

'What we plan to do when term ends. How we're going to apply what we've learned here to our everyday lives.' Bouncing out of bed, he flung open the curtains. 'Ah blessed sunshine and an almost blue sky.'

I glanced at my watch. 'Come back to bed, it's only six-thirty.'

'No, there's so much to do before class.' He danced to the washbasin, splashed water over his face, retrieved clothes from the back of the chair. 'Now for a walk in the garden before morning service. Come on, sleepyhead.'

I would have loved a hot shower and a change of clothes but felt reluctant to cause any delay. A caged animal, he paced back and forth as I eased myself out of bed and into crumpled clothes.

'Are you ready?' he asked impatiently.

'Yes.'

'Great, let's go.' He was out of the door and bounding down the stairs before I could goad my sluggish body into action.

———

The chapel was almost full; it seemed we weren't the only ones to be up and about early. Beside me, Jeremiah knelt on the cold stone floor, hands clasped, eyes shut tight. The intensity of his prayer enveloped me, and I gained a little comfort from its presence. Little by little confidence returned, so I attempted my own petition, but *my* prayer lacked substance and floated away through an open window. Determined to persevere, I kept trying until Choddy broke the silence.

'Thanks be to God for this new day,' he cried, raising his arms heavenward. 'May we go to our various tasks refreshed by the night's rest and secure in the knowledge he will guide us through the coming hours.'

'Thanks be to God for sunshine,' Benjamin added from the front pew.

'And blue sky with only a few clouds,' Jeremiah offered, his voice tremulous, his body quivering beside me.

'And Jeremiah's presence among us, healed by the grace of God,' Choddy exclaimed, his face suffused with joy. Arms outstretched, he hurried down the aisle, heading it seemed, for the pew where we still knelt, palms pressed together. Jeremiah leapt to his feet, pushed past me into a tender embrace.

Cradled in Choddy's arms, he sobbed loudly, shaking violently as though having an epileptic fit. Prayers swirled around the chapel, messages of hope for a pilgrim in distress. Slowly, the sobbing subsided and trembling ceased, leaving him limp as a rag doll reliant on strong arms for support. Silence hung heavy, other worshippers waiting, uncertain whether to stand up or settle back into prayer. Alert to his flock's indecision, Choddy gently raised Jeremiah's head and led him down the aisle. Sighs permeated the chapel, bodies relaxed, stretched, filed out into new day.

Taut as a drum, my body ignored my brain and remained fixed to the pew. Any semblance of prayer had long since departed, leaving me with a host of troubling thoughts. Jeremiah's outburst had caught me unawares. Fellow students and staff had thrown him lifelines of love, but I could only grip the pew in front and try to contain erratic emotions. All I had observed were Choddy's arms embracing *my* lover; all I had heard were *his* words calming a wounded spirit; all I had felt were *others'* prayers bathing Jeremiah in light. I could offer him nothing; the searing pain of jealousy had eclipsed all other thoughts.

So, Jeremiah had sought solace elsewhere, so, he was upheld by another's love. So what! Choddy was a man of God, trained to assist the spiritually troubled, how could he have ignored a cry for help? Would I have wanted him to push Jeremiah aside or the congregation to remain mute? A rational response echoed in my head. 'Of course not, love has many facets.'

Paul's words to the people of Corinth came to mind. 'Love is not jealous, or conceited or proud,' I said aloud, but my voice faltered before I'd reached the end of the verse, the lines I knew so well lost in mental mire.

'Help me, God,' I cried to the empty chapel, my plea striking solid stone walls before falling to the floor and shattering into dust.

Gravity had intervened; God the Father, God the Son and God the Holy Spirit remained an absent trinity.

Crushed, I propelled myself down the aisle and out of the chapel.

Outside on the path, I ignored gathering clouds and headed for the woods. I wanted to run, run as fast as I could, away from that seething cauldron where emotions boiled over. A place of peace, the brochure had proclaimed, a haven where faith flourished. 'Lies, all lies!' I shouted to the trees. 'This is no Eden; this is the wild land beyond the garden walls. There's no order here, all I can see is torrid desert and tangled forest and wind-swept tundra. I have been betrayed.'

My feet pounded the narrow path and before long I was out of the trees and racing towards the sea. I would find peace out on the ocean, that I knew for certain. Peace and the freedom to be myself again, to be in control, to determine the next step with rational deliberation. I had been betrayed but I would not surrender. In the name of God, I refused to fall into the soldiers' arms.

'And where are you going in such a hurry?' someone called behind me.

The question startled; I thought everyone else had returned to the house. 'The sea,' I answered without stopping, or turning to see who was there.

'Wait, I'll walk with you.'

I increased my stride.

'There's no boat today, Julia.'

Feet faltered, lungs heaved; I fell in a heap onto soft grass.

Choddy ran up the path and flopped down beside me. 'Running away never achieves anything,' he said, putting his arm around my shoulder. 'Troubles always follow. Besides, this isn't the time to leave, there's still work for you to do here.'

'I've had enough. I can't take any more of this place. It's impossible to live at fever pitch all the time. For Christ's sake, Choddy, I need a break. My emotions are shot to pieces. I can't think, I can't pray, I can't study.'

'Eden College has that effect sometimes,' he said placidly. 'There's nothing to worry about.'

'Nothing to worry about, are you mad? I came here a happy levelheaded person, my life was in order, not perfect I grant you, but heading in the right direction, following the right path. Ten weeks later I'm a total mess, no direction, no path, no God. I don't understand what's going on.'

'Don't you?'

'Choddy, have you been listening?'

'Oh yes, I've heard every word.'

'Then tell me what on earth's going on.'

'It's simple, Julia.' He looked in the direction of the sea. 'Islands are isolated places therefore they evolve differently. Surrounded by sea, nothing from outside can penetrate, so change has to come from within. In other words, one's real self surfaces and is exposed, warts and all. Initially, this can result in chaos, for we don't always like what we see. But we have to come to terms with who we really are, it's the only way out of the mess, the only way forward.'

'But I don't know where to begin?'

'Begin by sharing your hopes and fears.' He turned to face me. 'Perhaps you'd like to tell me what you see as the major stumbling block. I'm a good listener.'

'I know you are.' I took several deep breaths. 'Ok, I'll try, but I'm not certain it will make much sense. The main problem as I see it, is trying to comprehend my altered behaviour. After only a few days here I had jettisoned all my old ways of thinking. I was never a passionate person, but now I find my life dominated by passion. Here, every emotion is amplified. It's like watching life on a giant screen. I've had enough. I want to shrink the image back to normal.'

'Why?'

'Because passion is so debilitating. I've no energy left for just being.'

'I think you're mistaken Julia, passion is an important part of life. It allows us to feel deeply, to see the world in technicolour. I agree the images aren't always pleasant but, and here's the real blessing, because they're so bold, they evoke a reaction. They make us hurt, angry, sad, joyful and as a result we're able to change, not just ourselves but our world.'

'Do you honestly believe that?'

'Yes.'

'Then why did you leave South Africa, that's a part of the world in dire need of change? There's not much you can alter on a tiny Welsh island.'

He reddened and looked away.

I immediately regretted my harsh words. Atypical behaviour again, why on earth was I being so rude when he was trying to help? 'I'm so sorry Choddy. I had no right to say that.'

'It's ok, my problem. I'm still coming to terms with leaving. It's difficult being parted from loved ones.'

I envisaged a black woman and child waiting in Soweto. Why couldn't you bring them with you, I wanted to ask, then realised my total ignorance of South African laws on interracial relationships. 'Perhaps that's *my* problem,' I said instead. 'The familiar functions are irrelevant here. I'm no longer mother, wife, sister, daughter.' I paused. 'Yes, that's it Choddy, I've lost my identity. No wonder I'm confused.'

Leaning back, I lifted my face to the sun, relieved to have solved a problem.

'May I ask a personal question, Julia?'

Danger signs flashed before my eyes. He was going to ask whether my relationship with Jeremiah had altered now that I knew the truth. 'Of course,' I answered politely.

'How would you describe your marriage?'

A sigh of relief; I could cope with this question. 'Brian and I have a good life together. Would you believe we've never had a serious argument? He's a good man, helps around the house and he's a great dad to Stephen and Penny. He's supportive of my spiritual life as well, even though he doesn't feel any need for God. Oh, and we enjoy sailing together.'

'Where's the passion?'

Had I heard him correctly? A middle-aged couple married for twenty years; passion didn't come into the equation.

'We love each other, if that's what you mean, but ours isn't a passionate relationship, it never has been. Brian and I were friends first, we met at work and it sort of developed from there. After a few months, marriage seemed an appropriate next step. I don't regret it.' I relaxed, relieved to be in control. Back on an even keel, I could be nice, polite, happily married, middle-class Julia Mitchell. Nice husband, nice kids, nice house in the suburbs. Oh, and don't forget the boat, a trailer-sailer, nothing too ostentatious and easily towed by the Holden Commodore.

'But now that you've experienced life in technicolour, can you go back to pastel shades?'

Colour flooded my face, the core of my being exposed and subject to intense scrutiny. A crazy love affair was tearing me apart, no wonder I felt terrified. Jeremiah filled me with love and desire, irritated me beyond belief, stirred up the anger and jealousy in me, pervaded my dreams, my thoughts, my prayers. Even when we were apart, I felt tied to him, could still feel his hand in mine, see his face clearly, hear his words, sense his breath stirring the cool air. Day after day, night after night, my passion for him had propelled me towards a future I couldn't begin to envisage, in a land I had never seen, amongst people with whom I had nothing in common, not even the colour of my skin.

'Oh Choddy,' I cried, 'what can I do, I love Jeremiah so much?'

'Come back with me to the chapel,' he replied, taking my hand and pulling me to my feet. 'If you find it difficult to pray, I'll pray for you. God *is* there, believe me, even in our darkest hour he is there.'

We walked away from the sea arms draped around each other's waists. The warmth of his arm and the soft pad of midriff beneath my hand, soothed my troubled spirit and I surged with tenderness for this man of God who spent his life helping others. His past remained an unknown story, but his brief allusion to suffering had ironically, given *me* a spark of hope. Truth had smashed my islands dreams, but at least I could return to a loving family, re-take my place in a society that sanctioned every aspect of my chosen way of life.

———

Sitting beside Choddy in the chapel, I marvelled at the depth of his prayer. Prayer given freely just for me, prayer to lighten the sorrow shadowing my soul. The strength of his faith gave me courage and a modicum of peace, even though I still failed to sense a holy presence.

Soft silence descended after prayer and we sat for many minutes breathing in peace. Summer breeze wafted through open windows, shafts of sunlight warming aged grey stone. Reaching out, I grasped his hand to squeeze my gratitude. He responded with a radiant smile and quietly took his leave. Tranquil at last, I lingered, confident spiritual connection would return before too long.

CHAPTER SIXTEEN

A RUSH OF WIND CAUGHT ME UNAWARES AND DREW MY gaze to the open window at the end of the pew. Framed by grey stone, a female figure hovered, fragile as mist. Inexplicably, I felt unafraid, so remained seated, resolved to discover if she could be the apparition Jeremiah had seen on the cliffs. A face materialised: prominent chin, bony nose, thin lips, weathered skin etched with a web of fine lines, long strands of grey hair escaping from clips—an old white woman.

Sliding along the pew to gain a closer view, I discerned a startled expression, saw arms outstretched as though reaching for something or someone. Light dawned; she was no angry ancestor come to torment a troubled African in exile. Ghost of a Welsh islander, she was one of the people Choddy had mentioned, drowned when a fishing boat foundered on rocks. A restless spirit doomed to spend eternity wandering her native island. But why was she looking through the chapel window? I thought perhaps she sought salvation, sudden death having denied her the opportunity to make her peace with God. That could explain why she lacked the courage to enter the chapel. What did she want with me, I wasn't her descendant? I knew my paternal ancestors had been seafaring folk as far back as my great-great grandfather, but they had inhabited a different island, surrounded by a different sea. My maiden name might have been Evans, but no family member had ever mentioned a Welsh connection.

Comforted by rational explanation, I bowed my head and prayed for her release, but when I opened my eyes, she remained floating in the window, watching and waiting, a menacing presence now. Fear clogged my throat, at last I understood her purpose. She wanted me to join her, become another defeated soul.

Summoning all the courage I possessed, I leapt to my feet, grabbed the window latch and pulled tight. Metal rang on stone as it fell from my hands. Shaking, I sank to my knees, prayed hard for deliverance from doubt and despair.

When I left the chapel, I deliberately turned left and left again, counting casement windows until reaching the one where the old woman had lingered. Stretching up, I managed to press the tips of my fingers against the windowsill. The stone was warm and when I glanced up, the stained-glass panel gleamed in morning sunlight.

Back in the sanctuary of my room, I rejected the notion of a drowned fisherwoman and concluded the apparition had been nothing more than the product of overwrought emotions.

———

After yesterday's unnerving experiences in the chapel, I felt relieved when Choddy announced we were adjourning to the art room to experiment with clay and paint. Although I found artwork of any kind challenging, daubing paint or making a sculpture would be a welcome respite from complex and confronting spirit-work. Before long we were settled at trestle tables replete with paper, paint pots and lumps of clay, waiting patiently for instruction. My spirits fell when Choddy informed us the day's task was to mould our faith or paint its myriad colours.

'I would prefer you to disregard any preconceived ideas,' he added, following a glance at his watch. 'This is to be an exercise of the spirit. And no talking please until everyone has completed either a painting or a sculpture.' Turning on his heel, he retired to the plastic chair in a corner.

I contemplated a lump of reddish-brown clay and quickly rejected sculpture. The pot I'd made during a previous visit to the art room had been a complete failure. So, I reached for a paintbrush, wavered a moment before dipping it into a paint pot. The thick brush felt unwieldy, but I remained determined to paint as directed, so allowed my hand to be guided across the paper.

After a while, I noticed Choddy had risen from his seat and was ambling around the room, inspecting each piece of faith-art. When he reached my table, a surge of embarrassment flushed my cool cheeks. My painting resembled a pre-school child's effort: a rectangular red house with square windows, surrounded on three sides by green shapes vaguely resembling trees, a yellow circle sun with uneven rays in one corner. The painting made no sense to me, I had imagined a seascape would emerge, blue-green ocean and a red boat with trim white sails. Fortunately, Choddy soon moved on.

The bell announced lunch break just as purple flowers began to bloom in front of my little red house.

'Time to finish,' Choddy called from his corner. 'You can collect your paintings and sculptures after lunch. They will have dried by then, so you can take them back to your rooms for further contemplation. I trust you all found this a helpful exercise.'

So that's it, I thought, grateful we weren't expected to share an interpretation of our work, but all the same, wishing for a little guidance.

————

Pinned on my noticeboard below family photographs, the mystery painting proved a constant distraction during afternoon study. Was I afraid it would fade in summer light? Surely not, primary colours had depth and Welsh sun remained gentle. My eyes alighted on the triangle apex and I realised that unlike the simple drawings illustrating the mostly British books of my early childhood, this house had no chimney. I had drawn a tropical dwelling, a contemporary Queensland low-set, my home in a bayside suburb. Pushing back my chair, I moved over to the noticeboard and reached up to touch the painting. Pale against the red house, my fingers appeared thinner than usual and my watchstrap slipped a little. There was no longer a white line around my wrist.

Washed-out woman. Faded faith.

Back at the desk, I extracted a red felt-tip pen from my pencil case and opened my journal. Red seemed an appropriate colour for the day's reflections, strong enough to marshal my wandering thoughts.

————

Engrossed, I failed to notice the door open.

'Too much study makes Julia a dull girl,' declared a familiar voice. The pen hit the desk and rolled onto the floor as Jeremiah kissed the back of my neck.

'What are you drawing?' he asked, leaning over me.

'Who knows, I usually express myself in words not images.'

He slid his index finger over the paper. 'Um, red triangles. Are they going to be more houses?'

'Unlikely.'

'Faith?'

I shrugged.

Easing his thin backside onto the desk, he traced triangles with a fingertip. 'Three sides, equal distances.'

'Trinity,' I exclaimed. 'Father, Son and Holy Spirit.'

He bent to kiss my forehead. 'A brilliant deduction, my love! Now will you come into the garden; this fine weather is too good to waste?'

———

Hands behind our heads, we lay on lush lawn, delighting in the warmth of the long afternoon. If I extended my arm, I could touch him, but his presence seemed sufficient. Conversation had been spasmodic since we chose a spot by the lake, we remained content to listen and observe. Among nearby reeds, ducks dived repeatedly, ruffling the lake's smooth surface. In the distance, sea-birds called.

'This spirit-art fascinates me,' Jeremiah remarked, rolling over onto his stomach. 'Two colours dominated my painting, red and black. When I studied the painting back in my room, I noticed there were equal numbers of red and black circles and triangles. Weird eh? I've been trying to think what they could mean.' He picked a nearby daisy and twirled it between his palms before tickling my cheek with soft petals.

Laughter shot into a pale blue sky.

'Your laugh is a bell,' he said softly. 'A little silver bell.'

My circle mouth dissolved into a crescent smile.

'Your smile is a ray of sunshine.'

A broad yellow band lingered on his lips, but I could see shadows in his eyes. Slivers of Welsh light were insufficient; he needed a golden globe to burn away the clouds.

'Sun, moon and stars,' he said, tilting his head to the late afternoon sky. 'He placed the lights in the sky to shine upon the earth, to rule over the day and the night, and to separate light from darkness. Day and night, the sum of our lives.'

'Like red and black shapes?' I suggested tentatively.

'My thoughts exactly, and now I must learn to accept both colours. Day and night, tears and laughter.' He stroked my cheek with the tips of his fingers.

'You will,' I replied and almost added, 'with me beside you.' But that would have been a presumption and how could I supplant the Holy Spirit.

'With God by my side,' he said, looking down at me.

———

After supper, we walked with Hannah and Benjamin to the tiny beach near the jetty. No old dinghy lying on the sand waiting for would-be escapees; she had been towed back to shore by a gleaming white speedboat, most likely destined for firewood. Prior to our rescue, I hadn't seen a speedboat anywhere near the island and still had no idea where it was berthed. Martin had known how to handle it, proving he wasn't the semi-recluse I had envisaged at the beginning of term.

Sitting in a row on the sand, all four of us kicked off our shoes and wriggled bare toes in the sand. Waves lapped the shore, sea-birds bobbed on a slight swell. Benjamin began to sing, his voice rich bass, the lyrics rolling from the back of his throat like ocean waves. Soon, Jeremiah and Hannah joined in, harmonising effortlessly. I longed to participate but sensed my white skin was an impediment. How could I meld with an African trio without diluting their powerful intonation?

'Come join us, Julia,' Hannah said, when the song had finished. 'I know you can sing. I've heard you in the chapel. I'll say the words slowly.'

Grateful, I watched her wide brown mouth.

'Soyiwela silwele ikulu le ki Africa. Got it?

I repeated the words.

'Right, let's try it together and then in parts.'

We sang together in perfect harmony.

'What does it mean?' I asked when we were silent once more.

'We'll struggle and struggle until Africa is free.'

Benjamin reached out to take her hand. 'It may be a long time coming but she will be free, and all her children will join hands and dance to celebrate.'

'And I shall play my drums,' Jeremiah cried, 'all through the victory night.'

Hannah seized my hand and pulled me to my feet. 'Come dance, Julia, the drums are calling.'

On and on we danced, pummeling sand, slapping our hands together, spinning around and around until we lost our balance and fell together arms hugging.

———

Evening song echoed in my head as I mounted the stairs to my room. Once inside, I went through the usual nocturnal routine and was about to climb into bed when I noticed my journal lying open on the desk. Red triangles snaked across the day's page; no room left for words. Somewhat relieved, I glanced at the morning's effort, illuminated in the soft glow of the bedside lamp. My little red house seemed to reflect all the warmth, love and laughter experienced on the beach. Calm and content, I slipped beneath the bedclothes and turning off the light gave thanks for the friends I had made during weird and wonderful weeks. And as I settled back on the pillows, the residue of black despair dissolved into night.

My dreams were full of triangles. Inverted triangles, red, black and white like Give Way signs at crossroads, T-junctions, intersections and roundabouts. Scattered across my dreamscape, they dominated the route, every sign damaged, the metal twisted, paintwork cracked or daubed with graffiti.

CHAPTER SEVENTEEN

RAIN FELL STEADILY ALL MORNING, THE LAKE STAYED shrouded in daybreak mist, woods and cliffs a distant memory enveloped in low-cloud. Reluctant to risk grey gloom, I arranged to meet Jeremiah in my room after lunch. He offered to make coffee in the diminutive room located at the end of my corridor, known as a 'tea spot.' Like similar spaces dotted around the building, it contained a sink, a tiny fridge and electric kettle, plus tea and coffee making supplies.

He took his time. Impatient, I tapped the desk with a pen and stared out of the window at a leaden sky. At last, the door opened but I remained seated, head bent over imaginary work.

'Close your eyes and don't open them until I say so,' he said behind me.

Mugs clinked on the desk; the smell of strong coffee wafted over my face.

'Hold out your hands.'

I complied, and he placed a small flat object on my cupped palms. It felt like something wrapped in paper.

'You can look now.'

I opened my eyes. 'Chocolate! Great, I haven't had any for weeks. Where did you get it?'

'Elizabeth sent it.'

'How?'

'In the post, of course. Don't tell me you fell for that rubbish in the brochure about contact with the outside world being detrimental to spiritual study?'

'I must admit I did.'

'Oh, good Lord you're so gullible!' He collapsed on my bed, his whole body shaking with laughing.

Annoyed, I studied the chocolate wrapper: Cadbury, made in Bournville, England. A suburb of Birmingham, from what Choddy had said. Unwrapping, I broke off two squares and began to chew thoughtfully.

'Good?' he asked.

'Delicious, I adore chocolate.' I held the wrapper up to the light. 'I'd be as big as a house if *I* lived near the Cadbury factory.'

'Who told you?' he demanded, sitting bolt upright and swinging his legs over the side of the bed as though about to leap up and grab the offending wrapper.

'Never you mind.' I slipped the wrapper under my notebook.

'How long have you known?'

I hesitated, contemplated whether to explain why I had waited two weeks to confront him. I should have challenged him straight after my meeting with Choddy. Trepidation had been the impediment, I couldn't face probable consequences, the immediate ending of our unstable relationship. 'Why the lies, Jeremiah?' I asked, ignoring his question.

He hung his head. 'I thought it might help.'

'Help what, seduce me? Africa the dark continent,

exotic, mysterious. I must admit it does sound more romantic than an industrial city in the middle of England.'

He looked up. 'You misunderstand, give me a chance to explain.'

I ploughed on, determined to have my say. 'You've done enough explaining or should I say spinning tales. I got sucked in all right, same as I did about the ferry not returning for three months and no contact with the outside world. But I don't like the word gullible, Jeremiah, I prefer trusting. I believed you because I love you and wanted to help make your African dream come true. Why didn't you trust me, I would have kept your secret?'

He sighed deeply and looked over my head to the window. 'I wanted to forget that dark winter, when I saw nothing but grey inside and out and heavy cloud pressed against my head squeezing my life into darkness. I wanted a new beginning and Eden seemed like a good place to start.'

'The garden of Eden is another fable.'

'There's always a grain of truth in legends,' he said defensively, turning away from the window. 'Anyhow, I felt safe within the garden walls. At least I did until that damn woman tried to lure me over the cliff. But I defeated her, didn't I and you won't catch me standing on the edge again, throwing gifts into the sea.' He thumped the mattress with his fist.

'You'll have to leave the island soon.'

'Yes, but it will be an easy journey this time. It's only a few miles to the harbour and we'll be in a seaworthy boat.'

'It's a long way to Africa, Jeremiah.'

I waited for a response, but he turned away, swung his legs back onto the bed. Hugging his knees, he rocked slowly back and forth, lowering his head with each movement, until the tip of his beard became sandwiched between his legs.

'You are still planning to go?' I asked, instantly regretting the question.

The rocking resumed.

'Oh Africa, my Africa,' he lamented, his voice hollow as a vacant shell. 'A dazzling memory I repeated to myself when cold wind whistled around our English house and rain beat against the grimy windows. She wouldn't tell me the stories anymore; she bought British books, made me read tales of Robin Hood and Long John Silver.'

He rocked faster and faster, his words a torrent plunging over a steep precipice.

'Each night we prayed to the white man's Jesus, pale-skinned prophet smiling down from the picture above my bed. Father, a true Yoruba, wanted to keep his options open, but she would have none of it. "There'll be no tribal gods in our nice semi-detached," she said, "we have British passports now. Look at the mess Nigeria's in, freedom didn't last long. We had to leave everything, get out quick. Thank God, thank Jesus for Uncle Isichei. We'd have been rotting in the earth if it hadn't been for him. You don't hear him talking about 'home' as if Nigeria is some sort of beautiful dream. He knows, and I know, that country is nothing but a nightmare. Safe dreams here, Jeremiah, safe dreams."'

He fell backwards, curled foetal fashion, cried softly.

A whimpering child, I enfolded him in my arms. 'The nightmare's over Jeremiah. You can return anytime. It's simple, go to Heathrow and buy a ticket. You'll be in Lagos in no time. Blue sky, hot sun and warm earth beneath your feet.'

'There's nothing left for me in Lagos.'

'The country's still there.'

He looked up eyes awash with tears. 'You don't understand, my past has been trampled by the thousands fleeing for their lives; it sank into that warm earth and decayed. It didn't take long, only cold preserves. The life I knew has gone.'

'Then make a new life, you said just now you wanted a fresh start.'

'But there's no path to guide me.'

'Follow the sun.'

He blinked, managed a small smile. 'I see rays of golden sunshine and a deep blue sky.'

I held his head tight against my breast.

'I feel heat and moisture.'

'See, you've already started the journey.'

'I emerge from the earth,' he declared pushing out of my arms. 'What a fool I was to forget that seeds need darkness.'

'And then light.'

He cradled my face in his hands. 'My journey began in a dark place, then light blazed, and I caught a glimpse of Eden.' He trembled and dropped his hands. 'But what if the vision fades before I can grasp it?'

'Africa isn't a vision,' I reassured, reaching out to stroke his woolly head. 'It's jungle and mountains, deserts and rivers, places and people old as time. Human life began there, dig deep and you will surely find Eden.'

'No Julia,' he said quietly, 'you misinterpret my words. The sunshine I see is your golden hair; your sapphire eyes are summer sky. *You* are long hot days and sultry nights.'

He kissed my cheek so gently, I felt as though a feather had brushed my skin. Then, without a word or smile, he moved to the end of the bed, tilted his head and stared at the ceiling. Century-old plaster, cracks concealed by blobs of white paint. 'But soon you will fly away to a land I can't even begin to imagine.'

Goosebumps erupted on my bare arms. 'I can make a fresh start, if you want me to.'

He shifted his gaze and studied my face as though from a vast distance. 'Talk is easy, words are weightless, they float before our eyes. But behind them lie solid blocks of life: children, spouses, homes, jobs. Words cost nothing, but life is an expensive exercise.'

CHAPTER EIGHTEEN

HUDDLED UNDER SEVERAL BLANKETS, LISTENING TO interminable rain, I began to draw deserts in my mind, sketched red sand into dunes, peppered the sky with black and white wings. A gecko darted across the sand and I smiled, reminded of the television programme, Quantum, one of Brian's favourites. 'A quantum leap,' I said aloud, envisaging a flight over deep ocean, a landing on foreign soil. *Feet first or head first,* I pondered? Reluctant to know the answer, I returned to windswept dunes and the sure-footed gecko. Warmed by Australian sun, I stretched pale limbs, wriggled cold toes in hot sand. Sleep enveloped me, black velvet, a clear desert night.

'This desert isn't the dead heart you feared,' Aunt Muriel said in my dream, reading from a letter she had written to me twenty-five years earlier. *'There's spinifex and tufts of yellow grass and insects buzzing. If I dig into the red earth, I'll find seeds waiting for a summer storm and if I stay long enough flowers will emerge and dance in the breeze. Desert nights are cold, but a brilliant canopy of stars shields me from*

harm. In the mornings, I walk along a nearby ridge and watch the wind sweep sand into new patterns. At noon, I sit in the shade of a mulga tree and listen to the silence.'

Swaddled in my narrow island bed, her words were tight in my head. The year I turned fifteen, she had asked me to accompany her on an outback odyssey, but I could see no purpose to such a journey and refused to turn my back on the sea. Twenty-five years on, her bones were brittle, dry as the bull dust that once coated her ancient Land Rover. The women died young in my family, unwilling perhaps to witness sagging suntanned skin or faded blonde hair. How many years before I joined them?

Pulling the bedclothes tighter, I pushed away life-span speculation and closed my eyes. Grey island light retreated; I slipped into Brisbane sunshine.

Dreaming back the decades, I saw a Give Way sign leaning precariously towards a patched bitumen road, its paintwork faint and peeling. A cracked concrete footpath bordered by clumps of nut-grass surrounded the twisted sign, an adjacent picket fence had several palings missing and the house behind was in need of a coat of paint. In the garden, a middle-aged woman waved to a girl mounting a red bicycle. The girl freewheeled down the hill that led to a broad esplanade and Moreton Bay.

The panorama altered, and I stood watching a heavily-laden truck accelerate up the same street. When it reached the intersection, a tyre exploded, sending the vehicle careering through the old fence, killing the woman as she tended her narrow strip of garden. The old Give Way sign toppled into the road. Only the house survived, saved for the girl, for her future. Life is an expensive exercise.

I awoke drenched in perspiration and threw back the covers to gulp fresh morning air. As my body cooled, the traumatic past receded and present obstacles evapourated, leaving a future clear as island streams. No impediments, Jeremiah. Why on earth hadn't it occurred to me before? I would write to our solicitor immediately and instruct him to put my house on the market. It shouldn't take long to sell, being in a good location close to public transport and shops. Sure, the house needed a bit of work but that didn't seem to deter buyers of old property. I could already see the advertisement in the Courier Mail:

Turn of the century worker's cottage. 2 bedrooms, bathroom, lounge/dining, sep. kitchen, large rear garden. Renovate and reap the rewards of heritage living.

The housing market had been buoyant for some time and my tenants' lease would expire within months. The timing couldn't have been better.

Liberty Jeremiah, true liberty! Airfares to Lagos, a Land Rover to take us into the interior, equipment to help Yoruba villagers! My little red house will supply all we need.

All through the day I hugged this knowledge to me, conscious I must wait for the right moment to break the news. In class I was bright and attentive, my mind unclouded as desert sky. Black cockatoo and red kangaroo, I soared and bounded across the arid land. Seed beneath the sand, I had become a future flower, a smiling golden face.

By late afternoon the rain had cleared, so Jeremiah and I walked over to the jetty, where we sat on damp timber throwing conversation into a choppy sea. He told me about the concert to be held on the last night of term, expressing delight that he'd been asked to play his drums.

'I'll need to practice,' he said, tapping the jetty rail with his fingers. 'I haven't played for weeks. I must ask Martin if I can use one of the classrooms in the evenings, preferably a good distance from the sitting rooms. I wouldn't want to disturb anyone.'

'The storeroom would be fairly soundproof,' I suggested, forgetting the rhythm of his drums could disturb *me* long after his fingers were still.

'The acoustics would be terrible in there. Besides, I'd feel claustrophobic.'

'What about outside in the garden?'

'In this climate, you must be joking?'

I slipped my arm around his waist. 'Imagine playing in a jungle clearing beneath the tropic night, dancers swaying to the rhythm, bewitched by your music.'

'Sometimes I hear drums in my dreams. The beat soothes me, transports me back to when life was simple and all I had to worry about was the next game of football.'

'The magic of childhood,' I murmured.

'I'm a spectator now,' he mused, gazing out to sea. 'I stand on the sidelines shouting encouragement to my boys. Matthew is a brilliant footballer but Luke, ah Luke's a dreamer. He doesn't concentrate, runs around the pitch without any real sense of direction. It's the same with his schoolwork. He's a clever boy but so easily distracted. His last school report was appalling, particularly his math. When I asked him why, he said, "well, you see Dad, there's a tree outside our classroom window with a nest in it and I've watched all the baby birds hatch and they're beautiful."' He turned to face me. 'What can you say to that?'

I shrugged, had no idea if he expected an answer.

'It's another matter with music,' he continued, turning back to the sea. 'Luke plays the drums brilliantly. He has natural rhythm, long sinewy fingers.' Jeremiah flexed his own fingers. 'He can sing too, perfect pitch. It transports me to another world.'

'Africa?'

'It doesn't have a name. It's a place of tranquillity where my troubles fade away. When he sings, I can forgive him anything. How I wish he could stay a child forever, wide-eyed and innocent, my beautiful boy soprano.'

'We all have to grow up.'

'Not too soon though, not too soon.'

He moved away from me, not far, just a few centimetres, but our thighs no longer touched, and I knew he was miles away in that grey industrial city, back in the bosom of his family, husband and father, respectable British citizen. Distressed, I struggled to suppress the emotions swirling like bands around my heart. Tighter and tighter they bound me, until pain seared my chest. I couldn't breathe, soon I would fall, drown in cold green water. Heavy with jealousy, how could I float?

'Oh Julia,' Jeremiah said, patting my hand. 'I forgot to give you Hannah's message. She's organizing a group to sing at the concert and would like you to be part of it. If you're interested, meet her in the small sitting room tonight after supper.'

The bands began to slacken. African faces swam before my eyes, African voices sang struggle, sang liberty, their continent, their song. 'I'm not sure I can sing in front of the whole college, it's different with a few friends.'

'You'll be fine, just imagine you're on a beach singing to the sea.' He kissed me lightly before jumping to his feet. 'Come Julia, it's time to go back. I don't want to miss supper. I need plenty of energy for drumming.'

I reached out, waiting for arms to encircle my waist. He

lifted me gently and then his lips found mine, his tongue pushed between my teeth, his legs pressed against mine.

Drums throbbed in my head; songs crooned in my heart. Elated, I drifted on warm currents, watertight, light as balsawood.

CHAPTER NINETEEN

AFTER SUPPER EACH EVENING, HANNAH'S CHORAL group—four women, two men, six nations—practiced in the chapel well away from Jeremiah and his drums.

During the initial session, I completely forgot my earlier apprehension, Hannah a born teacher, recognising our different talents and carefully melding them into a harmonious whole. Melody filled my head with the unfamiliar sounds of African languages as we learnt four songs for the concert. Jeremiah had agreed to provide background music for one item; we would be having a few joint rehearsals before long. Term finished in a couple of weeks, sand had already reached the narrow hourglass neck.

Fourteen days until we departed these shores, a sliver of time in the scheme of things, yet so many plans remained to be made, so many details to be considered. His life, my life, separate selves uniting to face a future beyond our, or at least my, wildest dreams. Soon, I would have to relay the message imparted through art and dream and prayer. Oh, I had prayed hard, tested the validity of dream in chapel and on cliff top. No ghosts haunted either space now, only a cold stone floor, chill wind and churning water. But beyond grey seas, high on a hill overlooking blue ocean, sat the solid substance of dreams, faded weatherboard and corrugated iron, my little red house.

Twilight slipped into night as I sat at my desk, disclosing the day's events to my journal. Love and laughter rang in my ears, spirit sang in my heart, crossing boundaries, breaking down barriers. Father, Son and Holy Spirit were leaping from the pages and I was filling fast with faith. Faith full.

The elusive trinity had returned.

———

Still awake at midnight, I left my bed and wandered over to the window behind my desk to draw back the curtains. For the first time in ages, night sky remained clear and the lake shone in pale moonlight. I listened for night-sounds, an owl or a bat, but all stayed silent, waiting like me for dawn. How I longed to sleep curled into Jeremiah's thin back, but we had abandoned the idea of spending anymore nights together. Island beds were definitely designed for one. Soon, I told myself, soon we would be together every day, waking, sleeping, eating, working. God bless you, Aunt Muriel, no need to sell either of our family homes, no need to uproot any of the children. Unencumbered by excess baggage, I would carry my single suitcase, hoist my back-pack and begin again in Africa.

Night air wafted through the open window and I shivered in my thin nightdress. Leaning over the desk, I pulled the window shut and returned to bed.

I slept deeply for what seemed like hours, but when I awoke the bedside clock flashed 02:00. Annoyed, I turned to face the wall, tried to conjure up African nights, the heady smell of tropical blooms, insects buzzing, still humid air. I envisaged us lying under a mosquito net waiting for a cooling breeze, perspiration warm and wet on the back of our necks.

Restless, I turned on my back, watched my travel clock flash 03:00.

Over the next hour, I sang concert songs in my head, hymns, Waltzing Matilda and anything else I could think of that might induce sleep. When that failed, I tried counting sheep, kangaroos and elephants.

04:00.

Drumbeats resounded through the night like distant thunder. I danced towards them, feet pounding the earth, hands slapping the air.

'Julia, Julia,' the drummer called.

'Here I am, my love, here I am.'

And then he was standing beside my bed, wrapped in the red blanket, his face glistening with sweat.

'Hold me,' he begged, 'I am afraid.'

I held him close, eased the nightmare from his body. At dawn, he slept.

———

I surfaced into daylight, my travel alarm clock confirming the passing of early morning prayers and breakfast. Cramped against the wall, I tried to shift position without waking Jeremiah, who remained stretched out beside me. The manoeuvre failed; half-asleep, he nuzzled my neck and mumbled something unintelligible. I kissed his head.

His eyes opened. 'Julia? What am I doing here?'

'You came to me before dawn.'

He looked puzzled, then nodded. 'That's right, I had a bad dream. Someone took my drums away, said the music was inappropriate. I looked everywhere but I couldn't find them.'

'Your drums are safe,' I reassured, tapping his chest lightly with my fingertips. 'I heard them in the night.'

Moist lips brushed my cheek. 'Oh, Julia you are a great comfort to me. I can forget my fears in your arms. You understand, more than anyone I've ever known.'

Understand you Jeremiah? Never, your multifarious temperament overwhelms me most of the time. I stroked his cheek.

'You understand about Africa,' he whispered, as though afraid someone out in the corridor might overhear. 'When I speak of my country's beauty, her poverty, her corruption, you listen, not out of politeness but with your whole being. You are there with me, living it. Don't you think that's odd, considering you have never been to Nigeria?'

'Perhaps Africa waits for me too?' I whispered in his ear.

He answered with a kiss, soft and warm as sun-washed sand. Limbs entwined, windblown ridges smooth and silky. Beneath the dunes, I was a rock pool waiting for high tide; Jeremiah a wave inching up the beach, almost there then retreating. Impatient, I rippled my surface, but he teased again, rising falling rising falling. Sediment stirred, I clouded over, failed to notice the colossal breaker heading towards me. Gaining momentum with every roll, it pounded rock and sand. Breached, I lay helpless as he surged through me, thick foam.

Afterwards we lay listening to the sounds of morning: voices in the corridor, feet running down stairs, doors slamming, a distant bell ringing.

'Sanctuary,' he murmured, 'a place of peace.'

'Yes,' I answered, unsure whether he was referring to me or the island or the moment.

'I wish this inner calm could last forever. It doesn't happen often, most times I just turn over and go to sleep. But occasionally it is there, and life seems crystal-clear.'

'My life has been crystal-clear for several days.'

'Tell me your secret.'

'Clarity came early one morning when a nightmare woke me.'

He propped himself on one elbow. 'You're not making much sense, Julia. Care to explain?'

I took a deep breath, eased myself onto pillows. 'Remember the painting I did in the art room the other day?'

He nodded and looked towards the noticeboard. 'A house, trees and flowers.'

'Don't forget the sun.'

'A golden sun to burn away clouds.' Shoulders slumped, he sighed deeply.

'Simplistic images that should have been easy to interpret, but unlike your red and black shapes, they stumped me. It took a nightmare to reveal the truth. The house is mine. Not the one I live in, the one I inherited from my aunt. I've owned it for years, Aunt Muriel died when I was sixteen. It's rented out; the income enabled me to come to Eden College. If I sold it, there would be sufficient funds for both of us to travel around Nigeria, helping the poor in rural villages.'

Still focused on the painting, he pushed back the bedclothes and sat up hugging his knees. 'I am an engineer from Birmingham,' he stated in a voice devoid of emotion. 'I have a wife and two children, an enormous mortgage and a ten-year- old car that has seen better days. I haven't worked for six months due to,' he hesitated. 'Due to my illness. Fortunately, I'll get my job back. Great Uncle Isichei will see to it.'

I stared at his naked back and reached out to touch him, but something stayed my hand. Once more on the outside, I was an Australian on long-service leave, a stranger in these islands. What had happened to our intimacy, the safe haven he found in the after-glow of love?'

'One thing I've learned here,' he said, turning his head to address the wall, 'is that Nigeria is an old story. There's nothing I can do to resurrect those days, so I must look forward.'

'That's what I'm trying to say. The new Nigeria needs people like you, intelligent, educated, cosmopolitan.'

He swung around. Black eyes burned through me and I shivered.

'Almost white you mean.' He spat out the words. 'I'd soon knock those Third World blacks into shape.'

'You're twisting my words.'

'I'm reading your mind.'

Shoving me back against the pillows, he leapt out of bed, grabbed his red blanket and wrapping it around his waist, tucked in the end securely.

'Jeremiah, I just want to help you turn a dream into reality. Does it matter where the money comes from?'

Exhaled breath struck my face as he grasped my left wrist and pulled me roughly to a sitting position. I shuddered as he loomed over me, spread my fingers with his free hand and wrenched off my gold wedding ring. Wincing in pain, I glanced at his scowling face. The tension between us grew rapidly, he tightened his grip on my wrist, jerking my shoulder. Fearing a blow to the face, I raised my free hand but all of a sudden, he released me and stepped away from the bed.

Still scowling, he held my ring up to the light for an instant, before placing it between his teeth. Then, inhaling deeply, he drew in his lips and expelled the ring. I watched it spin around and around on the floor.

'The taste is intolerable,' he said, backing towards the door. 'Intolerable and unacceptable. I spit out your white-country money.'

———

Naked, cold and alone, I sat on the edge of the bed, too traumatised to weep. Low tide had left me high and dry.

CHAPTER TWENTY

His drums remained silent. I listened for them every night for a week, kept my window open even though I shivered, and the endless rain blew in and soaked my desk. Most nights, dreams unfolded but lacked substance, empty shells they held no music, no echo of his hands. I knew he was practicing; I had seen him carrying his drums into a classroom after supper, but I couldn't hear them, not even a murmur.

Our choral group continued to rehearse songs in the chapel each evening. Hannah was delighted with our progress and said we were sure to be a hit at the end of term concert. Immersed in song, I could forget the chapel was a place of praise and prayer. I still attended morning prayers even though Choddy's words failed to reach me and my own plaintive petitions fell on deaf ears. As far as I was concerned, the invisible but ever-present deity had departed, forever and ever Amen.

So why did I keep turning up, why kneel on the cold stone floor, head bowed? Was I hoping against hope for a faint signal? No, I had moved beyond optimism but still wished to give the impression of enduring devotion. Appearances counted, not to God, I knew, who could easily peel away my thin veneer of faithfulness, but to my fellow students. Reluctant to cause distress, there seemed little point in declaring my loss of faith one week before the end of term.

Classes were informal during those last days; all written work had been completed, individual presentations given. Our tutors encouraged discussion of the term's study, the experience of living in community, what we had gained, if we considered our lives had been altered. When it came to my turn, I employed metaphor and allegory, deliberately avoiding personal pronouns. Choddy nodded and smiled at my comments, accepting no doubt that it was too late to change my mode of expression.

Late at night before the blissful release of sleep, I tried to come to terms with the ending of my long-term relationship with God. It felt as though I had lost a family member or close friend through sudden accident or illness. There had been no time to prepare for the absence, no time to say goodbye. Here one minute, gone the next, leaving me with a host of unspoken words that coated my tongue and clogged my mouth.

> *'Death I cannot swallow you*
> *bitter you rest heavy on my tongue*
> *sweet sugar will not dissolve you*
> *nor strong spice disguise you'*

Words I had written at a kitchen table in a silent house, words I had whispered at an open grave. A poem composed when I'd lost not only an aunt but a good friend. Aunt Muriel had listened to my adolescent verbiage and understood, Dad far too busy running a business and bringing up two girls single-handed to give me the extra attention I craved.

I was so angry when she died, so full of hatred. The night after her funeral I climbed out of my bedroom window and marched up the hill to her home. The runaway truck had ruined her front garden; I wrecked the back. Fuelled by intense grief, I yanked flowers out of the earth, slashed trees with the axe she kept by the shed and gauged holes in the lawn.

When my father discovered the vandalism, he blamed the local Aboriginal kids. 'They have no respect for other people's property,' he'd said, 'or even their own judging by the state of their houses down by the railway line.' He reported the vandalism to the police, but they showed little interest, maintaining it was impossible to convict unless the culprits were caught in the act. Consumed by remorse, I kept my eyes fixed on the floor whenever Dad retold the tale of destruction to friends and neighbours.

A few months after Aunt Muriel had been laid to rest in the windblown cemetery on the hill overlooking the bay, I was loitering outside the small weatherboard church at the end of Flinders Parade, trying to think of something to do with the rest of my day. It was the long Christmas school holidays and my best friend had gone south with her family to visit relatives. My sister Karen had left the house early to spend the day at a friend's place and everyone else I knew had gone away. Adjacent to the street, mangroves and mudflats exposed by low tide stretched far into the bay, ruling out sailing for hours. I could have ridden my bike to a nearby sandy cove but lying on the beach surrounded by hordes of small children chucking sand around and squealing, did not appeal.

A sagging timber fence surrounded the church. I kicked it idly and wasn't surprised when several weathered palings toppled to the ground. Through the opening I could see a row of hibiscus shrubs, their huge flowers dominating the narrow strip of earth between fence and church. Slipping through the gap, I picked the nearest flower and placed it on my palm. The petals were slightly puckered, reminding me of the seersucker dresses Aunt Muriel had favoured in summer because they didn't need ironing and she hated anything that kept her in the house. As I stroked the pale pink petals, I noticed a splash of dark red decorating the flower's centre as though someone had spilt a drop of blood. *An indelible stain,* I thought, recalling tyre tracks gouged in green lawn, flattened flowers, uprooted shrubs. A sea of bloodied blooms surged in the wind and the flower fell to the ground. Reaching forward, I grabbed the nearest branch and began to tear the blooms to shreds.

I had no idea how long the man had been standing there watching me destroy the hibiscus flowers, but he gave me such a fright when he wished me good morning, I simply looked up, stared hard and forgot all about running away. A small man wearing old boots, baggy shorts, torn shirt and a battered straw hat, he stood on freshly turned soil leaning on a spade. *Oh shit,* I thought, *I'm in big trouble now. It's the bloody gardener.*

'Don't you think it's a bit selfish to pick them all for yourself?' he asked.

I hung my head, too appalled by my actions to answer.

'Come inside and have a cold drink,' he continued. 'It's awful hot today.'

Meekly, I followed him into a small room at the rear of the church.

'Sit yourself down.' He indicated a stool near the open

door. 'I won't be a minute with the drinks. Lemon cordial, do you?'

I nodded, still too shocked to speak.

We sat in silence drinking weak cordial from pink plastic tumblers. On the opposite wall, an old wooden clock ticked away the seconds reminding me that before long I would have to explain my destructive behaviour. The gardener finished his drink and bent over to put the tumbler on the ground. I shivered when he straightened up, even though he smiled at me.

'I don't often have visitors on a Monday,' he said, 'what with the kids at school and the mums busy cleaning up after the weekend.'

I shuddered and burst into tears.

'Oh dear, was it something I said?'

'I haven't got a mum or a granny or even an aunt,' I spluttered between sobs. 'They're all dead.'

'Dad?' he asked hopefully.

'Yes, but it's not the same and he's always too busy and anyway Karen's his favourite.'

'Karen?'

'My sister.' I looked down at the petal stains on my hands. 'I was Aunt Muriel's favourite, but she died in her garden. All her flowers crushed and blood on the grass where the truck hit her. Now I'm alone, abandoned.'

'You haven't been abandoned,' he said gently. 'If you open your heart to the truth you will hear God's message of love.'

I sniffed, uncertain how to respond. No one had ever spoken to me like this before.

'It seems to me you could do with a good friend.' The gardener removed his hat and scratched his head, bald in the middle with tufts of grey hair sticking out behind his ears. 'I know someone you can take your troubles to, he's always willing to listen and never too busy or too tired.'

I looked up. 'Who?' I asked, curiosity getting the upper hand.

'Jesus.'

'Jesus?'

The gardener beamed. 'Yes, he's my best friend.'

'Really?'

He nodded. 'He pulled me off the scrapheap and helped me regain my self-respect. And he never deserted me even when I was too busy for him.' He looked over my head to the garden framed in the open doorway. 'He led me here one day and I've never looked back, this place is my life now.'

Following his gaze, I looked out at flowering shrubs green lawn and what appeared to be vegetables in neat rows. *Fancy planting vegies in a church garden,* I thought. 'Do you talk to Jesus when you're gardening?' I asked tentatively.

'I sure do. When I'm kneeling on the soil planting seedlings or pulling out weeds, I can feel his presence all around.' He turned to face me. 'It's a sort of warm comforting feeling, the kind you get as a kiddy when you hug a favourite teddy.'

Jesus a teddy bear, this man's weird. 'Must go now,' I said, rising from the stool. 'Thanks for the drink.'

'Would you like to see the church, it's awful pretty?'

I hesitated but his smile was so warm and comforting, I thought what the hell, no one was waiting for me at home. 'All right, show me around.'

The first thing I noticed was the simplicity, plain wooden pews and a polished timber cross hanging on white-painted walls. There were no stained-glass windows or pictures of Mary and Jesus, the sort of things I had expected to see. The churches I'd attended for the occasional family funeral or wedding had been huge ornate places, candlesticks and statues and men dressed in long flowing robes. Then I saw the flowers floating in a dish set on a small table. They were hibiscus, blood red.

'I only pick a few,' the gardener said softly as I bit my lower lip. 'They don't last you see but I love the way they cast a warm glow.' He sat down in the front pew. 'It's peaceful in here especially on Mondays. Such a crowd on Sundays, sometimes we have 'em standing in the aisles and the doorway, but he doesn't mind, the more the merrier and so many youngsters it does my heart good. It just goes to show you can't believe all you read in the papers.'

What on earth was he talking about? 'Papers?'

'All that rubbish they write about God. God is dead, no place for religion in a modern world.' He scratched his chin. 'Them journalists should come here one Sunday, soon change their minds.'

I studied faded paintwork, worn benches, salt-splattered windows. Could Jesus really be here, not ten minutes' walk from my home? But even if he were, I reasoned, he wouldn't want to listen to *my* troubles.

'Do you think Jesus would forgive my sins? I asked in a small voice.

'Of course he would.'

'Are you certain, it's a terrible sin to ruin a church garden?'

'The flowers brought you in here,' he answered. 'I call that a little miracle, don't you?'

'I guess so.'

'Why don't you come to the service on Sunday,' he

suggested, getting to his feet and stepping into the aisle. 'Hey, I don't even know your name.'

'Julia,' I muttered, 'Julia Evans.'

He extended his hand and shook mine. 'Alf Burnes.'

'Pleased to meet you Mr. Burnes.'

'Call me Alf, everyone else does.'

'Ok Alf and thanks, I'll see you Sunday.'

'Good. Come at eleven. You won't regret it, Julia.'

We walked out into the garden where he picked one of the few remaining hibiscus flowers and tucked it behind my ear. I smiled my thanks and walked down the path to the street. On the footpath, I hesitated a moment before turning right; not the shortest route home but no way could I face the fence palings lying on Flinders Parade. At the end of the church grounds, a battered wooden noticeboard leaned against a fence post. Curious, I paused to read the faded letters:

Cliff St Baptist Church
Sunday Services 11a.m. and 6.30p.m.
Pastor: Rev. Alfred Burnes

'Oh shit,' I said aloud and began to run.

———

A small weather-beaten church, a small weather-beaten preacher and for me, a new and very different life. Worship on Sunday, youth group on Friday evening, weekend camps, discussion groups; the list seemed endless. Preoccupied with all these activities plus year eleven homework, I scarcely had a spare minute to ponder Aunt Muriel's untimely death or my mother's lost battle with cancer a few years earlier.

Reverend Alf possessed a simple faith, grounded in love of God, the natural world and all people. He spoke of God, Jesus and the Holy Spirit as if they were personal friends, often beginning a sermon by recalling a recent 'conversation' with one of them. 'So, I said, sorry God, but I'm not going to use that text today,' he told us one Sunday morning when winter rain lashed the windows, 'though I do appreciate the suggestion. You see there's too much sadness in the world, so I want to preach something cheerful. Miracles are the way to go today.'

Leaning on the old wooden lectern, he began to speak of loaves and fishes, water into wine, Lazarus rising from the dead. I heard the words, but their meaning failed to register; I was too busy contemplating his refusal to use the recommended text. Obedience to the word of God seemed paramount and I knew if ever I received a missive, I wouldn't dare disobey.

———

What would the Reverend Alfred Burnes say now if he could see me sitting at my Eden College desk, journaling the death of a twenty-four-year old faith? Innumerable sermons, delivered by a host of preachers, hymns sung, prayers offered and all I had left was a mélange of words that rattled around my empty shell. No way could I go to church when I returned home; the other worshippers would soon see through my façade of faithfulness. And how could I answer their loaded questions, give my opinion of island reflection, preaching, prayer?

If only I had a dinghy, a craft I could handle on my own.

I would turn her into the wind and we'd dance over the water, far away from land's discordant song.

———

On the cliff top, I stood facing the sea, a defeated woman huddled in a thin jacket. Rain fell steadily, wet hair clung to my scalp, drops of water ran down my neck. After fleeing my room, I'd trekked to the cliffs intent on hurling unanswered questions into the sea, convinced forceful action would dislodge the thick plug of gloom blocking coherent thought. I had been standing on the edge for what seemed like hours, yet words remained imprisoned inside my zipped-up mouth.

A yellow daisy caught my eye. Kneeling on drenched earth, I brushed bright petals with damp fingers. *Pick it,* said a voice inside my head, *take it back to your room, a flicker of light to challenge the darkness.* The daisy slipped from my fingers; I couldn't deprive others of its beauty. Getting to my feet, I wiped wet hands on damp denim, but the flower-force remained on my fingertips, gleaming golden, a glimmer of hope. Thankful, I raised my head, tried to look beyond grey sea and leaden sky to a sun-drenched land, fringed with clear blue water.

A sudden burst of rain blurred my vision. I blinked, saw the old white woman floating before me, too far away to touch but near enough to see the outline of her face. One small step and I could have seen the colour of her eyes, known for certain if the apparition was a future self, shrivelled by innumerable years. I inched forward. She stirred in a gust of wind and I noticed her arms were raised level with her chest, the fingers curled as though she was gripping something or reaching out for someone, arthritic fingers locked in a mock-embrace. My gaze shifted to her mouth, a thin red circle cracked at the edges. Wary, I hesitated before looking higher.

Her eyes seemed too bright for an elderly person. I had caught her at a moment of panic, she stared straight ahead, terror snap-frozen in brilliant blue. What did she see that filled her with dread? Turning with care, I peered through a curtain of rain. Nothing had altered, windswept grass and a trampled yellow flower the immediate environment.

I dug my heels into the grass, confirming my existence in the here and now. An Australian woman standing on the edge of a Welsh island, looking out to sea. Saturated chalk began to crumble; I sprang forward onto solid ground.

CHAPTER TWENTY-ONE

NEXT MORNING, I OPENED THE WARDROBE DOOR AND peered into its mirror: forty-year old face, pale with faint creases clustered above the top lip. Blonde hair brushed narrow shoulders, but a closer look revealed a smattering of grey close to the scalp, promise of faded years to come. Only the eyes remained bright, intense as summer sky. Queensland summer, not the weak cloud-filled season I could see from my window. It was time to return to my own land. The future might be bleak but at least the sun shone on *my* island.

But before departure, I needed to forget wounded pride and apologise to Jeremiah. I had been a doubting Thomas, demanding to see the evidence with my own eyes, my white-country sophistication seemingly impervious to ethereal beings. Scepticism had vanished out there on the cliffs. I had crossed the boundary, experienced first-hand the world of spirits, a world *his* people knew existed long before the advent of a Christ.

A bell called the faithful to morning prayers. From my window, I watched them stream from the house and cross the lawn. Jeremiah emerged a few minutes after the others, walking slowly, hands in pockets, head bowed. If only I could sit beside him in the chapel, the emptiness would be bearable, but each morning he sat wedged between Hannah and Benjamin, his hands locked in theirs. African solidarity, no place for a white colonist. I have been dismissed. I lie on the floor gathering dust.

On this penultimate morning, I felt no compulsion to enter the chapel, fall to my knees and feign faith. I wouldn't be missed; all eyes would be on the invisible deity. *Christians too,* I reflected, *stretch the boundaries of rational thought every time they pray.*

Alone, I would walk in the garden or sit by the lake and ponder a way to approach the affronted African.

Clouds parted as I stepped from the house, sunshine warmed my back and I lifted my face to welcoming light. By the lake, reeds swayed in morning breeze. Sitting beside shimmering water, I watched ducks feed in the shallows, brown beaks dipping and rising. Repetition soothed me, I floated easily, an autumn leaf released for flight.

Later, much later, I became aware that someone was stepping over the lawn towards me. Disposed for company, I prepared to smile.

'Julia,' Jeremiah called, 'may I sit with you?'

Words scrambled in my head.

He took my silence for consent and sat down beside me. 'It will be over soon,' he said, eyes focused on the water. 'Lake and sea and house all part of the past. Sure, we'll have things to remind us of our time here: notes in an exercise book, photographs, snippets of song and conversation recalled as we go about our daily work. But we'll have moved on, as is only right.'

He turned to face me. 'I came here to escape the dark

side of myself. Left it behind in the city I call home. At least I thought I had, but I know now you can't discard the bits you deplore like a crab throwing a claw. Accepting who you are, warts and all, that's what it's about.' Suddenly he jumped up and twisted around, graceless movements that seemed at odds with his usual agility. 'May I present the complete Jeremiah Ajuwon,' he said, giving a small bow. 'Christian, husband, father, engineer and sometime psychiatric patient.'

He had forgotten lover. I wanted to remind him of this oversight but forced myself to smile instead as he flopped back on the grass.

'So, you see I'm ready to get on with my life. All my spiritual and cultural baggage, my unresolved childhood terrors have gone, back where they belong in the bloody past. Christ has freed me from superstition and false gods. The white woman was a test, my devil in the desert.'

'No, you're wrong,' I cried, 'she's a future me.'

He reached out to clasp my hands. A friendly gesture meant to comfort. I trembled at his touch.

'See how you shake at the thought of her. What can I say, except I'm sorry for filling your head with my demons? Come with me to the chapel. Christ will enter your heart and dispel this fearful apparition.' He released me.

'No one there for me now.'

'A temporary absence,' he reassured. 'Remember my despair when I felt abandoned by God? All will be well, my friend.'

'Friend?'

'Well, I hope we're still friends. I reacted badly the other day. Pride I suppose. Forgive me?'

'Of course.'

SUE PARRITT

Inclining his head, he kissed me lightly on the lips. An insubstantial kiss; his arms remained by his side.

'Dear Julia, my dear friend,' he said calmly, his breath warm on my cheek. Then he scrambled to his feet, shook grass from his jeans and tossed me a friendly smile.

I watched him stride towards the house, head held high. Cool as an English summer day, facing the rest of his life with a stoicism, I found difficult to accept. How I wished I could rekindle hot African fire.

The complete Jeremiah Ajuwon. I didn't believe him for a moment, the description merely sounds easily expelled, demanding nothing. 'See how self-possessed I am, how confident of a bright future,' they appeared to be saying. Brave words uttered to convince both speaker and listener of their inherent truth. How long before the mask cracked, the myth exploded?

I would never know. Within hours, I would depart this place of dream and nightmare, return to my own sweet-slumber land. All I could be sure of was my own fragmentation. A shattered mirror, my shards glinted on moist island soil.

———

The concert was a great success, adrenalin fuelled, we sang and danced and listened to the Word and fell to our knees in prayer. Drums, piano, three guitars and a flute created a sumptuous symphony; each instrument played with skill and passion.

Each time Jeremiah's slender fingers caressed taut skins and drumbeats hovered in the evening air, I drew them into me until they coursed through my veins, molten magic. Oh, they had bewitched on that first night, dislodged me from a familiar world, pulled me towards an unknown continent, a place I would see only in dreams.

After the concert, I retired to my room but found it difficult to concentrate on journal writing, my thoughts drifting away before I could commit them to paper. I understood the reason. Words could be written during the long journey home but there remained one final opportunity to contemplate what remained a special place. In the morning, I would be too busy packing to stand and stare. So, standing by the door, I gradually absorbed the space I had occupied for twelve momentous weeks. Desk, chairs, washbasin, wardrobe, bed; I committed them all to memory. Smooth timber worn by countless hands, porcelain riddled with tiny cracks, a faded cushion propped in the easy chair.

On the desk, lay a gift from Donna, her wooden bracelet I'd often admired and a hand-drawn card thanking me for friendship. Next to them, a book from Hannah and Benjamin containing all the songs we had sung together. A tiny handwritten book, each page illustrated with bright African patterns.

Eventually, my gaze fell on the noticeboard, every inch covered with drawings, poems, photos and passages from the bible copied out on scraps of paper. How bare it would look when I took them all down.

Looking away hurriedly, I focused my attention on the circular motif stuck to one corner of the small window above my bed. A rainbow, clouds and flowers, they glowed on bright mornings when light struck that side of the building. Who had put it there? Did they want to ensure a part of themselves remained here forever?

What could I leave behind, a drawing, the little koala, my name scratched on the desk? No, all I could leave was the intangible concept called faith. Perhaps, I'd needed to discard it, perhaps it was time to move on, seek some other solace for my soul? The initial almost intolerable pain of loss had eased a little to become a dull ache, bothersome but bearable. In time no doubt, the ache would disappear, and I would wonder what all the fuss was about, how an invisible deity could have had such a hold over me for so many years.

The other loss I couldn't begin to come to terms with, even though I accepted that for Jeremiah, passion and love had died. 'Passion is a dangerous emotion,' he'd said once, an opinion I hadn't shared at the time. Now, I agreed with him, although I mourned its departure with every part of my battered body. My grief, my intense grief, was for the kind of life I could never have imagined in pre-island days, when I was sensible, secure, complete Julia Mitchell.

These past twelve weeks I had lived more than ever before; lived and loved and prayed and cried and smiled and laughed and shouted at God and despaired. At times, I had longed to escape, thought I'd go mad if I had to endure another minute in this passion-soaked place, but as the clock downstairs struck midnight, I wanted to cling to the final hours, thrust them deep into my body, steal their seed and propagate.

Dawn threatened; I must face her and my own sad sterility.

CHAPTER TWENTY-TWO

WEDGED INTO FERRY SEATS, WE SUMMER TERM students craned our necks for a last look at our temporary island home. Figures on the jetty had already receded into noonday haze; the house was a red-brown smudge on an evergreen canvas. The ferry increased speed as we headed into the channel. Reluctantly, I sat back in my seat.

Beside me, Jeremiah pressed his thigh against mine. 'Africa out there across the wide ocean,' he murmured.

'You'll get there someday, if you have faith.'

'Oh, I have faith in abundance.'

Enough for me as well, I wanted to ask?

'I'm brimming over too,' Donna exclaimed, reaching over to seize my hands and squeeze them hard. 'Thank the Lord I came to Eden College, I'll never forget this special time, nor you special people, not my whole life long.'

I blinked back tears. 'I'll write Donna, I promise.'

'And pray, don't forget to pray for me, I'll need your prayers back in New York City. Oh, am I gonna come down to earth with a bump, I can almost feel that concrete on my butt.'

'It won't be easy for any of us,' Jeremiah said thoughtfully. 'We've been living in a protected environment.'

'Yes, but we couldn't stay there forever,' I answered curtly. 'Eden is a beginning not an ending.'

In the row ahead, Martin stirred and turned around. 'Be gentle with yourselves, take time to adjust to life on the outside. Don't be surprised if initially you experience a degree of culture shock, it *is* a different world out there. But remember, the world didn't stop spinning while you were on the island, family and friends will have moved forward too.'

Jeremiah looked puzzled. 'What do you mean?'

'They'll have changed as a result of life-events while you were at Eden College. They might want to tell you about these experiences, so try not to bombard them with island talk. Listen and acknowledge the validity of *their* lives.'

Donna grinned. 'Mom won't waste any time telling me to shut my mouth if I act too self-centred.'

I envisaged Brian sitting on the old sofa in the family room, listening politely, turning the pages of my photograph album and asking the occasional question. Could I really sit beside him and remark nonchalantly, 'Oh that's Jeremiah, a Nigerian student?' How could I disguise the colour of my passion when it was daubed all over my face?

'Luke will be pleased to see the drums return,' Jeremiah remarked. 'Twelve weeks is a long time to a child.'

Questions scattered as I pushed that other island into tomorrow.

Conversation continued, but I detached myself from the group to float with the current, scud with the clouds. Away from the immutability of earth and rock I felt untethered as the gulls wheeling overhead, no fixed address, travelling wherever wind and tide took me.

A shout jolted me back to the ferry. The harbour was in sight; heads had turned to view the Pembrokeshire coast.

Martin got to his feet. 'Please stay seated until we dock and once on shore, wait near the end of the jetty while we unload the luggage. Then we'll split you into groups according to destination. Mini-buses are waiting to take you to either London, the North or the South.'

Summer term students nodded obediently.

Jeremiah took my hand and held it against his breast. Beneath my palm, his heart pounded, churning the life-blood. How I longed to embark once more, range over smooth skin, explore broad nipples, the slight indentation of navel, the black hair curling around his abdomen and upper thighs.

'Julia,' he whispered in my ear, 'please stay a little while after the others have disembarked.'

I squeezed his arm with my free hand. 'Yes, this is a good place to say goodbye.'

'A good place,' he repeated dreamily and turned to the window.

———

Tears dried fast in warm summer air, but his kisses scorched, salt and heat fusing on my lips. Reluctant to leave, we clung to one another as though our last embrace would endure forever, if only we could hold on and never ever let go.

'Thank you for loving me,' he whispered. 'I won't forget our time together.'

His words floored me. There was so much I wanted to

say in these final minutes, yet so much that could never be said. 'Thank you,' I stammered, immediately regretting my choice of words. A puny phrase, two little words lacking substance. The sentences I yearned to speak crowded in my head, trapped behind tears.

'Don't cry,' he said, wiping my eyes with the tips of his fingers. 'You'll set me off and that would never do. Stiff upper lip and all that. I'm British you know.'

Somehow, I laughed, and we rocked together, holding fast to an impossible dream.

'Come Julia,' he said, when laughter had died and tears crusted our cheeks. 'It's time to go.'

Head bowed, I followed him out of the cabin, taking care not to slip on damp decking.

When we reached the gangway, Martin interrupted suitcase stacking to look up and smile. 'May God hold you in the palm of his hand,' he said, and stepping forward, embraced us both.

Jeremiah smiled his thanks, but impulsively I reached up to kiss Martin on the lips. He blushed as though he'd never been kissed before.

Arms around each other's waists, Jeremiah and I walked along the jetty, cherishing the last steps of our shared journey. The time for conversation had passed; we moved forward into blessed silence. A few paces from land, he stopped, cupped my face in his hands and kissed my lips tenderly. Then he departed, and I was left watching his thin figure stride towards the northbound bus, hands in pockets, eyes fixed on a future I couldn't share. Gravel crunched beneath my feet; gulls cawed overhead. In between, I walked sluggishly, trapped in the hush of goodbye.

————

After what seemed an eternity, the London-bound bus crawled away from the harbour. The northbound bus had departed ten minutes earlier and was no longer in sight as we turned onto the narrow coast road. I had waved but Jeremiah, deep in conversation with Ruth, hadn't returned my final communication. In the seat beside me, Donna sat stiffly, clutching my hand, between us a heavy silence I wanted to break, yet felt reluctant to risk more words when everything important had already been said. Her warm hand soothed, I sensed the force of her friendship trying to moderate my pain. Gradually, we both relaxed, dropped hands and rested our heads on the back of the seats.

Our bus was travelling straight to Heathrow; no Swansea stop on this return journey. By nightfall, all of us would have left Britain and be winging our way home to culture shock and kisses. Tomorrow remained a distant horizon; the present a whining engine and conversation drifting around my head.

Before long, dialogue ceased as fellow-travellers settled down to sleep away the boredom of motorway travel. I stared at the seat in front, willed tired eyes to close.

———

When Donna stirred beside me, I waited until she appeared fully awake before reaching out to squeeze her hand. 'Thanks.'

'For what, I can't even find words to comfort you?'

'For being here, it really helps.'

'Are you sure?'

'Absolutely.

'But what will happen when we're no longer in the same place?'

'I promised I would write, remember?'

'I'm a poor correspondent. Will postcards do?'

'Anything just keep in touch. I can't bear to think this is the end.'

'It isn't, you know, Julia. There is life after Eden.'

I managed a thin smile. 'I should have been a better student. I had such good intentions, then it all went haywire. Why on earth did I fall in love with a crazy Nigerian, I should have known better?'

'You needed it.'

'Like a hole in the head!'

She grinned, then leant towards me. 'It let out the steam.'

We laughed together, good friends sharing a private joke.

———

Lukewarm airport coffee, a plastic table smeared with sugar crystals and screwed up biscuit wrappings. Around us, small children bawling, weary parents attempting to pacify. An elderly man knocked against the table, spilling our coffee.

Donna grimaced. 'Let's get outa here.' She stood up, grabbed her hand luggage.

We pushed towards the relative quiet of a wide corridor where a row of plastic seats lined the walls.

'A far better place,' I remarked, anticipating talk of children, jobs, and the weather back home. Idle chatter to pass an obligatory final hour when both of us would have preferred to be strapped in our seats hurtling through a cold night sky.

Donna sat down heavily and stretched out her legs.

Fingers lightly tapped her thighs, but she said nothing, contemplating reunion perhaps, mother waving from behind a barrier, twins shouting out her name. My own reconnection with family would be problematic, guilt already rising to the surface. Utterly absorbed by an African odyssey, I had disregarded their feelings. How had I become such a cold-hearted woman, a woman willing to toss aside half her life as though it had been of no consequence? The questions remained unanswered, Donna suddenly turning to me, her expression sombre.

'Now I hope you don't take what I'm going to say the wrong way, Julia and I assure you it's said in love.'

'I promise not to take offence.'

Her face softened. 'I've been thinking about this for a while. You're forever berating yourself. It's all, 'I should have' or 'I shouldn't have' with you, even little things like suggesting a drink at that noisy café. My advice is ditch the 'shoulds' and 'shouldn'ts,' accept who you are, don't be forever looking backwards wishing you'd made a different decision. Past is past, my friend, the present is all that matters.'

Truth stung but I refused to hide behind tears; she deserved a response. 'How about every time I'm tempted to speak those words, I pretend I'm writing them instead, with a pencil? That way I can grab a rubber and erase them before they do any harm.'

She flung her arms around my neck. 'A brilliant solution. Well done, girl.'

After a lingering hug, we went our separate ways.

———

Doors closed behind me at the entrance to my departure lounge. There was no going back, no possibility of a different destination. Nearly two hours before boarding, there were plenty of empty seats, so I chose one as far away as possible from two hyperactive toddlers, retrieved a paperback novel from the depths of my daypack and attempted to block out high-pitched screams.

Chapters later, I became aware of movement around me, seats were filling fast.

'Joseph look out for the lady's bag,' a female voice called. 'How many times do I have to tell you to look where you're going? Come here and sit still for a few minutes.'

'Sorry Mamma,' a small boy answered.

I heard him flop into the seat beside me, but kept my eyes fixed on the book, wanting to appear undisturbed. Almost as soon as he sat down, the boy began to swing his legs backwards and forwards, speed increasing with each movement. Mesmerised by skinny denim-clad legs and bulky brown boots that seemed far too big for him, I forgot about reading. Mamma's slap jolted us both to the surface.

The boy grinned at me, mischief brimming from wide brown eyes, his face round, smooth, gleaming. And black. I returned the smile as he tucked his legs under the seat. Less than a minute passed before he started to drum on the arm of the seat, flexible fingers dark against rigid orange plastic.

'Joseph, stop it at once.' Mamma looked in my direction. 'I'm so sorry. Lord knows what I'm going to do with him on the plane.'

'Don't worry, he'll probably sleep most of the way, it's getting late.'

'Pray God he does.' She settled back in her seat.

On the other side of Mamma, I noticed a girl of about twelve quietly reading a book and next to her, a man staring serenely at the ceiling, his hand on the child's knee. African faces, African legs, African arms, no escape from poignant reminders, at least until we boarded and even then, the family could be seated close by. It would be discourteous to stand up and walk away; they would think it was Joseph's fault. Quiet now, he sat with thin arms folded against his chest, bottom lip protruding in a pout. *Like a younger Luke Ajuwon,* I imagined, wishing I could reach out and give him a hug.

'Qantas flight zero zero nine to Singapore now boarding,' the flight attendant announced.

Joseph jumped to his feet and raced to the departure gate.

'Kids, who'd have 'em?' Mamma exclaimed.

We exchanged knowing smiles; two strangers bonded briefly by shared experience.

———

From my window seat, I watched the lights of London glitter below. Then, we were over the Channel and all I could see was a never-ending sable sky.

CHAPTER TWENTY-THREE

FLYING ACROSS THE GLOBE, CROSSING INVISIBLE borders. Sleep intermittently and dreams, vivid, disturbing, places and faces competing for attention, stretching arms, legs and mind until I screamed in agony. Waking with a start in the darkened cabin, I worried that someone had heard me but a quick look around reassured. Heads lolled on tiny pillows and there was no sign of a flight attendant.

In an attempt to banish night terrors, I retreated into daydream, but no matter how hard I tried, I failed to conjure up the beloved face. All I could see was the back of his head, tight black curls flat against his scalp, smooth neck, head bowed in prayer. Chapel, prayer, God, why did I have to be reminded of all I had lost? Why couldn't I picture him on the cliffs, in the woods, in my arms?

Yesterday, or the day before, I had calmly imagined God-grief to be almost over, a manageable state. A few more weeks and I would have tucked it away in my past along with adolescence, babies, mother and aunt. Absurd naiveté, memory never allowed me to forget, repeatedly lured me into the nucleus of long-discarded days. Every November I blushed when the first hibiscus flowers bloomed in the church garden, every year I paid two visits to the wind-blown cemetery high on a hill overlooking the bay. Mother faced the sea, the wide blue ocean that separated her from the Mother country, the 'home' she never knew. Three rows down, Aunt Muriel slumped into sandy soil, her headstone tipping drunkenly. A demise that would amuse her, although I felt certain she would have preferred to be buried in her beloved garden or beneath the Land Rover still rusting quietly on her friend's farm.

Church and State compel us to conform, insist we deposit our dead in the correct location, intone the right words to ensure them, so we're told, a place in the afterlife. But what happens to the disbelievers, do they return to the earth from whence they came, or are they doomed to wander eternally like the old woman he, I saw on the cliff top? Jeremiah threw gifts to the long dead, to pacify and keep them in their place, but when one of them materialised, he could only blanch in terror, certain she would lure him to his death, his premature death. Why do we consider threescore years and ten or more to be an absolute right?

Hurtling towards tomorrow, I clung to the language of yesterday and gained a small measure of comfort. God-grief, like the other, would be a long time leaving. I must exercise patience and be gentle with myself.

'Can I get you something?' a flight attendant whispered over the heads of my sleeping neighbours.

'Pardon?' I queried, confused by her presence.

'You pressed the button. Is everything all right?'

I blushed. 'Oh yes, sorry. It was a mistake.'

She retreated up the aisle.

Back in the land of the living, reinstated by a tiny plastic button. Shoving my pillow into the window frame, I made myself as comfortable as possible in the cramped quarters of economy class and sank into slumber.

———

Changi Airport was hordes of weary travellers, gleaming tiles and polished plate-glass windows. I passed the two hours between flights window shopping and trying to restore circulation to swollen feet. My wallet contained fifty pounds but there was nothing I wanted to buy. Stephen and Penny were far too old for tee shirts emblazoned with gaudy images of Singapore, although I felt guilty returning without gifts. I should have purchased some of the paintings on display in the foyer that last week, simple images of island flora created by a former student and sold to raise funds for the college. Oops, there goes another 'should.' Too late, I reach for the eraser.

Seven hours to my homeland; a short flight compared to the thirteen-hour haul from London, yet I found it difficult to envisage her white beaches, her lush rainforests, her empty heart. Australia, the long years of my four-decade life, family and friends, work and play but also past tense. No way could I recapture before-Eden life; I had been irrevocably altered. I presented the same face to the world, but behind that façade, everything had been torn down and remained under construction. The new lacked profundity; I was raw as Queen Street buildings, gleaming paint and steel behind heritage facades.

'New York Hotel,' I exclaimed, remembering Brian's favourite after work watering hole and hurried into a shop to purchase a bottle of Johnnie Walker black label.

———

A spectacular spread of golden light announced sunrise over the Northern Territory. Below, unseen by aircraft passengers, the luminous red of Uluru and the purple silhouettes of the Olgas. Beautiful photographs I had only seen in books. I knew so little of the vast continent I called home, so little of her heart.

Beyond the desert, we passed over rolling plains, then the Great Dividing Range and forests of grey-green euca-lypts. Nearer the coast, trees retreated into a cloudless winter sky and I stared in disbelief at cleared ground, iron-roofed homesteads, narrow road ribbons. In a few minutes, we would be over familiar ground, wide rivers, pine planta-tions and my blue Pacific. I strained to catch a glimpse of ocean, then realised I was sitting on the wrong side of the plane. My view was houses, highways, the inevitable Hills' hoists.

'Is that Brisbane?' my neighbour asked in accented English.

'Yes.' I leant back to give her an unimpeded view.

'You live there?' the girl in the aisle seat asked.

'All my life.'

'Is it at a good place?'

'Yes, a good place.'

The plane banked and turned towards the mouth of the Brisbane River. Cargo vessels slid towards the sea, in the distance, I saw a few white sails.

'Good morning ladies and gentlemen, we will be landing in five minutes,' the captain announced. 'Local time is 6.20 am. The weather in Brisbane is fine and cool, ten degrees Celsius.'

'Ten degrees,' I exclaimed. I hadn't packed a jumper in my daypack and had no wish to rummage in my suitcase.

Perhaps one of the kids' old sweatshirts would be lying in the back of the car?

All at once, I understood that tomorrow had dawned. Ready or not, I must face not only husband and children but also my own altered future.

———

Moving mechanically, I hauled my suitcase from the carousel, loaded it onto a trolley and set off for customs' queues. Once verified and stamped, I approached the automatic doors leading into the arrivals' area, my stomach churning, beads of perspiration dotting my forehead. Thin layers of steel and paint were all that separated me from loving embraces and dreaded questions. The doors opened; I pushed forward into a sea of waiting arms.

CHAPTER TWENTY-FOUR

Kisses warmed, and love soothed sensitive skin, our embraces brief, a crowded airport no place for lingering hellos. Brian quickly organised Stephen to push the trolley, Penny to carry my backpack. Behind our teenage children, Brian and I walked hand in hand.

'Good flight?' he asked.

'Fine, tiring though, I feel half-dead.'

'You'll soon buck up when you get home, especially after a decent cuppa. They serve lousy tea on planes.'

'Lukewarm and weak.'

'Karen will be around this afternoon. She wanted to be here to meet you, but they're short-staffed at the surgery, some virus or other.'

'Have you been well?' I asked, grateful for something innocuous to say.

'Never better.'

'And the kids?'

'Penny had a cold back in June but nothing since.' He turned his head slightly. 'I must say you look great.'

He must be joking! I haven't slept properly for forty-

eight hours my hair's a mess and I couldn't see any point in applying lipstick before we landed. Pushing aside negative thoughts, I smiled up at him.

'We all missed you so much. The worst part was not being able to write or phone. A peculiar rule, I reckon.'

'I misread the paperwork. It was just a suggestion not a rule, although the phone was off-limits except in an emergency.'

He frowned, no doubt wondering why I hadn't written when I discovered my mistake.

Ahead, Stephen and Penny left the concrete path, my trolley clattering as it descended to patched bitumen.

'Do be careful, Stephen,' Brian shouted, saving me from invented explanation.

'No worries, I know what I'm doing.'

'How's Dad?' I asked before Brian could return to the nuances of Eden College rules.

'Good. He's coming down tomorrow.'

Ahead, Stephen lurched to a halt.

'Hey Stephen,' Brian called. 'Pay attention will you or you'll damage the paintwork. Just wait until I open the boot.'

Incredulous, I stared at a brand-new red car gleaming in early morning sunlight. Brian dropped my hand to fumble in his pocket. Pulling out keys, he pointed them at the car. Lights flashed.

'I got a great deal on the Commodore,' he remarked nonchalantly. 'This one's got the lot: central locking, air-conditioning, power steering.'

'But what about the boat, this car won't be any good for towing?'

'I was fed up with towing. I've leased a berth at the marina.'

'But I thought you didn't like...' My voice trailed off as Penny opened the front passenger door for me.

'You'll love the leather seats, Mum, real luxury.'

I eased myself into the plush interior.

Cruising north through sleepy suburban streets, I began to wonder if the house would look the same, but when we entered the street, I saw that nothing else had changed. Second in the cul-de-sac, number four remained as expected: winter-thin lawn, swept paths and neatly trimmed shrubs, garage door closed against the continual onslaught of gum leaves. But as we turned into the drive-way, Brian retrieved another gadget from a dashboard compartment and pointed it at the roller door.

'Very useful when it's raining,' he remarked cheerfully.

Queensland was enduring the worst drought in living memory, but I nodded in agreement, unwilling to express my concern about the large sums of money he'd spent during my absence in this first hour of reunion. In the past, we had discussed substantial purchases at length, making sure they would not impact on the family holiday or prevent us paying extra off the mortgage. Although we were comfortably off, Brian insisted on preparing an extensive annual budget, which he would present to me with a seri-ousness comparable to that of the federal government trea-surer. Perhaps he'd decided on a half-year financial review and realised a new car was well within our means, or perhaps he'd had a pay rise? Turning towards him, I noted his self-satisfied expression as he silenced the engine, saw the fingers of his free hand caress the leather steering wheel cover.

Stephen opened the car door and offered a helping hand. Surprised by uncharacteristic attention—a typical teenager, he thought only of himself most of the time—I withdrew from luxury and walked through the garage, pausing to pat my faithful old Datsun. She had been washed and polished, but dents remained, memories of myriad journeys made over more than a decade. Moving on, I opened the door leading to the rear garden and stepped onto a patterned concrete patio. A short stroll and I would be inside the house, sitting on familiar furniture, drinking tea from a favourite mug. Back home, back where I belonged. I headed for the swimming pool instead.

'Have a good look around,' Brian called. 'I'll go and put the jug on. Stephen get a move on with that luggage.'

'What's the hurry?' I heard Stephen retort.

Opening the pool gate, I stood on neat brick coping, gazing at chemical-clear blue. Below the surface, a kreepy-krawly trawled for any leaves that had escaped daily netting, nothing allowed to sully the pristine water. The orderly environment reminded me of Brian's workplace, where every task was performed according to a complex set of rules. He had been part of the public service machine since leaving school; a good profession, well paid, plenty of leave and secure, or as secure as anything in the post-recession nineties. A section-head now, Brian had gained promotion the hard way, studying at night school three times a week for years.

Initially, we had worked in the same office, but within a year Brian had moved up to a higher floor and a higher grade. At the time, we had already taken the first tentative steps towards a serious relationship, so although I missed his cheerful company in the office, I only had to wait until five o'clock to resume private conversation begun that morning. The drive to and from the office in his shiny HG Holden, became the best part of my working day. In Brian's company, I could forget the monotony of clerical work, the petty rules and an overbearing supervisor. I was definitely not public service material. I asked too many questions and made suggestions to improve workflow, serious misdemeanours for a first-year clerk on probation. The supervisor could hardly contain her delight when my marriage and pregnancy followed in quick succession.

Maternity leave didn't exist in mid-seventies Queensland and it was considered bad form to leave babies in a crèche all day, so there was no chance of returning to the Organisation and Methods Department. Brian earned sufficient income to enable me to stay home with the children and I was content to devote myself to domestic duties.

After a few years, Brian left the old brick building we both had known and moved across the street to a modern glass-fronted high-rise. His new position demanded far more time and energy, and then there were the weekly evening classes at a city college. When he wasn't attending classes or preparing assignments, Brian slumped in front of the television after dinner and often fell asleep before ten, leaving me bored and lonely. Before long, I began to question why I had abandoned my adolescent dream of spreading God's word in the wide world for the unrelenting monotony of marriage and motherhood in an outer Brisbane suburb. My life, my could-have-been vibrant twenties revolved around housework, playgroup and the occasional afternoon tea with other mothers and their pre-school children.

Eventually, to compensate for lost opportunities, I approached Reverend Alf and offered my services as a Sunday school teacher. Thereafter, Sundays became a time of agitated activity, as I struggled to teach young children who would no doubt have opted for the beach if given a choice. Six months later, my sense of purpose began to erode, and I questioned my role in the faith community. Teaching Sunday school and baking for the monthly church stall seemed a poor contribution.

'Nonsense, Julia,' Alf responded when I mentioned my concerns, but he found a job for me all the same.

I loved books and I loved God, so the part-time position in the church bookshop suited me well. At last I had a mission, at last I could begin spreading the good news. Selling books in a suburban shopping strip seemed a far cry from the role I'd envisaged years before, but I felt certain God understood the difficulties facing a young mother with two children under school age. So, three half-days a week I deposited Stephen and Penny at the local childcare centre and walked down Brighton Road to sell the word of God.

Five years ago, I became the bookshop manager, charged with selecting, ordering and stock control, accounts and supervising three part-time staff. Since then, I have expanded our stock, adding colourful posters, tee shirts emblazoned with pertinent messages, books that address contemporary issues and modern sacred music on tape and CD. Changing beliefs and tough economic times had compelled modernisation, spiritual literature, prayer books and bible story picture books no longer sufficient. Most years we made a reasonable profit, which was ploughed back into the church to fund social concerns.

I had never looked elsewhere for employment; the work was enjoyable and rewarding. Adolescent dreams had long faded, God's island-hopping messenger securely anchored in a Brighton Road shop, berthed like our trailer-sailer.

'Julia, tea's up,' Brian called from the house.

'Coming.' I walked away from past regret, pausing a moment to peer through the tall gates next to the garage, where until recently, our boat had been stored, her white sails hidden beneath green covers, her blue bow jutting into a garden bed. A hollow space confronted me, stray leaves on grey concrete, black garbage bin hard against the garage wall.

The family room remained unchanged, for which I felt intense relief. Slumped in a comfortable cane chair, I swallowed strong hot tea, Stephen and Penny arranged at my feet like small children waiting for a story or treat. The moment I put down my mug, they began to fire questions like bullets, point-blank range, no place to hide.

How did you find living on a small island?

What were the other students like?

Did you make any special friends?

Was the study interesting?

What was your room like?

How did you cope with the weather?

Was the course worth it?

The well of thought cracked, wounds oozing unspoken words. I considered taking refuge in metaphor as I had for months, but quickly rejected that approach. Family members would soon see through any attempt at subterfuge.

'Hang on a minute.' Brian admonished. 'Give Mum a chance to relax first, she's had a long flight.'

'Sorry,' they chorused and retreated to the sofa.

I endeavoured to shape a suitable response. 'I think jet lag has addled my brain,' I said after several minutes. 'How about you two telling me what you've been up to?'

'Boring,' Penny replied with a toss of blonde hair.

'That's not what you said about Michael last week,' Stephen contradicted.

Penny blushed and kicked her brother's shin. 'I told you not to say anything to Mum.'

'Who's Michael?' I asked innocently.

'Penny's boyfriend,' Brian informed me. 'He seems a pleasant young man.'

'Friend, Dad,' Penny insisted. 'We're just friends.'

Brian suppressed a grin. 'Ok, have it your way.' He leant towards me, said solemnly, 'Michael is Penny's friend.'

Man, woman, lover, friend, remnants of language, fragments of island life loud in my head. Jeremiah had resurfaced, floated through my mind like a slow-moving swimmer. I tried to halt his progress, but he dived deep, disappeared into shadowy depths.

'Are you ok, Mum?' Stephen asked. 'You've gone all pink?'

'Hot tea,' I mumbled, 'it was lovely. Could I have another cup?'

'Sure,' Brian said, kissing each pink cheek before taking my mug.

————

By afternoon I was longing for Karen to arrive. Brian wouldn't let me out of his sight, he even followed me down the hall when I needed to use the toilet. Constant solicitude was entirely out of character. I had expected a little fussing, cups of tea, hugs and kisses but found it difficult to comprehend his obvious anxiety, his compulsion to please. Six hours after my arrival, he should have been watering the garden or sweeping up stray leaves; Stephen and Penny had long since departed to play tennis. I would have loved some time alone to potter about and get my bearings but clearly that wasn't on Brian's agenda. Earlier, when I had expressed a desire to look around the house, he'd accompanied me to each room like a real estate agent desperate for a sale.

I couldn't stay in the toilet for the rest of the day,

although I was tempted to exit quietly, tiptoe down the hall to the bedroom and lie on the bed feigning sleep. Feasible moves were soon discarded, Brian might sit on the end of the bed waiting for me to open my eyes. Perhaps I was being unreasonable; we had been apart for three months. The telephone interrupted futile planning. I hoped it was someone from the office calling Brian in for an urgent meeting. *Clutching at straws*, I thought, *the public service doesn't operate that way*.

'Julia,' Brian called from the family room. 'It's for you, Karen.'

'Coming,' I answered, escape thwarted.

After an effusive greeting, Karen went on to tell me that her employer, Doctor Bryant, had had an emergency and still had several more patients to see. In between asking after my health and the flight, she apologised at least tenfold for her non-appearance at the airport. Such overt civility seemed unlike her and I wondered why yet another family member was behaving oddly. 'Tomorrow will be fine,' I assured her, but she insisted on visiting after dinner.

Brian slid his arm around my waist as I hung up the receiver. 'I've got some good news.'

A promotion, I thought. *That would explain the new car and the berth at the marina.*

'I've managed to take the next few days off work. It was a bit tricky as we're in the middle of an audit but fortunately the other guys understood and offered to work back while I'm away.'

My spirits sank, time alone unattainable. Re-enter slowly Martin had said, take time to adjust to the wider world. Just landed, I was struggling with time itself and couldn't begin to embrace the intimacy of married life.

'Good,' I answered after flashing a smile, 'I don't go back to work until Thursday.'

'I know. So, tomorrow afternoon when your Dad's left, you and I are going up the coast.' He squeezed my waist. 'The kids are old enough to manage for a few days. I've booked a room at the Hyatt.'

'The Hyatt! We can't afford that.'

He kissed my cheek. 'You deserve the best.'

I managed to appear appreciative.

'How long is it since we spent quality time together?' he continued, leading me to the sofa where he sat so close, I could feel the car keys in his trouser pocket. 'We must think of ourselves for a change, the kids are almost grown up, they don't need us hanging around all the time.'

'How will Penny get to school?' I asked in desperation.

He ruffled my hair. 'It's school holidays, silly.'

'Oh yes, of course.' Needing time to digest his news and all it implied, I yawned repeatedly.

'Think of it as a second honeymoon,' he said, stroking the inside of my thigh. I inched away but he pulled me back, fondled a breast with his free hand.

'I bought a book the other day,' he confided, whispering as though the children were in the next room. 'You wouldn't believe some of the pictures and I don't mean drawings. Not like the coy sketches in that book we had when we were first married. I can fetch it if you like.'

Loud sighs replaced yawns. 'Not right now, Brian, can't you see I'm exhausted? What I'd really like is a rest before the kids get back.'

Brian quickly removed his hand. 'Sorry, honey, I'm getting ahead of myself.' He patted my knee. 'Go and lie down for a bit. I'll organise tea. Anything you fancy?'

'Something light please, they overfeed you on planes.'

'Sure.'

I got to my feet and tried not to run down the hall to the bedroom. Lying fully clothed under the duvet, my head refused to stop spinning and I pondered whether jet lag or confusion were to blame. Brian's odd behaviour must be the result of enforced celibacy if he'd been studying a new sex manual in readiness for my return. But why did he buy it in the first place, was our love life really so stale? Male menopause, I concluded, recalling his fiftieth birthday celebration a few weeks before my departure. He remained in good shape for his age; hair graying around the temples but still thick, laughter lines around the eyes. Sailing and walking kept his body trim while salt air and sun tanned his skin. An attractive older man, so why the flashy car and a lovers' textbook? I had no desire for an oversexed pseudo-adolescent, I needed a levelheaded fifty-year old to help me reclaim the still centre of my life. Tranquillity is all I ask, Brian. Please don't turn this world upside down, Australia is supposed to be a safe place.

———

'Julia, Julia, time to wake up otherwise you won't sleep tonight.' A pleasant voice, a hand warm on my cheek.

'Night shields us from harsh light,' I murmured, uncertain where I'd surfaced.

'Wake up, Julia.'

My eyes opened wide, stared blankly at the man bending over me.

'It's ok honey, you're home now. Come and eat.'

Released from confusion, I gave Brian my hand.

Conversation proved undemanding as we sat around the table eating the vegetable soup Brian had prepared. I felt pleased he had finally learnt to cook something other than beans on toast or the inevitable steak and sausages on the barbeque.

'It's delicious, Brian,' I remarked, when my bowl was half-empty. 'Where did you get the recipe?'

'From a TV programme, if I remember correctly.'

'Well, as far as I'm concerned, you can make it again anytime.' I reached for a slice of the crusty bread Stephen had bought from the local baker on the way home from tennis.

'I made a chocolate cake for dessert,' Penny piped up, not to be outdone.

'Thanks, darling, that's very thoughtful.' I beamed across the table at the teenage daughter who had never shown any interest in baking and only helped prepare dinner when I insisted. 'Why don't we leave the cake until Karen comes, I'm sure she would appreciate it as well?'

'Ok by me.' Penny turned back to her soup.

'I propose tea and cake in the family room,' Brian said brightly. 'We can use those tea plates that belonged to your grandmother and the silver cake forks, make it a bit of a party.'

Penny groaned. 'But we can't put those in the dishwasher.'

I chuckled inwardly. She *was* the same Penny I'd farewelled three months earlier.

———

After demolishing two pieces of cake, my sister Karen filled me in on neighbourhood gossip, especially the continuing saga of Doctor Bryant's battle with the council over the 'no parking' signs outside his surgery. Her laughter was infectious and before long the ball of tension that had pervaded my body all day began to unravel.

Opposite me, Brian lounged in his favourite chair, sipping a glass of red, his free hand resting lightly on his knee. The picture of contentment, as though he too had finally relaxed. I had misjudged him, over-reacted to his concern for my welfare. My absence must have affected him more than I'd anticipated. Perhaps, during the long nights alone, he had contemplated ways to revitalise our marriage and unsure how to proceed, reverted to youthful endeavours. Dazzle the girl with a shiny new car, smart clothes—I had noticed the new slacks and jacket in the wardrobe—a short holiday in a four-star hotel and inventive sex. Despite misgivings, I found myself warming to this middle-aged man struggling to regain the glories of his twenties. Our marriage must mean more than children, food on the table, clean shirts in the wardrobe. Ashamed, I sought his eyes across the room and signalled apologies. His response came immediately, a surge of love rolling towards me.

Karen continued her monologue and I began to think she was hiding something. Weary again, I wished she would go home. 'I think we've had enough of Doctor Bryant,' I interjected loudly. 'I want to know how things are with you. Why didn't Raymond come tonight?'

Her mouth snapped shut and her eyes darted across the room to exchange a knowing look with Brian. He tensed and turned his head, appeared to be studying the curtains. *Oh shit,* I thought, *I've put my foot in it. After five years of living together Karen and Raymond have split up, and just when I thought my sister had finally settled down.*

'Raymond had to go and see Maggie,' Karen said after an uncomfortable silence.

Maggie was Raymond's much younger sister. He

enjoyed playing the protective big brother, although I surmised she found his attentiveness annoying on occasion. 'All three of you could have come over, it wouldn't have mattered.'

'Family thing,' she muttered.

I nodded.

Silence descended. Karen and Brian gulped their wine, eyes focused on the floor.

'I'm going to have to throw you out, Karen,' Brian said, placing his empty glass on the coffee table. 'Julia needs some sleep; she's had a long day.'

Karen looked up. 'Sorry, Jules, forgot the time. We'll have another chat soon when you're over the jet lag. I'm dying to hear more about your stay on the island.'

She rose hurriedly, pecked me on the cheek and marched into the hall.

'Hang on Karen,' Brian called after her. 'I'll see you to the car. It's dark out there since the streetlight stopped working.'

After ten minutes, I gave up waiting for Brian and made my way to bed. Snuggling under the duvet, I relaxed in its warmth, confident my first night home would pass without undue intimacy. Heavy eyelids closed.

———

'They've fixed the light,' Brian announced gleefully from the doorway, 'Service at last.'

'Good,' I mumbled.

'It's a bloody miracle. I only phoned the council on Thursday.'

Through half-open eyes, I watched him strip off his clothes and pile them neatly on the bedside chair as usual.

'Bloody cold tonight, think I'll need to wear something.' He reached under the pillow to retrieve an oversized scarlet tee shirt.

'What happened to your pyjamas?' I asked when he'd pulled the shirt over his head.

'I threw them out.'

'Why?'

'Bit old hat.'

Yet another difference to absorb.

When he climbed into bed, his naked thigh touched my leg. 'You're freezing! I exclaimed. 'What on earth have you been doing all this time?'

'Talking to Karen.' He nestled in, wrapped cold legs around mine.

'What's wrong, Brian?'

'Nothing.'

'With Karen, I mean.'

'Nothing to worry about. Stupid argument that's all, they'll soon kiss and make up. Forget about Karen and Raymond.'

Lips brushed mine, kisses tender and undemanding. For tonight at least, he only wanted to hold me close as I slipped into slumber.

And tomorrow?

Tomorrow was another day. I would wake to familiar sounds and the crisp bright light of a Queensland winter morning.

CHAPTER TWENTY-FIVE

SAPPHIRE BLUE, FLAWLESS AS GEMSTONES CLUSTERED around a golden necklace. The sky I observed from my bedroom window might have resembled the manufactured hue depicted on postcards, but I knew from experience it was an authentic August morning, Brisbane style. No clouds to sully the canvas, no hint of rain or mist. Light breeze ruffled leaves on the large eucalypt shading the front garden, across the street a palm frond stirred. Bathed in winter sunlight, the house breathed peace. Alone in bed, I listened for the murmur of voices in other rooms and hearing nothing, wondered whether the children were still asleep. A glance at the bedside clock provided the answer. Ten-fifteen, I had slept for twelve hours. Dad would be arriving soon; I had just enough time for a shower.

I threw back the duvet, but the sky was a magnet drawing me away from windows and walls, the shuttered space of complex emotions. High above cool winter earth, liberty abounded, and I could shout my secrets without fear of discovery, no one around to read my mind or see the shadows in my eyes. A peopled Heaven had been an illusion, our heavenly father a mythical figure created to instill reverence and fear; I was no longer fooled by promises of eternal life. Against a perfect backdrop, the colours of my life appeared well-defined: the brown and yellow of discarded truths, the green of new unblemished growth. Why then did I ache with emptiness? Voices rose in greeting; I tumbled back to earth.

'Wake up sleepyhead.' My father's beard felt soft against my cheek, his hand warm on my shoulder. 'It's wonderful to see you, sweetheart.'

Lifting my arms, I pulled him to me.

'Hang on a minute,' he said, swaying above me. 'I'm going to lose my balance. Just let me sit down.'

'Sorry,' I murmured as he lowered himself carefully onto the bed.

'That's better. Now we can have a proper hug.'

Clinging to his familiar warmth, I inhaled the salt air pervading clothes and thick wavy hair. At seventy, he still explored his beloved bay in the boat he'd built decades earlier, his face nut-brown with deep creases radiating from blue-grey eyes, legacy of a lifetime spent squinting at the sun. Rough hands—I could feel the calluses through my nightdress—and I knew his fingernails were thick and yellowed. Close to his left ear, a jagged white line reminded me of the day we had almost lost the boat and his blood stained the turquoise sea. Beloved father, the one constant, the colour of my childhood.

Dad and I were close, the type of intimacy that developed between father and elder child when mother was no longer present. I had taken Mother's place at the helm, while Dad adjusted sheets and helped Karen with the jib. I had leant precariously over the bow to grab the mooring buoy, endured his irritation when I missed, and he was forced to turn around, approach it again. At home, I'd helped with the chores and tucked my little sister into bed. Every night Dad had read her stories and I would sit beside him trying not to fidget because I knew the words off by heart and wanted to be tucked into my own bed and kissed goodnight.

'So, how's my girl?' he asked, releasing me.

'Good, how about you?'

'Not bad for an old salt.' Tilting my chin with his fingertips, he looked directly into my face.

'Then why the clouds in your eyes, Julia?'

'Jet lag I suppose. Give me a go, Dad, I only arrived home yesterday.'

'Pleased to be back?'

'Of course.'

'You sure about that?'

I wriggled free. 'Yes, Australia will take a bit of getting used to that's all. It was a very different world over there.'

'Want to tell me about it?'

'Not right now, I'd better have a shower first, the day's half over.'

He levered himself off the bed. 'See you in a few minutes then. By the way, I was pleased to hear Brian's taking a few days break, works too hard he does. I hardly saw him while you were away.'

'He takes his job seriously, Dad, you know that.'

'Sure, but all work and no play make a man dull.'

'Brian doesn't seem dull to me. Quite the contrary, look at the new car.'

Dad snorted. 'I don't know what the hell he was thinking. Bloody thing won't even tow the boat.'

In the shower, apprehension crept over me, goose bumps erupted along my arms and legs and I shivered uncontrollably under a torrent of hot water. I had forgotten Dad could read me like a book; every word I spoke, every move I made would reveal more of the narrative. It promised to be a constant battle remembering to think before opening my mouth, repressing telltale body language and above all, avoiding his all-seeing eyes.

———

Comfortable in jeans and a light sweater, I strolled into the family room, double UV sunglasses clutched in one hand. 'Why don't we sit on the patio? I need to soak up some sun.'

'Good idea.' Brian looked up from his newspaper and smiled in my direction.

Hurrying across the room, I planted a friendly kiss on his cheek, then donned sunglasses and walked outside.

'I'll make coffee,' Brian called after me.

Moments later, Dad ambled onto the patio, sat opposite me at the white polyurethane table. 'Beaut day. God's own country this.'

'It's perfect. I must admit I didn't go much on the Welsh climate.'

'Too bloody cold, I imagine.'

'No, too changeable. Sunny and warm one day, cold and raining the next.'

'Sounds a bit like the sea, never know what she's going to throw at you. Keeps you on your toes though.'

'I guess it does.'

'You can't afford to become complacent out on the ocean.'

I nodded, images of my foolish attempt to flee the island in an old dinghy fresh in my mind.

He cleared his throat, drummed thick fingers on the table. 'Cat got your tongue?'

'No, I was just thinking.'

'About that Welsh island?

I looked up. 'No, this island continent.'

'There's nothing like home, familiar faces, familiar places.'

'Sure, but I know so little about Australia. I didn't realise just how ignorant I was until I travelled to another land.'

'Ignorant, how can you say that, you've seen a fair bit?'

'Only around the edges. I've never ventured far inland, seen deserts or ancient rock formations.'

He grimaced. 'Why bother, there's nothing much beyond the range.'

'I don't know that; I've never been there.'

Leaning across the table, he patted my hands, resting on the table in anticipation of coffee. 'Well you won't get Brian to agree to an outback trip. He's thinking of the Whitsundays next.'

'I could go alone, Muriel did.'

Brian appeared in the doorway, carrying a tray. 'Did what?'

'Went out west,' Dad replied. 'Julia's got this crazy notion of outback travel.'

'It isn't crazy. I saw the most fantastic sunrise yesterday over the Territory.'

Brian set down mugs of coffee and a plate of leftover chocolate cake. 'That sort of thing is great to see from a plane, honey, but you'd hate the flies and the dust.'

Fuming inwardly, I turned my attention to coffee.

The men talked sailing. I pretended to listen, nodding and smiling between mouthfuls of coffee and cake, all the while drifting in my head over vast expanses of desert dotted with terracotta rock. The arid land stretched to infinity; saffron sand sculptured by hot north winds. Nowhere to hide but that didn't bother me, I had nothing to conceal, hot sun had dried my dank abandoned centre. The dead heart held no place for tears.

'Another cup?' Brian asked, lifting my empty mug.

'Thanks, but I can get it, you don't have to wait on me.'

'No trouble, you stay and talk to Dad. I'm sure he's dying to hear about your trip.'

What about you? I wanted to ask. *Don't you want to know what happened on the island?* We had been together for twenty-four hours and apart from the smattering of information I'd given Karen, he had learnt nothing of interest.

'Don't worry about me,' he said, reading my mind. 'I've got the next three days to hear the full story.'

Dad leant towards me as Brian entered the house. 'I expected to be bored stiff this morning by talk of God and spiritual development,' he said in a low voice. 'You know my feelings on the subject, Julia, but I've never discounted your beliefs and I'd be the first to acknowledge what Cliff Street Church did for you. God knows I couldn't reach you after Muriel died. You shut me out, preferred to wallow in your own misery. It took a man of God to bring you back to me and even *I* got down on my knees and gave thanks.' He paused to take a deep breath. 'But now I see you putting up those same barriers again, avoiding my eyes, making small talk about Welsh weather, instead of saying what's really on your mind. For Christ's sake, Julia, what happened on that bloody island?'

I squirmed in my seat. 'Eden was no paradise,' I said at

last, my eyes fixed on the table. 'I tried to escape in a small dingy, but wind and tide brought me back to shore.'

Dad clasped my trembling hands. 'Why did you want to leave?'

'Silence, absence, emptiness.'

He frowned. 'What the hell do you mean?'

Slowly I raised my head. 'Somewhere on that island I lost my faith.'

Almost jumping to his feet, he enfolded me in his sturdy brown arms, dried my tears with a soft mantle of love. 'It's all right now, sweetheart, this is a safe place.'

When Brian returned with fresh coffee, flushed cheeks had faded, and I reached for the mug confident I could hold it still. Ever vigilant, Dad deftly steered the conversation away from a treacherous island coastline out into a benevolent bay where islands floated on cushions of soft sand.

———

Our first morning in the luxury hotel bedroom and my fears of sexual experimentation were drifting away on a gentle swell. Brian caressed me with exquisite tenderness, as though he could feel the fragility beneath my skin, and when he entered, I experienced neither sensation nor discomfort. Disconnected, I floated high above my body, while he whispered a few endearments and plunged deep.

'Sorry honey,' he murmured a few moments later, 'I couldn't wait.'

'No problem. It's been a long time.'

'Too long, don't go away again.'

'I don't intend to.'

'Not even to the outback?'

'You could come with me.'

'We'll see.' Rolling onto his back, he lay eyes half-closed, face flushed.

Vertical blinds swayed in morning breeze, sending strips of winter sun across the beige carpet. Shivering, I pulled up the rumpled sheet. 'How about a walk on the beach after breakfast?'

'Sure, the beach is a good place to talk.'

'About my trip?'

'Um.' A hand brushed my breast.

'Then we'd better get up.'

'You shower first.'

In the ensuite doorway, I paused to glance back at the bed. As expected, Brian's eyes were closed, and parted lips suggested he had already succumbed to post-coital slumber. A sporty red car and a new sex manual hadn't altered the habits of a lifetime.

———

Although the wind stayed fresh, sunshine warmed our backs as we walked along the winter beach and the exercise freed my mind from jet lag cottonwool. Conversation centred around my stay at Eden College, Brian's questions harmless, enabling me to answer comfortably. Together we laughed about the Welsh climate, my pitiful attempts at painting, the cold chapel floor. I managed to sidetrack the few queries concerning my spiritual life and he didn't pursue the matter. Jeremiah remained an unspoken name.

The beach stretched forever, a broad white band curving into a distant headland. I yearned to keep on walking, not just today but for the rest of my life, heading towards an elusive horizon, the song of the sea ringing in my ears.

'Let's sit down for a bit,' Brian suggested, all of a sudden.

'Are you tired?'

'No, I want to talk.'

'I thought that's what we were doing?'

'I want to talk about me.'

Too late I recalled Martin's advice to acknowledge the validity of others' experience. 'Sorry for hogging the conversation. How about up in the dunes, it should be sheltered there?'

Brian opened his mouth to speak, then nodded and inhaled deeply as though drawing words back inside. I noticed his lower lip was trembling. Silently, we traversed the beach heading for dunes fringed with waving grasses. Soft sun-warmed dune sand and clumps of coarse grass provided support for our backs. Brian stared at the sea, while I drew circles in the sand with a stick and waited patiently for speech to emerge.

'I don't know where to begin,' he said at last. 'That's the problem, it all seems so juvenile now.'

It's the car, I thought. Relaxing, I looked up, watched waves dribble over moist sand.

'I never thought I'd be tempted,' he continued. 'I feel such a bloody idiot.'

I turned my head. 'It doesn't matter, Brian, I quite like the Honda and after all we don't need a large car now; the kids rarely come out with us.'

'I wish it were as simple as that.'

What else, has he chucked in his job?

Swinging around, he gazed into my face. 'Oh God, Julia, I realise it sounds pathetic, but I don't know what came over me. I've let you down, I've ruined everything.' He looked down at the sand. 'I had an affair while you were away.'

Of course. New clothes, new car, new sex, how could I have been so blind?

'Is it over?' I asked, sensing he needed a response.

'Yes, yes, I broke it off when I realised I was getting in too deep.'

Curiousity compelled a somewhat futile question. 'Anyone I know?'

'Raymond's sister Maggie.'

'Did Karen know about it?'

He nodded.

'Well, that explains her edginess the other night.' Picking up the stick, I drew more circles in the sand.

'I understand that you're angry. What can I say, sorry seems such an insignificant word?'

'Surprised yes, angry no.'

'I feel such a shit. You over there communing with God and me over here screwing Maggie.'

'Is that all it was, screwing?'

'No, oh I don't know. At first it seemed like love.'

'And now?'

'Now it feels like a bloody stupid mistake, a typical middle-aged male thing. I guess I was flattered; she's an attractive woman and not even thirty.'

'I know how old Maggie is.'

'Say something Julia,' he pleaded after an awkward silence.

Uncertain what to say, I continued to stare at the sand.

'It says in your book to forgive those that sin against you,' he remarked quietly.

I stabbed the stick into the sand. 'Leave the bible out of it.'

'Why, it's always figured prominently in your life?'

Scrambling to my feet, I stood over him. 'I said leave it, Brian.'

'Sorry, sorry,' he said defensively, hands raised to shield his face. 'I know this has nothing to do with religion. You've had a shock. Would you like to be alone for a while?'

Backing away, I collapsed on the sand, spent minutes considering whether this was the right moment to spill my own secret. Confession might ease the ache, the emptiness within. Brian took my silence as desire for solitude, rose quickly and returned to the beach. At the water's edge, he picked up a flat pebble, skimmed it over undulating water. From my vantage point, I watched it bounce and sink. He threw another and another, seemingly oblivious to the waves washing over his trainers.

Minutes passed before I felt strong enough to join him. Walking slowly down the beach, I stood near him but not close enough to touch. 'I didn't intend to say anything, Brian but now I feel there should no secrets between us.'

He looked up and turned towards me, his face etched with misery.

The words stuck in my throat. Taking a deep breath, I blurted out, 'I've been unfaithful too.'

Tense shoulders relaxed. 'A fellow student?'

'Yes.'

'Where from?'

'Does it matter?'

'No, I'm just curious.'

'Birmingham, England.'

He sighed. 'Oh, I thought you were going to say some-where exotic.'

Like Africa, I thought, hugging the memory of Jeremi-ah's beautiful body.

'Did you love him?' Brian asked, looking directly into

my eyes. 'Oh God,' he said, before I had chance to answer, 'it was a man, wasn't it?'

'Yes, and yes to your first question.'

He studied salt water swirling around his feet. 'Never know what life's going to throw at you,' he said thoughtfully. 'Three months ago, I considered I had everything sewn up: a good job, happy marriage, great kids. Guess I had a few things to learn.'

'You weren't the only one.'

He reached for my hand as I moved closer.

CHAPTER TWENTY-SIX

Time alone at last, Brian had taken Stephen to soccer training and Penny had gone out with a friend. The first opportunity to open my journal since returning home. So many thoughts and feelings swirling on the surface of my mind, caught in a whirlpool unable to break out. I had no alternative but to dive deep, seek truth and direction in still waters. After staring at the blank page for what seemed like hours, I concluded it was far too soon to face the realities of infidelity, faithlessness and betrayal, decided instead to take the soft option and write of recent days.

"After the emotional exertion of confession, Brian and I took it easy for the rest of our brief holiday. Each morning we went for a leisurely walk along the beach, enjoying winter sunshine and fresh sea breeze. Sometimes, we ventured into the dunes and made love to the rhythm of waves. Sometimes, we sat staring at the ocean, arms around each other's waists. After dinner in the hotel restaurant, we wandered to the edge of the dunes, stood watching stars pierce a clear black winter sky. Between us, there lay a calmness and clarity, disclosure had erased the burden of guilt. Sun, sea and wind infused me

with hope and inner peace became a distinct possibility. I even found myself looking forward to the future.

One problem continued to niggle. I felt apprehensive about returning to work, uncertain whether I could continue to manage a Christian bookshop when I no longer believed in the product. My three assistants were all committed Christians and two of them worshipped at the little wooden church on Flinders Parade, which created a further dilemma, as I had no intention of returning there. Eventually, I hoped to pluck up sufficient courage to visit Reverend Scott, offer some sort of explanation for my absence.

One step at a time, I told myself that last day on the beach and decided to reconsider the employment situation after three months.

I need not have worried about work. My assistants, all three young women under thirty, were delighted to see me, there having been little levity during my absence. My temporary replacement, an older woman, had proven demanding, overly critical and dour.

On the first day, I bought doughnuts for morning tea and we took it in turn to sit around the tiny back room table, our mouths coated with sugar and laughter. The girls bombarded me with questions about my trip, but fortunately, were more interested in the people I'd met and the island landscape, than spiritual aspects. I promised to bring in my photos next week."

——

My journal safely returned to the old wooden box where Aunt Muriel used to store correspondence, I returned to the family room carrying the Kodak envelopes collected from the pharmacy the previous day. I had already purchased an

album with room for one hundred prints, its deep blue
cover overlaid with swirls of white. *Julia Mitchell's time
travels,* I mused, opening the first envelope. *Back to the
beginning where ignorance and innocence walked hand in
hand and glimpses of an old white woman were dismissed as
products of an over-active imagination.*

I leafed through prints, considering which to keep and
which to discard. When I came to a photograph of Jeremiah, my hands shook, so I quickly added it to the 'keep'
pile and turned to a group snapshot taken on the lawn the
second day of term by Martin. Every face except Jeremiah's
appeared out of focus. How long before he diminished?
How long before he retreated to the proper place of
memory?

Next, I turned to a beautiful shot of the lake in early
morning, dark water and dappled sunlight, a vision of
perfect peace. But I knew the camera deceived, soon ducks
would ruffle that smooth surface and wind whistle through
reeds.

An hour passed; discarded envelopes littered the tiled
floor. After stretching stiff limbs, I embarked on a second
classification:

Island lover
Island lake
Island house
Island chapel
Island woods
Island people
Collage of an Island interlude

The front door opened and closed. 'Hi, Mum, I'm back,' Penny called, her voice echoing down the long hallway.

Reluctant to share or offer explanations, I scooped up the photographs and rushing into the kitchen, retrieved a brown paper bag from the pile on the pantry shelf. Tomorrow, I would engineer more time alone, plead fatigue when Penny mentioned attending church, wish Brian and Stephen a good day's sailing as they set off for the marina.

———

My blue and white photograph album lay open on the coffee table in the family room; island life available for scrutiny. Penny knelt on the floor leaning forward slightly, her hands turning thick pages, while I sat on the sofa pretending to read a magazine.

'Who were your special friends, Mum?' she asked after a few pages.

'Donna, Hannah, Benjamin and Jeremiah.' I rattled off the names easily, even the last.

'Show me.'

Discarding the magazine, I flipped through the pages until I found a photograph taken at the concert. 'There we are singing at the end of term. Hannah's on the far left, then Benjamin, Donna and me. Jeremiah is the one playing drums.'

Penny peered at the photograph before looking up at me. 'Were they all from Africa?'

'Some were but Donna lives in New York.'

'Will you keep in touch?'

I shrugged. 'We promised we would, but you know how it is. Busy lives.'

Penny nodded and continued turning pages. 'The sea

looks rough in this one, Mum. I wouldn't like to chance it in a small boat.'

'Neither would I. There were treacherous rocks at the base of the cliffs on that side of the island.'

'Where, I can't see them, unless this fuzzy white bit is rocks?'

I looked over her shoulder. 'No, I don't think so, I didn't venture that close to the edge.'

'It looks a bit like a face,' she said, peering closer. 'It must be your thumb over the lens. Really, Mum, that was a silly thing to do.'

'No one's perfect,' I retorted, as the blur became a white face emerging from grey waves. Quickly turning the page, I remarked in what I hoped was an even tone, 'Look at this one of the lake. Don't you think I've captured the tranquillity?'

'Sure.' She looked up. 'Hey Mum, I didn't mean to upset you just now.'

'I know.' I patted her shoulder. 'I shouldn't have got so uptight. I guess it's because I'm tired. Work was a bit of a shock after a three-month break.'

'I know the feeling.' She closed the album and came to sit next to me on the sofa. 'I hate going back to school after the Christmas holidays.'

'This year will be your last long school holiday,' I remarked, relieved to have moved to safer ground.

'But I'll get longer breaks at uni.'

'You haven't got there yet.'

'No, but I will.'

'I sincerely hope so; you deserve a place after all your hard work. But don't be too disappointed if you're not offered your first choice. It pays to have an alternative plan.'

'Why, only a major disaster's going to stop me getting in to UQ?'

'The future is unexplored territory,' I said softly, but she chose to ignore my comment, launched instead into her plans for a career in journalism. Having heard it all before on numerous occasions, I spent the time trying to erase an aged, ashen face from the corners of my mind.

———

After dinner, Brian sat at the kitchen table, studying my photograph album. Fully occupied at the sink, I felt thankful for an excess of dirty dishes. The dishwasher was full and already whirring its way through the cycles.

'Picnic?' Brian queried above the clatter of saucepans. 'I thought you said the weather was lousy over there?'

'Not all the time.'

'The guy wrapped in the red blanket must have been cold.'

'Oh, he was always wearing that, security blanket probably.'

'Wasn't he the one playing the drums at the concert?'

'Yes.'

I heard the slap of thick pages. Good, he'd moved on.

'Beautiful drums, were they African?'

'Nigerian, he learnt to play in his village before the war.'

'Before the war, he doesn't look old enough?'

'The Biafran war. He was nine when his family were forced to flee the country.'

'Where did they go?'

'England,' I answered, aware too late I had revealed more than intended. Hands dripping suds, I crossed the kitchen and pointed to the photograph. 'That's Donna next to him.'

'Good looker.'

I slapped his wrist playfully. 'She'd soon put you in your place, Brian Mitchell, she's a New York cop.'

'Don't think I'll tangle with her then!'

We both laughed and the tension compressing my head began to slacken. Soon, he would reach the last page and I could redirect his attention to coffee or a glass of wine.

Back at the sink, clean water rinsed away the detritus of domesticity. A few minutes later, saucepans had been neatly stacked in the cupboard under the hotplates, cooking implements sorted and put away. Only my thoughts remained jumbled.

Tomorrow I would have to face the God-issue. This first Sunday I could probably plead tiredness as an excuse for non-attendance but there seemed little point in putting off the inevitable, Brian would soon realise something was amiss. *Perhaps he'll be pleased,* I thought, pouring myself a glass of red wine. I had often sensed his disappointment when the weather proved perfect for sailing, but I refused to accompany him, reluctant to miss Sunday morning service. Although he had accepted from the start that faith played an important role in my life, I was beginning to wonder whether my preoccupation with religion could have precipitated his affair with Maggie. A member of the yacht club without a boat of her own, she was always eager to crew for solo sailors. I gulped the wine. Deep down, was I afraid Brian would return to her arms once the glow of reunion had faded?

'Come and sit down,' Brian called from the family room. 'It's no fun drinking alone.'

I joined him on the sofa, thankful the photograph album remained out of sight on the kitchen table.

———

The alarm clock flashed four-fifteen. For a moment, I was back on the island, waiting for dawn and soft footsteps outside my door, but when I turned on my side, a shaft of moonlight drew my attention to the empty space beside me. Cold sheets confirmed I had been alone for a while, so I slipped out of bed, put on slippers and dressing gown and padded down the hall to the family room.

Brian sat huddled on the sofa, clutching a steaming mug.

'What's up?' I asked, sitting down beside him.

'I woke up and couldn't get back to sleep. Hope I didn't disturb you?'

'No. Come back to bed, it's cold out here.' I shivered, but not on account of the temperature; my photograph album lay open on the coffee table.

'In a minute.' He put down the mug, leant forward, lifted the album. 'This group photo, you all look so content.'

'We were. Eden College was a special place.'

'Are you happy here?'

Cold limbs stiffened. 'What sort of question is that, this is my home?'

'Would you have gone home with him?'

'He didn't ask me.' I answered truthfully, fiddling with the buttons on my dressing gown.

Beside me, Brian tensed. 'That's not an answer, that's an evasion.'

'I'm not obliged to tell you everything. Why are you so bloody inquisitive? I told you it's over, finished. Jeremiah's back in Birmingham with his wife and I'm back in Brisbane with you.'

'Jeremiah the drummer?' Brian queried in a low voice.

'Well, now you know. Satisfied?'

The photograph album sailed across the room, landed face down on the tiled floor. 'No, I want to know what the hell you thought you were doing?'

'Obvious, isn't it? Grow up Brian. I don't expect you to regale me with lurid details of sex with Maggie!' Shaking with fury, I retreated to the end of the sofa.

'How could you, Julia?' he pleaded in a little-boy-hurt voice.

'I could ask the same of you.'

'Answer the bloody question,' he demanded, striking the coffee table with his fist. His mug wobbled, sending globules of tea splashing over Australian Geographic.

'Don't shout, you'll wake the kids.'

'It might be a good idea. They should know their mother slept with a bloody black.'

Jumping to my feet, I scooped up the album and hugged it to my chest. 'Oh, is that what's bugging you. It wouldn't have mattered if he'd been lily-white, eh? You hypocrite, you bloody racist bastard.' I turned on my heel, but before I had taken two steps, he leapt in front of me and wrenched my left arm away from the album's protective armour.

'Don't you swear at me,' he blustered. 'I've every right to be upset.'

His grip tightened as I tried to free my arm. 'Every right?' I retorted, my spittle flying into his face. 'It's nineteen ninety-three, Brian. Mixed-race relationships are quite acceptable these days.'

'Not to me they aren't.'

'I'm sorry you feel that way but there's nothing you can

do about it. I had an affair and he happened to be black. End of story.' At last I broke free. 'I'm going back to bed.' I strode down the hall, but just before I reached the bedroom door, Brian grabbed me from behind and twisted me around.

'Oh no you don't. You can sleep in the family room for the rest of the night.'

'Let me go.' I pushed the photograph album into his chest. He released me at once and for a few moments we stood stock-still, our mouths open gasping for breath. I yearned to discuss his phobia in a rational manner, but when I looked into his eyes they were laced with loathing.

'And tomorrow,' he declared, spitting disgust, 'you can get your black-loving arse out of this house!'

CHAPTER TWENTY-SEVEN

ALL MORNING KAREN HAD BEEN LISTENING PATIENTLY to my sorry tale, her hand resting lightly on my arm, giving me space to spill. Only after prolonged silences had she injected her own thoughts and feelings. How I wished I shared my sister's optimism. She remained convinced Brian would soon recover from his fit of pique, come around full of apologies and beg me to return home. Racism was prevalent in older Australia males, she maintained, and went on to tell me about an article she'd read regarding the increasing numbers of Australian/Filipino marriages, where older, usually divorced men, 'met' young women twenty or thirty years younger than themselves through introduction agencies based in the Philippines. Karen asserted that such marriages—the media referred to the women as 'mail order brides'—were a form of racism, but I saw them more as determination on the women's part to escape from poverty and political unrest. Besides, I had no desire to debate mixed-race marriages. Expelled from my home, I felt distressed, confused and angry. All I wanted was somewhere to hide, a safe place to lay my aching head.

Waiting on the balcony while Karen fetched coffee and cake from the kitchen, I pondered whether I had divulged too much, infidelity not the only subject of my lengthy monologue. I had also poured out loss of faith and island apparitions. Her reaction had surprised me, no hint of the skepticism or derision I normally associated with my rational sister. Instead, she had offered reassurance and confirmed the validity of all life experiences.

———

Two weeks passed. Brian didn't visit or telephone or write. Several times I tried phoning but if he happened to answer, the receiver was slammed down the moment I spoke. Messages left on the answering machine were also ignored and a letter sent via Karen returned unopened. Most hurtful was the discovery this afternoon that the locks had been changed. I'd called to collect some more clothes and had to wait in the front garden for Penny to return home from school.

Distraught about the separation, Penny had spent the last half-hour pleading with me to stay and persuade her father to see sense. But how could I stay, new locks had convinced me he wasn't going to change his mind.

'Please Mum,' she called after me as I hurried down the hall, intent on grabbing clothes and departing before Brian came home from work. 'Don't you see Dad's just being pig-headed? It's the fragile male ego, he can't bear to think his wife slept with another man.'

In the bedroom, I tossed clothes in my suitcase, crammed shoes in a large plastic bag, make-up in a toilet bag. I'd almost filled the suitcase when Penny flew through the door and flopped on the bed, where she leant against the headboard, twisting the ends of her long blonde hair.

'I know about Maggie, Mum,' she said after a few minutes silence. 'It was painfully obvious.'

I stopped packing, looked over at her pale face.

'I mean since when has Dad ever shown any interest in clothes or wanted a trendy car or said he enjoyed Shakespeare?'

'Shakespeare?'

'Karen had to work back, so Dad agreed to go to the theatre in her place. The Tempest, I think. He got home really late, after midnight. Next morning, I asked him what he thought of the play.'

'What did he say?'

'Reckoned he'd changed his mind about theatre. Said at last he understood how meaningful live performances were and how privileged he was to live in a place where the arts are promoted.'

I shook my head in disbelief, knowing how much Brian disliked theatre and driving into the city centre.

'Bullshit, I said, but he didn't even tell me off for swearing, he was too busy raving on about Maggie's knowledge of the theatre. They went every week after that. He called it his cultural awakening. Funny name for an affair, eh Mum?'

'Did Stephen know what was going on?' I asked quietly.

'He didn't want to know, typical male response, of course. He told me I had an over-active imagination and if I were more mature, I'd realise it's possible to have platonic relationships with members of the opposite sex. You're kidding yourself, I said, open your bloody eyes.' She paused for breath.

I shoved the dress I was holding into the suitcase and closed the lid.

'Do you know what he did, Mum?'

'No.'

'He hit me, the bastard hit me across the face!'

I decided to ignore her bad language. 'I trust he apologised.'

'No.' She stuck out her lower lip like a child and sniffed loudly.

She was inviting more than verbal commiseration but my thoughts remained with her brother. Stephen hadn't spoken to me since the break-up and was always conveniently out when I telephoned. Earlier, Penny had told me he seemed indifferent, carrying on with his life as though Brian and I had been separated for two years not two weeks. One-parent families seemed to be the norm among his friends, so perhaps his attitude was understandable. 'When will Stephen be home?'

'About five, I think. Why don't you wait for him? I'll make some tea while you finish packing.'

I glanced at my watch. An hour and a half before Brian was due to arrive home. 'You're right, I should stay and talk to Stephen. And I'd love some tea.'

She slid off the bed, left the room with her customary haste.

Alone, I took a long hard look at the intimate space Brian and I once shared, so many nights, so many mornings. As usual, everything was neat: curtains pulled back evenly, matching cane chairs positioned either side of the bedside cabinets, his and her library books lying next to terracotta table lamps. Moving to the left-hand cabinet, I picked up my book. It must be well overdue. Creases marked the bedspread where Penny had sprawled. Automatically, I smoothed out the fabric, told myself it was sheer madness to discard a long-term marriage. Perhaps Brian would reconsider if I expressed remorse and said the affair with Jeremiah was a horrible mistake brought about by circumstances beyond my control.

Considering such blatant untruths, I recalled my initial experience of shame and how I'd hated myself for succumbing to lust. But somewhere along the way, guilt had vanished, and love grew so bright it arrested all other emotions. Even now, in the midst of extreme trauma, I couldn't think of Jeremiah without experiencing intense pain. No, I could never envisage falling to my knees, begging Brian to forgive me and take me back.

A door slammed in another part of the house and I heard Stephen greet his sister.

'Hi Steve,' Penny answered, 'you're home early. Want some tea? I've just made some for Mum.'

'Mum?' he queried, his voice shrill. 'Oh shit!'

I listened carefully for further conversation, but all I could hear was the family room door opening and closing. *Stephen will speak to me when he's ready*, I thought, lifting the suitcase off the bed and wheeling it into the hall. I left it by the front door and went to say goodbye to my daughter.

'What the hell are *you* doing here?' Brian demanded the moment I entered the family room.

'Just collecting a few clothes.'

'You should have phoned first.'

'Why, you won't speak to me when I do?'

'I've got nothing to say to you.'

He stepped forward, blocking my path to the door.

'Would you mind letting me pass?'

Penny rushed over from the kitchen and grabbed Brian's arm.

'Please Dad, talk to Mum.'

'Oh, if you insist,' Brian said, staring down at her.

Our offspring soon made themselves scarce, but not before Stephen had hugged me and apologised for not phoning. Brian sat in his chair, endlessly stirring a mug of tea, his head bowed. Clearly it was up to me to make the first move.

'We have to think about the future, Brian,' I began tentatively. 'If this is a permanent separation, we'll need to see a solicitor, work out where Penny and Stephen are going to live, sort out finances.'

His teaspoon clattered to the floor. 'I wish I'd never met the damn woman. I wish you hadn't gone to that bloody island.' He placed his mug on the floor, then turned to me. 'Have you prayed for forgiveness? I have, over and over again. Prayed to a god I hadn't acknowledged since childhood. Have you been to church?'

I shook my head.

'Why not?'

'I can't go to church yet,' I answered carefully.

'It's not a Catholic church. You don't have to enter the confessional and confess your sins to Reverend Scott. Keep the issue between you and God.'

Needing something to hold, I lifted my mug of tea and drank deeply. How could I tell him loving Jeremiah wasn't a sin?

Brian leant forward. 'How about I come with you?'

Astounded by his offer, I could only stare open-mouthed.

'I'd like to come with you.'

The mug wobbled as I placed it on the coffee table. Taking a deep breath, I turned to face him. 'I can't go to church anymore, Brian, I no longer believe in God. I've lost my faith.'

'Oh my God,' he exclaimed, jumping to his feet. His

245

mug flew towards the window, shattered on the tiled floor well clear of the glass. Shards of yellow china glistened like sand-islands in a dark brown sea. 'I don't believe it,' he shouted, 'I bloody well don't believe it! You've just spent three months and five thousand dollars on a spiritual retreat and you're telling me you no longer believe in God! Have you gone bloody mad?' He raised one hand as if to prevent my response. 'No, don't answer, I've got it plain as day. It's that bloody Nigerian, isn't it? He persuaded you to worship some primitive idol. Sacrifice yourself, did you; offer him your body because his gods demanded it? I've seen the way that bloody voodoo affects them.'

'Jeremiah is a Christian,' I said, trying to remain calm. 'His church sent him to Eden College because he'd been ill, a breakdown. His pastor thought it would help.'

'Oh Christ, he's crazy as well.'

'As well as what?' I asked innocently.

He shifted from one foot to the other. 'You know.'

Anger welled up inside. 'Say it Brian. Say you don't like the colour of his skin, say you don't like the thought of a black man screwing your white wife.'

'Don't talk like that.'

'Why not, it's the truth.'

He studied his feet. 'I don't know you anymore, Julia.' Then, he began to pace, broken china crunching under his shoes. 'Where's the woman I've been sharing my life with these past twenty years, the mother of my children, the one I promised before God to love forever?'

I clutched the edge of the sofa to still my shaking hands. 'I'm not the woman you married. I was twenty years old then with very little experience of the world. An innocent.'

Striding across the room, he skidded to a halt in front of me. 'So, you decided to make up for lost time, eh and jumped into bed with a crazy Nigerian the moment we were apart? Was it different, was he good; rumour has it they're well hung?'

'Do shut up, Brian, you sound like a jealous adolescent.'

'Perhaps you did it for excitement then? Boring old Brian, levelheaded, steady job, sensible clothes. Did he wear that bloody blanket when you made love?'

Exasperated, I leapt from the sofa, landed centimeters from his crimson face. Clenched fists struck my ribs; I stepped back. 'If you say another word about Jeremiah, I'm leaving, and I won't be back. It's past history. We need to talk about the present, about us.'

Chastened, Brian returned to his chair and sat staring at the floor. The silence grew oppressive. Was he waiting for me to broach the subject of reconciliation? Or divorce? Perhaps, but I refused to be responsible for launching so crucial a conversation. Resuming my seat on the sofa, I pressed my back against a firm cushion, folded my arms against my chest and waited.

After a few minutes, Brian raised his head. 'Julia please listen to what I have to say,' he began, his mouth softening with each syllable. 'I appreciate it's been a difficult time for you, but I'm not a complete bastard you know. Forget all this nonsense about losing your faith and come home. When you're ready, we can go to church together. Soon, you'll be singing and praying and wondering what all the fuss was about. Everyone questions at times, it's only natural. I reckon you were saturated with God at that college, so it's not surprising you need a break.'

His warm smile seemed genuine, but I felt compelled to speak truth. 'My faith is dead, Brian, not on holiday, of that much I'm certain. As for our marriage, perhaps we can begin again, but only if you accept me as the person I am now.'

'Oh God, won't you even try?'

'Try what?'

'To be the Julia I knew, the Julia I loved.'

I sighed loudly. 'You haven't heard a word I've said.'

'I hear you I hear you,' he snapped, 'but I don't understand how my wife can go on a spiritual retreat run by a reputable Christian group and return with her head screwed up. I've a good mind to contact the media and expose the place.'

'This has nothing to do with Eden College, the course was excellent.'

He slapped his knee. 'Oh, Christ why I'm I being so dense? It's not over is it; you came back to settle up, get your fair share? Then you'll return to him, a devoted disciple armed with a wad of cash!' Leaping to his feet, he raced to the sofa and grabbing my shoulders, yanked me to my feet. 'Go on, go on deny it!'

My head spun, wisps of thought twisting and turning into nothingness.

'Answer me, woman,' he demanded, shaking me violently. Answer me, damn you!'

I remained mute, as if all the words I had ever possessed had been spoken and new vocabulary was unattainable. There could be no more dialogue. Post-island, I spoke a different language.

CHAPTER TWENTY-EIGHT

My little red house became vacant at the end of the month. Small and furnished, it would suit me perfectly. It was also close to the children—I harboured no illusions about where they would choose to live—and within walking distance of the sea.

The real estate agent expressed surprise when I advised her new tenants wouldn't be required, but she didn't press me for an explanation, and I offered none. After thanking her for managing the property efficiently, I settled the account and left the office, the keys to an inconceivable future tucked in my pocket.

Ownership of the house wasn't a problem; my name alone adorned the title deed. 'To my niece, Julia Ann Evans, I leave my property...' Black type on cream parchment detailing an aunt's wishes. My sister Karen had received the contents of Aunt Muriel's savings account, later used to purchase her first car and an overseas holiday. Marriage had changed nothing, Brian considering it a better tax option to keep the house in my name. At least I couldn't be accused of creating further stress for Stephen and Penny by forcing the sale of the family home.

Penny didn't share my enthusiasm for my new home. 'It's a dump,' she remarked when I showed her around a few days after moving in. 'The tenants only stayed because the rent was so cheap. Why don't you sell it and buy one of those smart apartments on Flinders Parade like Karen and Raymond?'

'I don't want an apartment,' I replied, steering her away from dingy bathroom to sun-drenched back garden.

'But what about me?' she persisted. 'This place is at least three kilometres from home.'

'It's only a short bike ride.'

'I wouldn't be seen dead on a bike.'

'Take the bus then.'

'And walk all the way up the hill?'

I resisted the urge to tell her the exercise would be beneficial; she spent far too many hours in front of the TV.

'Oh, why did this have to happen?' she groaned, flopping onto a plastic garden chair. 'It's not fair, it's just not fair.'

———

'Life is never fair, Julia,' Aunt Muriel replied, lifting her left hand from the steering wheel to stroke my cheek, 'and it's no use blaming anyone. The doctors did all they could for your mother. Would you have wanted her to go on suffering?'

I sniffed. 'No of course not.'

'Then dry your eyes.' She pointed out of the window. 'We'll stop over by that creek and have a swim before lunch.'

Hot and humid, it was typical February weather. After a week of torrential rain, earth and atmosphere exuded moisture. Clothes stuck to damp skin, which in turn stuck to the vinyl seat. All morning, the ancient Land Rover had slithered over narrow muddy tracks—my aunt avoided bitumen roads—and on several occasions I'd gripped the seat convinced we were about to turn over or career into the bush. I would have preferred to spend the day sailing, but Dad had taken Karen to the dentist and for some reason said I couldn't take the dinghy out by myself. At thirteen, I felt affronted by his sudden lack of confidence in me, so stormed out saying I was going to Aunt Muriel's place where at least I wouldn't be treated like a baby.

Muriel swung the wheel hard, only just avoiding a fallen branch and we came to rest among dripping trees, a short distance from the creek.

'Perfect,' she said, silencing the engine. 'Plenty of water, bit of sunshine, bit of shade. 'Coming?'

'I'll get a towel first.' I reached over and lifted a towel from the backseat.

'Last one in buys the ice-creams this afternoon,' she announced and leapt from the vehicle.

Aghast, I watched my middle-aged aunt plough through the trees, stripping off clothes and flinging them to the ground with no regard for modesty.

'I win,' she yelled moments later from the middle of the creek.

At the water's edge, I faltered, even though rough stones pressed into my bare feet and mosquitos buzzed around my face. Beneath the towel, I wore only brief undies, my swimming togs still hanging on the washing line under the house. Newly pubescent, my ripening body troubled me. Pert breasts strained against school shirts and black pubic hair threatened to peep from my togs during swimming lessons. I understood what was happening to me; Aunt Muriel had explained everything in her no-nonsense schoolteacher tone, but I was still surprised by monthly bleeding and dreams that filled my head with curious longings.

On the far side of the creek, Aunt Muriel clambered onto a rock, shook herself like a dog and stretched out her legs. I couldn't help staring at her heavy brown breasts and the bush of black hair curling between solid thighs. There was no doubt she felt comfortable with her body.

'Don't be such a sook,' she called out, 'it's not that cold.' And as if to convince me, she slipped off the rock and disappeared under the water.

Taking advantage of her momentary absence, I flung the towel aside and raced into the creek.

Before long, she surfaced, hair streaming. 'Marvellous,' she declared, 'absolutely bloody marvellous.'

'What if someone comes?' I asked, standing waist deep, arms folded across my tiny breasts.

'No one would venture out here today, only an old fool like me would drive in such appalling conditions.'

I glanced at her smooth tanned face, bright eyes and thick brown hair. 'You're not old, Aunt.'

She extended her hand and pulled me into the centre of the creek. A rush of cold water streamed over thighs and through thin cotton, invading my smudge of dark hair. Shivering I pushed through the chill to her warmth.

'Silly goose, it isn't that bad,' she said, enfolding me in her strong arms.

Comforted, I closed my eyes and listened to the buzz of insects, wind in the trees, water lapping against our cool bodies.

'We'd better get out and sit on the bank for a while,' she

said, breaking the spell. 'Your Dad would never forgive me if you caught a chill.'

We swam to the bank, climbed out and unfolded the towels on a patch of grass beneath shady trees. Lying quiet beneath dense foliage, my head grew heavy with humidity. Toes and fingers warmed but still seemed numb and refused to move. Languid, I succumbed to the drowsy day, nestling into damp earth like a bush creature.

Midday sun woke me, a torrid burst of heat that squeezed through clouds, leaves and branches to hang over my body like a hot wet towel. Moisture crept over warm skin, threaded through curls, crawled into crevices. Sensation swamped me as if another sun blazed somewhere deep inside. I shuddered, sat up and stared at the creek.

A loud sigh directed my gaze to my aunt lying close by in dappled shade. 'Ah, this is how God intended us to be,' she called on noticing me, 'unfettered, untroubled, children playing in his garden.'

'Then why did he have to go and ruin everything?' I asked petulantly.

'My dear Julia,' she replied, raising herself on one elbow. 'God doesn't ruin things, people do.'

———

Muriel's words echoed in my head as I picked up a second plastic chair and positioned it close to my daughter. 'Life isn't fair Penny,' I began, but she interrupted before I could offer my own explanation.

'I suppose it's too much to expect you to answer Mum, you probably don't understand what's going on either.' She hesitated. 'Have you, er, have you considered this separation could be a test?'

'What sort of test?'

'You know, God testing you. A way to bring the sheep back to the fold.'

Light dawned. 'Is that what Reverend Scott says?' I asked warily.

'No, he hasn't mentioned either you or Dad to me, although he did ask where you were the other Sunday.'

'What did you tell him?'

'I said you were busy fixing up the house.'

I reached over to pat her arm. 'A good answer, Penny. Truthful but unlikely to fuel gossip.'

'Oh, there's plenty of gossip, Mum. I've heard it after church when everyone's hanging around in the garden. Silly old women jabbering away and giving me strange looks. They think I can't hear them, but they forget I'm not the one wearing hearing aids.'

'What are they saying?'

She fiddled with her hair. 'Are you sure you want to hear this?'

I nodded.

Penny leant towards me. 'One of them, I couldn't see who it was, said evil has entered your soul and pushed out Christ, condemning you to eternal darkness and damnation. What a load of crap, I thought. Just because you haven't been to church since you got back, doesn't mean you're a pagan like I heard another woman say last week.'

'A pagan, where did she get that from?'

Penny shrugged. 'No idea but it's pretty bloody difficult when my best friend says she can't come out with me because her mother's afraid I'll be a bad influence, as if paganism is some sort of contagious disease. I told Kelly all that nonsense went out centuries ago and anyway there's no actual proof you worshipped primitive gods. I mean, just because all your friends at Eden College were African and played drums and stuff. I reckon you're just upset about you and Dad and want to hide away for a bit while you sort yourself out. I would for sure, especially when I think how these so-called Christians are carrying on. How would they like it, everyone makes mistakes and it's not all your fault? And what about forgiveness, have they forgotten what Jesus said?' She paused, eyes pleading for comfort, but I had no words to ease her pain. Resenting my silence, she tugged at my arm like a small child craving attention.

Instead, I thought about Ororun-baba, the god Jeremiah had said lived in heaven and almost spoke the name out loud, wanting to tell her there were many names for God and Christians had no right to presume theirs was the only true deity. 'Forgive them their ignorance,' I murmured at last.

Tears tumbled down Penny's flushed cheeks. Holding her hand, I let the weeping run its course, determined not to interject with words that might make matters worse.

When they subsided, I walked my troubled daughter into the kitchen and sat her at the old wooden table while I made tea. I half-expected her to run out on me, but she stayed seated, sniffing and wiping her eyes on her sleeve. When the tea arrived, she drank it noisily, retreating when the mug was empty, behind a wall of adolescent babble. I answered her questions in monosyllables, or nodded and smiled, aware she felt compelled to erase all traces of her recent outburst. She returned the smiles, seemingly unaware of my virtual silence. At last, nervous energy dissipated, she slumped over the table and laid her head on folded arms. Leaving her alone, I headed for the lounge and a library book.

———

Footsteps surprised me, and I looked up to see Penny walking towards my chair, her arms outstretched. Then she was hugging me, so close I could hardly breathe. Afterwards, she clasped my hand, led me to the front door and out into the winter garden. 'Thanks for giving me space,' she said as we reached the rusting gate. 'It was just what I needed.'

I squeezed her hand. 'Sometimes we need a little silence. It helps put things in perspective.' I opened the gate.

'Next time I visit, I promise not to sound off like a little kid having a tantrum. I'll think before I open my mouth.'

Out on the footpath, we embraced again, and she kissed my cheek, something she hadn't done in a long time. Leaning on the gate, I watched her race down the street to the intersection.

'See ya, Mum,' she called, pausing briefly to swing around the Give Way sign.

———

Day stretched into evening as I sat at the kitchen table following the antics of a pair of magpies. Strutting across the lawn, they prodded the soil for grubs, turning periodically to peck one another. Were they implying there was insufficient space in my back garden for two?

Around me lay the remnants of my solitary meal. Crumbs dusted the gingham tablecloth, scarlet soup dregs clung to white china. How strange to acknowledge there was no reason to get up quickly, no need to wash and wipe. I had all the time in the world to watch other creatures go about their business, all the time in the world to ponder the altered pattern of my life.

I had never lived alone before, never possessed the luxury of self-time. Father, sister, husband and children, each and every one had soaked up my days and weeks and years. Comfortable with my lot, I rarely sought solitude apart from daily devotions and even then, there was no sense of isolation. God was all around, listening and giving direction; such security, such a solid existence.

Faced with the prospect of boundless liberty, I felt uncertain what to do next. Decision-making didn't trouble me, rather the fact that my actions wouldn't affect anyone else. Who cared if I cleared the dishes today or tomorrow? Who cared whether I stayed up half the night reading or ate peanuts in bed? Did I care, or had I slipped into a bottom-less pit of lethargy?

Becalmed, I bobbed on still water in no hurry for wind. Thankful for respite, my mind emptied of thought and fears. My heart, it seemed, had already sloughed off its heavy load. Twelve days I had lived in my new home and not once shed tears or felt a lump in my throat or an ache deep in my chest.

CHAPTER TWENTY-NINE

Days stretched into weeks. Early one Saturday morning, instead of loading the washing machine, I packed an overnight bag and drove away from my bayside suburb towards the city centre. After negotiating a plethora of road signs—I couldn't remember the last occasion when I'd driven through city streets—I located a freeway on-ramp and found myself driving southwest. I hadn't planned the weekend away, just needed a break from the monotony of everyday existence. The small town where I stopped to buy petrol possessed only one motel, old-fashioned but well-kept, so I checked in, dumped my bag in the room and set off to explore the surrounding area.

A few kilometres out of town, I made my way up a steep winding track halfway up a hill, parked and climbed to the summit where I sat on a patch of grass watching October sun fill the Dividing Range with gold. Around me, nothing stirred save ribbons of grass clinging to the hillside and a tiny yellow flower poking its head out of a rocky crevice. I couldn't think of the flower's name and immediately regretted my ignorance. Negative thoughts surfaced as I recalled other plants whose names remained a mystery and a land I would never know where a boy named Jeremiah had laughed and played. Tears threatened; I dug fingernails into raised knees in an effort to forestall them. Soon, hilltop breeze blew away clouds and I raised moist eyes to a cloudless blue sky, grateful for restored calm. I had spent too many hours brooding over lost love. Jeremiah belonged in another time, another place and if I spent every day looking over my shoulder, the future would pass by unnoticed. Why cling to the past, as if those three months had been the only significant time of my life? I should have been weeping for the death of marriage, the demolition of family, the departure of faith. Karen said I was being too hard on myself, too impatient and must realise it would take months to unravel my tangled emotions. Months, years, decades, what difference did it make? I had all the time in the world.

As I contemplated distant mountains, the fog of lethargy experienced since moving into my hill-top home, began to lift, revealing clear expectant space. Unforeseen tranquillity, the bliss of inner peace, a turning point.

'I am alone, and it is right,' I said aloud. Scrambling to my feet, I descended the hill with ease, feather-light and free.

———

A new and delightful experience, this vista of grey-green gums bordering straw-coloured pastures and placid brown water. Above my head, the mottled dome of sky threatened rain, but I continued to sit by the dam even though my showerproof jacket lay forgotten in the motel room and I had eaten the sandwiches purchased earlier at a general store further west. A weathered tree stump provided a comfortable resting place and afternoon warmth soaked into winter-pale skin.

Around and over the dam, the hum of constant activity: cows grazing, water birds nose-diving, a lone fisherman casting a line. Nearby, a willy wagtail swooped over tall grasses searching for insects. All of a sudden, he alighted on a stem of dry grass less than a metre from my feet and swung in the sun like a child. I marvelled at the intricate pattern of feathers, the keen eyesight; never before had I taken the time to observe a wild bird so closely.

A rural landscape pleasing to the eye, an environment I had rejected in my eternal quest for the sea. Beyond the mountain range lay more unknown territory: parched plains, dried-up rivers, wind-blown earth, Aunt Muriel's glorious outback. Did I possess sufficient courage to face the desert, the empty red centre? Later, I told myself, there's no hurry.

Cloud began to cover the range, a thick curtain of grey obscuring detail, yet I felt no yearning for visual clarity. The tree-filled slopes remained extant and even if I closed my eyes, I knew now the shape of leaf and trunk.

———

Weeks stretched into months. Late one afternoon, I planted a hibiscus in the narrow strip of soil adjacent to my back door. A healthy specimen, it had glossy green leaves, a straight trunk and several tiny buds. Before long, my view from the kitchen table would incorporate new growth and I could watch scarlet flowers unfurl. Magnificent blooms, they only lasted a day, a brief but beautiful existence.

The plant was a gift to myself to celebrate the end of interior painting. Penny had been absolutely right when she said the house was a dump. Years of neglect—for which I blamed myself as much as the tenants—had resulted in a dingy, uncared for space.

The garden remained a disaster: weed-choked, sagging fence, overgrown trees, a lop-sided Hill's hoist half-buried in shrubs run rampant. February was the wrong time of year to be working outside, the heat oppressive and mosquitos voracious, but on waking this morning, I couldn't bear the thought of another day indoors. Sick of the sight of paint and putty, my pale body yearned for sunshine. There had been little opportunity for sunbathing since November, painting having taken up almost every weekend. Clearing and replanting the garden would be another lengthy task. I didn't expect to accomplish miracles overnight, but the hibiscus was a colourful beginning.

Aunt Muriel would not have approved. I envisaged her solid brown legs planted on freshly turned earth, hands on hips, lips curled in disgust. 'Australian plants belong in Australian gardens. None of your foreign flora, bringing exotic diseases and sucking the soil dry. Take that bloody lantana for instance, running riot all over the country strangling native plants. Bloody noxious weed and all because a stupid Englishwoman thought it would look pretty in her colonial garden.'

I looked out at the darkening garden. 'Forgive this one indulgence, Aunt?' I pleaded in mock-serious tone, then turned my attention to the tea stewing in a thick brown mug.

'Just this once, my girl,' came the curt reply and I leapt to my feet half-expecting to see her standing in the doorway, a middle-aged ghost keeping watch over the property and me.

'Muriel?' I queried timidly.

There was no sound except the drip, drip of spilt tea on faded linoleum.

'Come back Muriel,' I cried to empty space. 'Nothing has changed you'll see. This is still your home, paint and new curtains a veneer. Believe me, the heart remains untouched. I've laboured long, but not for myself alone. It was, it is a labour of love. Can't you see I'm trying to thank you? Not for the house, though don't get me wrong, I really appreciated the gift and financial security enabled me to spread my wings, even if it did take me twenty-four years to get off the ground. But now I'm flying, can't you see it will take more than dollars to keep me in the air. I need your words of wisdom and your friendship. I've travelled far from troubled adolescence, but I still need your unconditional love.'

Again, there was no response and I felt foolish standing in the doorway waiting for ghost words. Was she hovering above my head, laughing soundlessly at my feeble attempts at flight?

Suddenly my knees buckled. Clutching the doorframe, my fingernails clawed new paint. 'All right you win,' I answered, sinking to the floor. 'Yes, yes, I'll go west, in the winter when the roads are dry. I'll hire a Land Rover, take a tent and tramp over blood-red soil. Yes, Yes, I'll go alone, I promise I'll travel to the desert on my own.'

———

Yesterday, I plucked up the courage to leave the camping ground, drove beside the shrinking river and pitched my tent on the bank opposite one of the few remaining water-holes. At dusk, several wallabies arrived for a drink and a flock of cockatoos squawked in the branches of a tall gum near the riverbank. Anxious not to disturb them, I waited for darkness before lighting a fire and preparing my simple evening meal.

Later, well fed and cradling a tin mug of sweet black tea, I sat on bare earth in front of the fire gazing at the night sky. Even out at sea, I had never seen such brilliance, the sky resembled a black velvet cloth decorated with innumerable diamonds. The night air was cold, and I could feel its fingers pushing through thick layers of clothing. Skin cooled; toes became numb. Part of me wanted to extinguish the fire and retire to the tent, where I could snuggle into my warm sleeping bag, but somewhere inside, a voice, definitely not Muriel's, urged me to sleep under the stars. I resisted for a while, the sensible me asserting it could be dangerous. I might roll into the fire, be bitten by a snake or a mosquito carrying a deadly tropical disease. At last, I capitulated and dragged my sleeping bag from the tent. Then, after smothering my face and neck with insect repellant, I settled down to sleep.

Just before dawn, I woke to the soft sound of wallabies padding past me on their way to the waterhole. Soon, smudges of pale pink light appeared low in the sky and a dawn chorus erupted from the tall eucalypt. Snug in my sleeping bag, I lay a long time gazing at the receding night sky, even though a cold breeze wafted over my exposed face every now and then.

In the minutes it took to dress, light the fire and put the billy on to boil, the cockatoos departed, and wallabies bounded away. For the first time in forty-one years, I understood the true meaning of solitude, understood the words Muriel had written to me all those years ago, when she sat alone by a campfire because I had refused to accompany her to the desert. Looking up at the cerulean sky, I spread my arms wide, called out to my absent aunt. 'I did it, Muriel, I turned away from the sea. I faced the desert, the heart I thought was empty and dead.'

Alone in the red centre, I felt truly alive and determined to make the most of the rest of my life.

CHAPTER THIRTY

WE HAVE ENTERED THE THIRD MILLENNIUM. Fireworks and champagne saturated that last night of the terrible twentieth century but dawn engendered little change other than numerals on calendars and computers, the feared Y2K bug proving a harmless creature, quickly relegated to a few brief paragraphs on Wikipedia.

I saw in the new century with a group of friends at the Southbank Parklands on the banks of the Brisbane River. Towards midnight, we selected a good viewing point and along with the thousands of others gathered to celebrate, cheered and applauded as the millennium drew to a close. Multi-coloured stars exploded high in the night sky, illuminating towering office blocks on the opposite bank, smoke ribbons trailed over the wide river, toddlers, frightened by the whoosh of rockets, bawled in parents' arms. Plastic glasses and Brut champagne emerged from backpacks and baskets and on cue, endless toasts added to the uproar. In the early hours, I farewelled my friends, walked through the gardens and caught a train home to my bayside suburb.

The following morning, after a late breakfast, I pottered

in my garden for a while before deciding to drive up the coast to Bribie Island for a swim ocean-side. I still enjoyed the rough and tumble of surf, the sting of salt on lips and eyes, the pull of tide and current. Over on the passage side the water remained silky smooth, a safe place for small children to splash in the shallows or timid adults to cool off.

Driving back over the bridge after a long swim and short sunbathe, my thoughts turned to other islands, some detached from land like Moreton and Stradbroke; others like this one tethered to the motherland. Inevitably, the distant isle that once had promised spiritual development swam into view and I had to grip the wheel with both hands to keep my attention focused on the road. Only the night before, standing in the crowd at Southbank, I had resolved to slough off the old century, concentrate on newborn days and months and years. So, why on this first day of the untried, untested twenty-first century, had I hurtled back to a period best left undisturbed between the pages of my island and post-island journals?

At the end of the bridge, I pulled off the road onto a patch of grass and after calming myself with a mantra learned in yoga class, concluded it was time to reflect on the almost six years since I had chronicled thoughts and feelings. The task seemed monumental until I acknowledged there was no need to write a novel-length narrative. If I made a list of key events, tackled each one in chronological order and wrote succinctly, the memoir wouldn't take long. Then, I could file the past in the depths of my new computer, keyboard and hard drive having long ago replaced pen and paper. Perhaps after that, I would be able to embrace the new century with open arms and cleared mind space.

What to call this one-off account, I pondered, as I

continued my journey south along the highway. The date alone, as written above each entry in my old journals, seemed inadequate; I wanted a descriptive heading.

Wheels rolled over bitumen and concrete, bush and pine plantations giving way to cleared ground, the ubiquitous quarter-acre block replete with brick-veneer box and newly-laid lawn. Only when I'd turned off the highway and was driving towards the long-established bayside suburb I called home, did I remember Donna's wise words as we sat on plastic chairs in a Heathrow airport corridor. 'A Journey of Discovery,' I said aloud, 'or, How I Learnt to be Myself.'

Although the title sounded like that of a nineteenth-century novel, it mirrored my experience, so, on the first evening of the first day of the new millennium, I keyed the words into a new document and pressed save.

At first, I wrote dates followed by headings in bold, followed by notes, but soon scrapped that methodology; the document resembled a research project rather than personal deliberations. Unsure how to begin again, I decided to kick-start the file by recording what paths others' lives had taken in the preceding six years, the twelve months following my eviction from the marital home already documented in my post-island journal.

Journey.doc

After a year of silence interspersed with violent outbursts whenever we met, Brian agreed to a truce and we set about formally ending our marriage in a civilised manner. Unlike me, the single life didn't appeal to him and six months after the Decree Absolute, he married a placid woman, fifteen years his junior. They had met at the sailing club, where she mixed cocktails behind the bar on weekends to supplement her income. A year after their marriage, she presented Brian with identical twin daughters. Occasionally, I see them shopping with their mother in Brighton Road, two dark-haired little girls wearing matching outfits.

I have no idea whether at fifty-three, Brian welcomed the arrival of twins. Apart from Stephen and Penny's welfare, the subject of children was never raised during our infrequent post-divorce meetings. Probably, like many men of his generation, he left ninety per cent of the twins' nurturing to his new wife. I couldn't imagine him changing nappies and bathing babies in the manner of a New Age man.

Soon after the twins' birth, Maggie, the one extravagance in Brian's modest romantic career, married a wealthy businessman, thirty years her senior. According to her brother Raymond, who still lives with my sister Karen, Maggie seems perfectly content to play the role of glamorous hostess and has no plans for motherhood.

In recent years, my children have spread their wings wide. Despite the upheavals during her final year at school, Penny secured a place at the University of Queensland, but abandoned journalism studies two years later to backpack around Europe. I felt disappointed but nevertheless empathised with her need to flee the sickly smell of milk-fat infants. For some unexplained reason, she refused to come and live with me. After six months travel, she landed in London and decided to settle there. Nowadays, she works as a legal secretary and cohabits with a well-heeled Scottish accountant who adores her laidback manner and broad Aussie accent.

Conversely, my son Stephen doggedly pursued his university studies and graduated two years ago with Bachelor and Masters' degrees in computer science. At present, he works for a Swiss company and lives in a picture-post-card village on the shores of Lake Lucerne, a short ferry ride from the city. Snow skiing and water skiing occupy his leisure time during winter and summer and, according to his emails, a string of pink-cheeked Swiss girls flit in and out of his apartment at any season.

Since my children departed these shores, I too have delighted in overseas travel and crisscross the globe whenever time and funds permit, content to sleep on my children's sofas or bunk down in a backpacker hostel. High-speed trains whisk me across continents, cut-price airlines carry me over oceans, mountains and deserts. Sometimes, I venture into remote locations, taking a local bus or taxi. Travelling alone doesn't faze me, I relish the opportunity to engage in conversation with strangers, learn about different cultures, experience different foods, try my hand at different languages. No longer confined by wind and moon tides, I am free to wander far from homeland waters and the surf-ringed islands of my first four decades.

Last year, I finally accepted Donna's long-standing invitation and crossed the wide Pacific. After a brief stopover in Los Angeles, I caught an internal flight to New York. Although we had kept up snail mail, email and the occasional phone call, I worried that the firm friendship established at Eden College might have eroded, but my concerns proved unfounded. From the moment we embraced at La Guardia airport, Donna and I reconnected as though time-travelling back to summer term ninety-three. Wrapped in the warmth of enduring companionship, we strode arm in arm through New York streets, sharing laughter and conversation. Evenings we spent at her apartment, deep in discussion over generous home-cooked meals. When the time came for me to leave, we promised to meet again before too long.

Relationships with work colleagues failed to survive the immediate post-island period and early in ninety-four I secured a manager's position at a city bookshop. The Christian work environment had become extremely uncomfortable, especially after my resignation from the church. However, I must record that on no occasion did Reverend Scott pressure me to leave my employment, insisting my sudden loss of faith was no impediment to managing a church bookshop. But later, I heard from Penny that he believed I'd suffered a mental breakdown on the island and could no longer distinguish between reality and illusion. Perhaps he'd heard rumours of my conversations with a long-dead and longer lapsed member of the local Anglican Church? Once, in a moment of levity, I suggested to Muriel that she haunt his house, but wisely she rejected the idea.

Ghosts and God ought to be compatible, both are invisible to the untrained eye, both invoked by faith alone. I would have welcomed a discussion on the subject during that last meeting with Reverend Scott, but he refused to be drawn, his mind and spirit focused on my errant soul. Perched on the edge of Muriel's ancient sofa, he spent hours imploring me to return to the fold, his face awash with concern, his normally calm voice high-pitched and quavering. He was a good man and I wanted to thank him for the years of solace in that sacred space, thank him for coming when my letter of resignation had made it clear a visit would not be appreciated. But, as the minutes passed, his surfeit of words flooded my mind drowning all thought, so I remained a silent non-combatant in the battle for my soul. Eventually, accepting perhaps that I was a lost cause, he stood up and extended his hand in farewell.

'Julia my dear,' he said, 'remember the grace of God. He understands your dilemma. We all make mistakes such is the nature of humanity. Should you decide to re-embrace Christianity, I assure you God will welcome you back with open arms.'

A response struggled to the surface. I determined to tell him I wasn't the miscreant in this sad affair, God had left *me* not the other way around. 'I'm the victim here,' I spluttered when we reached my front door. 'Can't you see that?'

'There's nothing more I can do for you,' he said sadly and walked out, shoulders hunched.

'That's right drive away without a backward glance,' I cried, flinging words at his retreating car. 'Leave me alone to face the world.'

Alone. Thou art *not* with me; thy rod and thy staff *do not* comfort me.

———

I grieved a long time, not only for the loss of faith but also for loss of innocence, the naivety that had protected me for so many years. How ill-prepared I had been for life in the complex environment of late twentieth-century Western culture. Inevitably, time dulled the pain and I began to focus on reconstruction. Desperate for respite from emotional trauma, I decided henceforth to erase passion of any flavour from my life and risking dullness, retreated to cool calm detachment.

Passion remains a distant memory and I have long since ceased to question why God departed from my life in the middle of a spiritual development course. The search for explanation only led to further confusion and threatened to destroy my hard-won tranquillity. How could I begin to fathom the mind of God when I knew so little of *my* heart?

Red heart, empty heart, dead heart.

———

My life continues to be untroubled by complex relationships. I have many friends, a comfortable home, a fulfilling job. I have chosen to remain single, although not always celibate. Sexual energy isn't easily ignored and even if it were, I have no wish to suppress it entirely. But consciously setting out to acquire a sexual partner is not my way. If I meet someone and we find we are sufficiently attracted, we become lovers, usually without a long, involved preamble. It's as though there's an unwritten code each adheres to, a desire to avoid the cloying intimacy of commitment. My lovers and I regard the world through clear glasses; rose-tinted illusions have no place in our relationships. Life is transitory; we know our planet spins inexorably towards the sun.

Yellow sun, giver of life, giver of death.

———

But what of my island lover, Jeremiah, troubled Nigerian in exile, has he proven expendable, along with passion and faith?

During the initial post-island period, I regularly received letters postmarked Birmingham England, detailing his plans for a Nigerian future. After a while, it became apparent he'd changed his mind about building bridges and sinking wells, intended now to enter the political arena and fight the corruption plaguing his homeland. Supported by his wife Elizabeth, who took on extra work to maintain the family, Jeremiah began a full-time university course in political science. Delighted to hear his life had direction at last, I wrote back echoing Elizabeth's words of encouragement.

After two years, the letters stopped and were replaced by postcards of the countryside around Birmingham. Each contained a similar message: a few words of greeting followed by a quote from the Book of Jeremiah. There was no mention of politics, at least not contemporary politics, although invariably the quotes concerned destruction, sin and punishment. Perhaps Jeremiah wanted me to read between the lines, substitute 'Nigeria' for 'Israel'? I pondered his need for subterfuge, did he really imagine Nigerian generals intercepted British postcards? My replies were secular, the sentences carefully selected. I had no wish to cause him further distress.

Months passed, the messages became transparent and I grew increasingly anxious about his mental state. Jeremiah had become his namesake the prophet; he was the chosen one who would lead his people out of poverty and corruption. At one point, I contemplated phoning Elizabeth to express my concern, but in the end, I couldn't face the possibility Jeremiah might lift the receiver. Despite banishing passion from my life, love lingered, locked in a corner of my heart. I couldn't risk releasing that intense pain.

The postcards became sporadic and three years after our island liaison they stopped altogether. I imagined Jeremiah had abandoned university studies and returned to engineering. Choddy was right, Nigeria had been a dream, desirable but not attainable. It was better this way for Jeremiah, the harsh reality of late twentieth-century Africa would have utterly destroyed him.

In the years since, I've made no attempt to revive our

correspondence. What could I say to an engineer from Birmingham? Occasionally, I wonder what he looks like now, if grey flecks beard and hair, if lines mark his broad forehead, if he's retained his slimness into middle age. Fleeting thoughts of a fleeting love affair, they quickly fade in Australia's harsh sunlight. I have no regrets.

———

Leaning back in my ergonomic office chair, I pushed bare feet against the plastic footrest and sighed with relief. Saved in a folder on my hard drive, the completed memoir resembled comments on journey steps, rather than the in-depth reflection I had intended. No matter, I felt content and ready to look forward, ready to live out the rest of my life undisturbed by lengthy soul-searching.

Postscript, 8 September 2001

I had taken a day off work—time in lieu of working the previous Sunday—so had only just finished dressing when I noticed a mail van parked parallel to my white picket fence. I heard the click of the gate latch and hurried outside. The following day was my birthday and Penny, unlike Stephen, always managed to send a gift on time. Accepting the large parcel with a smile, I quickly ripped off the customs slip, preferring a surprise present.

Minutes later, I was sitting at the kitchen table turning the parcel over and over in my hands. It hadn't come from London or Kussnacht, Switzerland. The postmark was Lagos, Nigeria, the sender Ajuwon.

A host of images tumbled through my mind as I recalled Jeremiah's damning portrait of that vast metropolis: palm trees and pollution, malnourished children weaving through traffic selling trinkets; a stinking stew of garbage and untreated sewage in the lagoon. The church built on its shore, Cherubim and Seraphim watching over the people, promising a future free from poverty and fear. 'Believe, believe,' they cried. 'Christ is your Saviour; he died that you might have eternal life.'

But who can hear their message? I asked, remembering Jeremiah's description of the relentless noise pollution present in Nigeria's largest city.

'They cannot hear your message, Jeremiah,' I cried, my ears ringing, my head pounding. 'They cannot hear you.'

Afraid of their loud indifference, I yearned to be by his side, sharing his mission. At the end of the day, I could ease the ache of failure with soothing words, draw away dejection with smooth fingertips. 'Hush I am here, come with me to another world where all is light and harmony. Take my words and let them quiet you, take my hand and let me guide you; enter in enter in, one body, one heart, one soul.'

I shuddered, and the parcel slipped from my hands. Lying on the floor, it posed no threat, was simply brown paper, white string and neat black letters. The contents remained invisible. I had a choice: cut, rip or leave it intact. Postponing the moment of decision, I got to my feet and spent the next few minutes making a mug of strong black coffee, which I carried to the open rear door. I sank down to the cold stone step. Hot coffee slopped over my hand and I cried out, dropping the mug. It shattered on cracked concrete, staining the swept path. Grabbing a nearby bucket, I poured rainwater over scalded skin.

Limbs shaking, I crawled across the kitchen floor to the abandoned parcel, struggled with knots and thick brown paper. The contents were soft with something hard in the middle. Red, the gift was red; not the brilliance of hibiscus flowers but the warm hue of sunbaked earth. A faded blanket unfolded in my hands, in the centre lay a small red bible. I held his blanket against my cheek, coarse wool and tears mingling, chafing my skin, the essence of his being woven into those thinning fibres. Wrapping him around my shoulders, I lifted the bible with trembling hands. A sheet of blue airmail paper fluttered to the ground. I grabbed it gratefully, news at last from Africa.

> *Federal Palace Hotel*
>> *Lagos, Nigeria*
>> *1st September 2001*
>> *Dear Julia*

> *It is difficult to write these words; I am still numb from the shock. Jeremiah wanted you to have his blanket and bible; I found a note in his suitcase. Perhaps he had a premonition, saw death skulking in these squalid streets.*

> *Thank God, he didn't suffer, it was too quick for that. Witnesses said the old woman suddenly lost control of her car and careered across the road, pinning Jeremiah to the side of the bridge. The police said she shouldn't have been driving at her age, foolish old white woman in her grand Mercedes. There is one consolation; he died in his own land.*

> *Jeremiah came to this appalling city to organise work in the interior. I was against it at first, but he persisted, said it was his last chance to fulfill the promise he had made to God all those years ago at Eden College. Hopefully others will come; this country desperately needs help.*

> *Thank you for being a friend to Jeremiah during a difficult time in his life.*

In peace,
Elizabeth Ajuwon

'Oh God, oh God,' I cried, invoking a name I had tried to forget, a language I had dismissed as irrelevant. 'Why have you done this, why did you take him away just when he had summoned up the courage to act? Why did you destroy his dreams, why do you always have to interfere?'

Roof iron creaked and groaned; my voice resounded through the house, plaintive cries and pointless questions trapped within static boundaries. Clutching the letter, I staggered to the doorway, forced myself out into open space where sound could float free over rooftops, continents and oceans. The blanket tumbled from my shoulders, lay crumpled on damp earth.

Storm clouds were gathering in the September sky. Forlorn, I watched their progress as seven-year serenity turned to dust, crushed beneath the stone of memory. Perfume hung heavy in the thickening air, scores of scarlet hibiscus blooms mocking my bleached and brittle bones.

'Jeremiah,' I called to the darkening sky, 'did the old white woman torment your waking hours and invade your dreams as you traversed the land of childhood terrors? Did she demand sacrifice for the sins of the fathers, the unborn frailties of future generations? Did you see her face in the yellow moon, feel her outstretched arms in the tropic night?'

The letter fell from my hands, became ensnared in hibiscus branches. Lashing out, I yanked the nearest flower from its calyx and ripped it to shreds. Shaking and crying, I stripped the plant, throwing each beautiful bloom to the ground.

A sea of torn petals lay dying on fertile black soil. Aghast, I stood before the carnage, chest heaving, bare toes scarlet-stained. Rain began to fall, huge drops splashing on to leaf and branch, hair and skin. Lifting my face to the sky, I drank deeply before risking the question looming large in my mind. 'Jeremiah, did you cry out in those last moments, "My God, my God why have you forsaken me," or did long-buried deities emerge from dank soil to reclaim your troubled soul? Answer me, answer me, I beg you.'

Glossy green leaves stirred as a wind blew in from the bay, a plaintive cry rolled across our wide blue ocean, leapt over our two large islands, surged through the breakers, raced over yellow sand.

'Olorun gba mi[1],' Jeremiah entreated, his voice resonating with the music of his majestic continent. 'Olorun gba mi...ii!'

I sank to my knees and the warm wet earth received me. 'Our Father which art in Heaven, hallowed be thy name,' I began timidly, my voice barely audible in the breaking storm. Wind gusts tossed leaves and branches, scarlet blooms flew through the air, anointing head and face and hands. I lifted my eyes unto the hills from whence came my help, heard a torrent of prayer spill from my ruptured mouth.

THE END

[1]Oh God please help me.

Dear reader,

We hope you enjoyed reading *Re-Navigation*. Please take a moment to leave a review, even if it's a short one. Your opinion is important to us.

Discover more books by Sue Parritt at
    https://www.nextchapter.pub/authors/sue-parritt

Want to know when one of our books is free or discounted? Join the newsletter at
    http://eepurl.com/bqqB3H

Best regards,

Sue Parritt and the Next Chapter Team

ABOUT THE AUTHOR

Born and brought up in Southern England, Sue worked in clerical positions within the civil service, firstly at an atomic power station and secondly for British Telecom. At nineteen, she married her childhood sweetheart, Mark and seven months later they emigrated to Australia, arriving in Brisbane, August 1970. After three and a half years working as a Library Assistant in a technical library, Sue became a stay-at-home mother to son David, now 44.

In 1978 Sue began a Bachelor of Arts degree at the University of Queensland, graduating in 1982 with majors in English Literature, Drama and French. One week after graduation, Sue secured a graduate position within the University of Queensland Library, where she worked until relocating to Melbourne with her husband in 1999. In Melbourne Sue worked for nine years as Acquisitions Officer at the Victorian College of the Arts Library, now part of Melbourne University, until taking early retirement to pursue her long-held dream of becoming a professional writer.

Since retirement Sue has written six novels: *Sannah and the Pilgrim,* first in a trilogy of a future dystopian Australia focusing on climate change and the harsh treatment of refugees from drowned Pacific islands, Odyssey Books,

2014. Commended in the FAW Christina Stead Award, 2014.

Pia and the Skyman, Odyssey Books, 2016. Commended in the FAW Christina Stead Award, 2016.

The Sky Lines Alliance, Odyssey Books, 2016.

Chrysalis, the story of a perceptive girl growing up in a Quaker family in swinging sixties' Britain was published by Morning Star Press in 2017.

Feed Thy Enemy, based on her father's experiences, relates a British airman's courage and compassion in the face of extreme trauma during World War II and his struggle to overcome Post-Traumatic Stress Disorder during his post-war life. To be published by Creativia, 2019.

Re-Navigation recounts a life turned upside down when forty-year-old Julia journeys from the sanctuary of middle-class Australian suburbia to undertake a retreat at a college located on an isolated Welsh island. Instead of spiritual sanctuary, Julia finds her long-held principles tested by a tumultuous love affair with Jeremiah, a Nigerian student, an unresponsive god and a menacing spirit-woman. Published by Creativia, 2019.

Sue's current project and seventh novel, *A Question of Country,* explores the female protagonist's lifelong search for meaningful identity through the context of country.

During Sue's employment at the VCA College, a lecturer in Film and Television read some of her prose fiction and suggested she consider scriptwriting as he felt her writing style lent itself to the screen. Using texts from the VCA Library, she studied screenwriting in her spare time, undertook a short scriptwriting course and subsequently, wrote a short drama script *Last Fling* adapted from her short story of the same title, published in 1996. The script won First Prize in the FAW TV Drama Award, 2009.

Since then, Sue has written feature film scripts based on her novels *Feed Thy Enemy* and *Re-Navigation*, plus a pilot episode for a tv series based on *Sannah and the Pilgrim*. So far, she has been unable to find a producer for her work but hopes publication of *Feed Thy Enemy* and *Re-Navigation* may assist in this endeavour.

Creative writing has been a passion since Sue's teenage years when she wrote poetry reflecting her feelings about social issues or newly discovered love. Her poetry has been published in Australian and UK magazines and anthologies and a book, '*New Flowering: selected poems 1986-2001*,' was self-published in 2001. She also writes short stories and articles. Short stories have been published in Australian magazines (print and online), anthologies and a US anthology. Articles have been published in Australian and UK journals.

Passionate about peace and social justice issues, Sue's goal as a fiction writer is to continue writing novels that address topics such as climate change, the effects of war, the treatment of refugees, feminism and racism. Sue intends to keep on writing for as long as possible, believing the extensive life experiences of older writers can be employed to engage readers of all ages.

Lightning Source UK Ltd.
Milton Keynes UK
UKHW022147260221
379474UK00003B/330